"I'm surprised to see you here."

Leif's smile reached his eyes. "But I'm glad you came."

If only.

Warmth dripped into Abigail's belly before she could strike the naughtiness from her head. What was wrong with her? Daydreaming about a guy like Leif? He was too different, too earthy and holistic and—

And standing there with the best smile in three parishes. He had a slight dimple in his left cheek and eyes the color of a fall sky. His jaw had a blockish quality while his lips were sensuous. How Abigail knew they were sensuous, she wasn't sure, but she was certain he could kiss her up one side of a wall and down the other... and make her beg for more.

Dear Reader,

Poor Abigail. The managing sister of the Beauchamp clan needs to chill. So I gave her the best thing an uptight, lonely woman needs—a laid-back, sexy Norse god. Leif's not your typical hero. He's vegan, plays the ukulele and wears natural-fiber clothing. He's a hippie... but a really fine one. And exactly what the buttoned-up PTA president needs to balance out her life.

Leif has come to Magnolia Bend with one purpose in mind—find his real father and clear his mother's name. He doesn't plan on breaking through the prickly Abigail's defenses or on falling in love with the passionate creature beneath the sweater sets. But when did fate ever care about plans?

Toss in a rebellious twelve-year-old, an ex-husband looking for redemption and the droll Hilda Brunet, and you have a story worth taking the day off for. So grab a glass of sweet tea and a couple of hours to fall in love with *Sweet Talking Man*.

I love hearing from readers, so give me a shout at liztalleybooks.com or friend me on Facebook (liztalleybooks).

Happy reading!

Liz Talley

LIZ
TALLEY

—

Sweet Talking Man

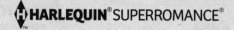
HARLEQUIN® SUPERROMANCE®

Recycling programs
for this product may
not exist in your area.

ISBN-13: 978-0-373-60896-6

Sweet Talking Man

Copyright © 2015 by Amy R. Talley

Printed in U.S.A.

A 2009 Golden Heart® Award finalist in Regency romance, **Liz Talley** has since found a home writing sassy Southern stories. Her book *Vegas Two-Step* debuted in June 2010 and was quickly followed by four more books in her Oak Stand, Texas series. In her current books, she's visiting her home state of Louisiana. Liz lives in north Louisiana with her hero, two beautiful boys and a passel of animals. She enjoys laundry, paying bills and creating masterful dinners for her family. She also lies in her biography to make herself look like the perfect housewife. What she really likes is new shoes, lemon-drop martinis and fishing off the pier at her camp. You can visit her at liztalleybooks.com to learn more about the lies she tells herself and about her upcoming books.

Books by Liz Talley

HARLEQUIN SUPERROMANCE

Home in Magnolia Bend
The Sweetest September

The Boys of Bayou Bridge
Waters Run Deep
Under the Autumn Sky
The Road to Bayou Bridge
Vegas Two-Step
The Way to Texas
A Little Texas
A Taste of Texas
A Touch of Scarlet
The Spirit of Christmas
His Uptown Girl
His Brown-Eyed Girl
His Forever Girl

Visit the Author Profile page
at Harlequin.com for more titles

To the girls who remember my first training bra,
my first kiss and my first Wild Thing
('cause I didn't like beer):
Dianna, Angela, Karen, Tina, Michelle and Heather.
I still think I look good in velour and twist-a-beads.

The oldest friends are the best friends!

CHAPTER ONE

August 1978

SIMEON HARVEY TURNED away from the open window noting the ceiling fan did little to relieve the discomfort of the sultry Louisiana night. He supposed he'd have to buy a damned air conditioner. Days ago, he'd discovered the humidity had damaged some of the priceless artworks hanging in the gallery. And that could not be.

He glanced at his grandnephew, Bartholomew Theriot Harvey, who sat in a chair in desperate need of reupholstering, fanning himself and sipping a gin and tonic.

"I don't know why you don't install air-conditioning in this old dump. It's hotter than shit in here," Bart said, wiping his brow with a handkerchief. He looked so much like his mother, Brenda, it was difficult to be angry at him...until he opened his mouth. "So why have I been summoned? Usually I call you. Regardless, you pulled the strings and the puppet dances."

Simeon stared hard at the boy. No, he wasn't a boy any longer, but rather a spoiled little popinjay of a man who'd turned thirty years old yet still acted like a frat boy, drinking too much, spending too much, ignoring his old uncle until he needed more funds.

Simeon itched to smack the boy, but he wouldn't. Simeon wasn't a man of violence.

"Pull the strings? That's the way you see it, eh?" Simeon asked, creeping painfully toward his recliner. His apartment of rooms occupied the upper floor of Laurel Woods, the historic plantation his family had owned for over a hundred years. Simeon seldom left his rooms, and his pride kept him from moving his bed into the downstairs parlor. He wasn't that damn old, but the rheumatoid arthritis had worsened over the years and he knew his ability to get up and down the staircase was nearly at an end. Yes, for a man who enjoyed the splendor of the natural world, accepting his limitations was a bitter pill to swallow. He missed the wind brushing his skin... not that there was a breeze tonight.

Simeon tucked his sateen robe around his legs, then adjusted his round spectacles. "And that is exactly why I asked you to come to Laurel Woods this evening. Those pesky strings."

Bart, whose gaze had traveled over Simeon's collection of beautiful things, jerked his head indicating the life-size sculpture Calliope had unveiled last week. "That thing is starting to give me a boner."

Simeon looked at the beautiful rendering of two lovers in a passionate embrace. The lithe female arched back, one arm lifted, as her lover suckled her breast. Folds of fabric fell from the bared stomach of the seductress. Diana, the huntress, captured in sensual pleasure.

"It's a work of art, meant to engage the senses."

"Well, if it does a better job, we'll both be embarrassed." Bart gave a dirty laugh. "Seriously, if people visit and see that, they're gonna think you're a perv."

Simeon took a few seconds to allow the disappointment inside him to settle. He still couldn't believe guileless Brenda had given birth to someone as low as Bart. The boy made him feel as if he needed to wash his hands. "Bartholomew, I'm sorry to say I've done you a great disservice all these years."

Bart's Adam's apple bobbed slightly as he swallowed. "A disservice?"

"Yes, a grave disservice," Simeon said, stroking the white goatee that brushed his knotted cravat, reaching for calmness, asking the gods to give him the right words.

Bart uncrossed his legs, adjusting his position in the chair. "What are you talking about?"

"I've provided for you because I loved both my sister and niece. Celeste and Brenda made mistakes in their lives, lives shortened by heartbreak, but each was free of selfish motive."

"Do you think I don't appreciate all you've done for me, uncle? Because I do," Bart said quite prettily, using a cajoling voice and a soft smile.

Trickery.

Bart had blown through half the money he'd inherited on his twenty-first birthday and came to Simeon several times a year to beg for more. His handsome great-nephew always brought presents, like the fine velvet pajamas or Victorian erotic art he knew his uncle treasured. He also exploited his uncle's loneliness by reminiscing about old times, times where laughter echoed through the halls of Laurel Woods. Though the boy was incredibly selfish and dissolute, he was hypodermically sharp.

"I care about you, Bart, and that's the reason I'm changing my will."

"Oh." Bart straightened, his eyebrows lifting. "Ah, what…" He paused as if unsure what position he should take. Buttoning his mouth, he elected to wait.

"You'll continue to receive the money remaining in the trust, but I've decided the estate will be given to the Laurel Woods Art Foundation on my death. I want the good work we're doing for artists and the community in general to continue after I'm gone."

Bart's eyebrows lowered. "You're joking."

"Not a joke. I firmly believe you'll never change, never grow up, as long as I continue to feed you money. You have two legs—it's time you learned to stand upon them."

At that moment his nephew did. Rising abruptly, Bart moved toward him, hand outstretched. As usual. "Uncle Simmy, please. I'm not a bad person. Didn't I bring you chocolates from the place on Magazine Street you like?"

Simeon looked at the box he'd already opened and sampled from. "A nice gift, Bartholomew."

"Yes, a nice gift," Bart said, dropping his hand. "And I think the art foundation is deserving of your generosity. But to give the whole estate to a bunch of fruitcakes who make crap—" he picked up a piece of driftwood carved to look like a sleeping heron "—is insane."

"I beg your pardon? *Insane?* What is insane about wanting to leave the world a better place?" Simeon cupped his hands over the recliner's arms, shifting his weight so he sat taller.

"Leave the world a better place with this stuff? You're mad."

Simeon chose to ignore that remark. *Keep to the course.* "I have an appointment with Remy Broussard tomorrow to make the changes. My mind is made up, but I thought it best to tell you in person. You deserved to know what to expect upon my death."

Bart turned. "I can't believe you would do this to me. I'm your own blood, the child of the niece who cared for you when no one else would. I'm a Harvey. You can't do this. You just can't."

"Of course I can. The estate belongs to me. The money you inherited from your mother was gambled away at the track. You think I don't realize why your hand is stretched out so often? You think I don't know about the people you owe money to? Dangerous people who would sooner slit your throat than piss on you."

His nephew jabbed a finger toward him. "I'll get an attorney and fight this. Harvey money belongs to a Harvey—not a nest of freaks."

"Do what you wish, but you'll lose. I know people whisper that I'm odd, and I suppose I am, but being different makes you more anticipatory. Think I'd leave any avenue open for you and some half-assed attorney? No, Bartholomew. I may wear silk underwear and eat macaroons, but my balls are steel." Power surged through Simeon. He hadn't felt this way in years. So alive. He had been a millionaire all his life, a burden, he'd often thought, but sometimes it felt good to exert the force his millions gave him.

"Don't do this," Bart said, his color fading, a look of panic emerging. "We're family. I'm—"

"Going to be better off depending on yourself rather than the money my father made. Trust me. You'll thank me one day."

A thump below drew their attention.

"Simeon?" a woman called out. "Are you presentable? I wanted to show you the new sketch for the library piece."

"I'm up here, Calliope," he called, turning to shoot Bart a warning. He didn't like to discuss personal affairs in front of his artists, especially the lovely Calliope. Of course, they weren't "his" artists, but they stayed at Laurel Woods because he fed and housed them, as well as commissioned their art for the town and surrounding businesses. The house and grounds his mother had loved so had been turned into a place of solitude, a place birthing beauty. It was a legacy that would continue with the huge allocation of resources upon his death. Until then, he'd continue to provide for the foundation.

"Oh, shall I come up?" she called.

"Make her go away. We're not finished yet," Bart said.

"No, we are finished," Simeon said, rising. He didn't want Calliope to see inside his rooms. Hattie hadn't come to clean in a few days because her grandson was ill. A pair of pajamas on the floor and rumpled bedclothes weren't an acceptable tableau for receiving a lady. "I'll come down."

Even if it meant another flare-up of pain.

"Is that the one the town says is after your money?" Bart asked, his voice low, still panicked.

"Pish posh, that girl isn't after my money. But Calliope is the person I've chosen to run the foundation. She's bright, talented and—"

"A whore. I've heard about her. Seducing all the men in town. Barefoot, no bra—she's a dirty heathen. And that's who you want to give the money to? Some fruitcake hippie who has slept with half the men in town?"

"Well, if it isn't the pot," Simeon said, picking up the ebony cane and moving at a turtle's pace toward the open door. "Seems rather a double standard from a man who's paid for two abortions."

As Simeon entered the upper hall, he caught sight of the loveliest artist he'd ever had the pleasure of hosting. She'd already turned and was heading down the stairs toward the marble-tiled foyer, her elegant hands gripping a sketch pad. She wore a broom skirt and her unbound blond hair just touched the curve of her buttocks. She padded barefoot, soundless on the curving staircase, a lithe sprite, full of energy and light. He'd never felt an attraction for a woman before, his tendencies leaning toward nubile young men, but he fancied he had a crush on the ethereal sculptor.

Something about her pulled at him.

Just as he reached the stairs, he felt Bart behind him.

"Please," Bart begged. "Please don't do this, uncle. We're family."

Simeon shook his head, turning back to tell Bart to stop groveling. Simeon felt his weight shift oddly, the foot that dangled over the first step downward found only air. He grasped for the banister, the cane falling from his hand and clattering to the tile below. And then he fell, slamming into the wall with enough force to make the sconce flicker, striking his head hard. Needles of pain flew at him from all directions as his body crashed down the marble staircase.

He heard the terrified scream and didn't know if it came from him or someone else. And just before he surrendered to the darkness coming for him, he saw the angel. Her eyes were wide, the color of the hydrangea still blooming at his door. Her silken hair, golden like the sunrise. She reached out for him, radiating comfort.

And then he was no more.

CHAPTER TWO

December, present day

ABIGAIL ORGERON GLANCED back at her twelve-year-old daughter as they approached the small white house located directly behind the antebellum home where they lived. Birdie resembled a prisoner sentenced to hang, trudging as if the happy cottage was the scaffold.

Birdie looked at the house with the stained glass and bamboo wind chimes, soulful eyes roving the charcoal shutters, regret shadowing her face. Not even the string of large-bulb Christmas lights could erase the dread from her face.

Well, Birdie shouldn't have stooped to spying on the lone occupant of the house if she didn't want to face the consequences of her actions.

"Please, Mom," her daughter said, her glance sliding to meet Abigail's.

"Sorry, but you must," Abigail said, her lips automatically dipping when she noticed the makeup Birdie had applied. Over the past year, her daughter had grown rebellious, doing things she knew her mother did not approve of. "Are you wearing eyeliner?"

Birdie looked away. "Yeah."

Since muttering *whatever* or giving the silent

treatment was Birdie's typical reply, Abigail counted herself lucky to get an actual response. Her daughter had tucked away the manners Abigail had instilled in her from the time she began babbling. "It's *yes, ma'am*, and I don't want to see that crap on your face again. You're too young."

"I'm not too young. I'm in the seventh grade. All the girls wear makeup."

"Except you."

Birdie made a great show of sighing and rolling her eyes. They were pretty green eyes, lined in black. She'd also managed to find some awful bubblegum-pink lip gloss. She looked like a little girl playing dress up, but maybe in Abigail's mind she always would look like her little girl.

"I can't believe you're making me do this. It was no big deal and you're making a federal case out of something stupid." Birdie stopped on the walk and crossed her thin arms. Pink stained the girl's cheeks, and Abigail was certain it hadn't come from the cosmetic drawer. She also suspected this was a bigger deal than Birdie wanted to make it. Birdie had told her she'd spied on Leif Lively only twice last month, but Abigail doubted her claim. The kid had gotten awfully interested in drawing birds from the perch in the big tree out back.

"Spying on people is a crime. It's called being a Peeping Tom…at worst, stalking."

"I wasn't stalking. Just, uh, looking a little. I didn't

intend to spy," Birdie said, not moving another inch up the walk.

"All you have to do is apologize. Don't worry. No beatings or stringing up by the toenails will commence."

Birdie shook her head. "Don't make me. He doesn't even know."

"That doesn't change the fact your actions were wrong. You have to apologize, Birdie."

"Stop calling me that ridiculous child's name."

Abigail sighed. "It's not a child's name. It's cute."

Birdie burned her with a laser glare. "I don't do cute, Mom."

No, she didn't. Not anymore. Birdie had gone from fluffy tutus and sparkly shoes to skinny jeans and a black hoodie. The one thing that hadn't changed was her size. Birdie may have been in the seventh grade, but she looked like a fourth grader. Slim, small and defiant, she had gone from funny Birdie to brooding Brigitte.

"Fine, *Brigitte*. Let's go apologize to Mr. Lively."

Birdie gave a short puff of aggravation. "Dad said I didn't have to if I didn't want to."

"Oh, did he? Well, since he's failed to be a parent for the past five years and doesn't even live in the state, his insight into the situation isn't va—"

At that moment the door swung open and there he was. Leif Lively himself…or, as Abigail had dubbed him, resident cuckoo bird. Okay, *sexy* cuckoo bird was a more accurate descriptor. The head of the art department at St. George's Episcopal School had flaxen hair that fell to his shoulders, bright blue Nordic eyes, a chiseled jaw and a body that made half the women in town salivate. He probably could make the other half salivate, too, but some women had principles and sense.

Like Abigail. She snapped her mouth closed and gave him her committee smile—the one that got things done.

"Ah, my neighbors," Leif said with a warm smile that touched those pretty eyes. "I don't see any casseroles in hand so I'm guessing you're not welcoming me to the neighborhood?"

He said it like a joke. He knew, of course, that Abigail would be the last person to welcome him to Laurel Creek, the new subdivision that had opened behind her historic Laurel Woods Bed-and-Breakfast in the small Louisiana town of Magnolia Bend. Abigail had vehemently protested the development behind her place of business. Laurel Woods, a plantation that had been around since before the Civil War, had always been surrounded by lush woods. The solitary, serene location was a main selling point for Abigail's business. But a planned patio community had taken away a third of the pines and hardwoods that lent peace to the bed-and-breakfast. Abigail hated the subdivision with every fiber of her being, but she hadn't been able to stop Bartholomew Harvey from selling the acreage to a developer.

She'd lost that battle, but she wasn't conceding to the hotness standing in front of her.

Wait. No. Not hotness.

She refused to think of the local artist as a sexual being…even if he made it difficult not to.

Chasing those thoughts felt too, well, dangerous.

And just why were those thoughts even in her mind anyway? She'd encountered Leif many times at St. George's and, though she appreciated his good looks and easy charm, she didn't consider him a prospect for anything other than an art teacher. In his eyes she'd seen what he thought of her as she organized wrapping-paper drives and delivered muffins to the teachers' lounge. Her dedication to being the PTA president amused him. He probably thought she was totally lame. Or at least she'd convinced herself that's what he thought of her. Either way, this man was on the other end of the spectrum from her.

"You've been living here for three or four months so I think the welcome period is over. I'm here on another matter entirely, Mr. Lively," she said.

"Call me Leif, and I'm just saying a casserole would have been delish," he teased, padding barefoot down the freshly painted steps, stopping way too near her.

He wore baggy cotton pants that gathered in at his waist. His bare torso belonged in an ad for suntan lotion, all bronze and free of chest hair. He looked like a man too comfortable in his own skin. Abigail swallowed, but refused to step back. "I thought you were a vegan anyway."

"Word gets around, huh? Well, vegans like casseroles," he said with another smile, craning his head around her to spy Birdie standing stock-still on the walk. "Hey, Birdie."

Abigail glanced at her daughter. The child's face was the color of the camellias blooming by the white picket fence. Good gravy.

"Hi, Mr. Lively," Birdie said.

"So what can I do for you?" Leif asked.

A naughty thought popped into Abigail's mind. Really naughty. But she flicked it away and cleared her throat. "Birdie has something to say to you."

"Oh." Leif's gaze swept down Abigail's body, taking in the clothes she'd donned for the open house held at St. George's Episcopal School earlier that day. She'd aimed for professional but suspected she looked overly conservative. But who cared? Besides it was winter, for Christ's sake. Leif needed to put on a shirt. What kind of man answered the door in such dishabille? Not any man she knew, that's for sure.

Abigail smoothed the wool slacks against her thighs before she could catch herself and turned toward her daughter with an arched eyebrow.

Birdie just stood there, looking scared.

"I hope you're coming to tell me you want to take the art class I'm offering at the community college next semester," Leif said, his eyebrows lifted expectantly. "I'm looking forward to having a talented artist in my class at school this semester, but it would be awesome to have you in the enrichment class, too, Birdie."

"Brigitte," her daughter said.

"Oh, of course. Brigitte, very French," Leif said, with another sweet smile.

Christ, why did he have to be so nice?

"Uh, I'm thinking about taking the course. Uh, if my mom will let me." Birdie turned pleading eyes on Abigail. Eyes that nearly swayed Abigail into scrapping the plan to make Birdie apologize. Abigail could always make up something about a dead branch on her property threatening Leif's back fence.

Wait. No.

She'd told Birdie she had to apologize. Children needed consistency. Every mother knew that. Still something pinged in her heart. Maybe if she bent just a little, Birdie would toss a piece of sunshine she hid somewhere beneath that awful hoodie Abigail's way. Maybe it would be a starting point to discuss why her daughter had spied on Leif in the first place. Obviously Birdie had questions about men, their differences and perhaps even—Abigail swallowed—sex.

"Mom?" Birdie waited for her to speak.

"We'll talk about art class later," Abigail said, giving Birdie the "go ahead" nod.

"Uh, I'm here because, uh—" Birdie dug the toe of her sneaker against the concrete walk. "Well, you see, I used to like to climb trees. For sketching. Uh,

Audubon once stayed at our house and, well, there are a lot of birds and stuff. I like to draw them and the best place to get a bird's-eye view is the old sycamore out back."

Leif held up a fist. "Mad props to our boy John James Audubon. He's one of a kind."

Birdie fist-bumped him. "Yeah, we have some originals. Two to be exact."

"You're kidding. I'd love to see them."

"Come over anytime," Birdie said.

Abigail started to shake her head, then caught herself. To be stingy with the original John J. Audubon watercolors would not do. Abigail had always welcomed anyone who wanted to take a peek at the tufted crane and the brown pelican the famed woodsman had created almost two hundred years ago. Leif Lively was no exception just because something about him made her...

Okay, fine. Abigail had a weird attraction to Leif that she'd never wanted to admit even to herself. When she dropped in at the school, she found her gaze hanging on him. And she hated herself for it. After all, she wasn't one of those women who fluttered, starry-eyed over the handsome artist. She wasn't like other room moms who cracked ribald jokes about Leif's ass.

Fawning wasn't something she did. Ever.

"I'd love to see the Audubon pieces," Leif said with another smile at Birdie...and then at her.

Christ, he smiled a lot. The Ryan Seacrest of Magnolia Bend.

Abigail nodded. "Sure, drop by anytime and Birdie can show you."

"Anytime? I could come now. It's about suppertime and I heard you're a good cook."

"Are you hungry?" Abigail had been knitted together with a strong thread of Southern hospitality so guilt pecked at her for not welcoming Leif and the other Laurel Creek residents with banana bread or cookies. But she was *not* inviting him for supper. The thought made her feel too warm...too nervous.

"I'm just joking, Abigail. You seem a little tense." His gaze moved over her once again.

Abigail tugged her cardigan closed and gave him the smile she usually reserved for her brothers. "I'm not tense. It just didn't sound like a joke. I grew up with three brothers—I know jokes."

"Well, I'll be more careful around you, then. Might end up popping open a can of snakes or sitting on a whoopee cushion." Leif's eyes danced, and even though she wanted to smile, she didn't. She held on to prickliness like a cape protecting her from being silly. She'd tucked away being lighthearted. Hadn't worked out for her. Besides the hot weirdo who strummed a ukulele at the local coffee shop and practiced tai chi in his yard wasn't the kind of guy to let her guard down with. Too different from her.

"Don't worry. I'm an adult and no longer put crickets in my brothers' trucks."

"Oh, that's a shame." He said it like he was truly sorry for her. Why? Because she didn't do asinine things anymore? Because she didn't crack jokes? Or wear flowers in her hair? She crossed her arms as he added, "I like your cardigan, by the way. Angora?"

"Are you making fun of me?" Abigail asked, a dart of hurt nicking her.

"No. Why would I?"

"Because I'm wearing… Because I don't frolic in my underwear."

Birdie closed her eyes. "Oh, God."

Leif's eyes widened. "I don't frolic in my underwear."

Abigail opened her mouth, then shut it. Silence as comfortable as a prostate exam descended. Not that she knew about prostate exams…but she could imagine.

Just as she was about to prod Birdie again, the squeal of tires sounded. All three turned their heads to see a bright red Mustang hurtling down the street. Another squeal of tires and the vehicle swung into Leif's driveway, halting with another screech.

"What the—" Leif muttered as the tinted driver's window rolled down to reveal a pretty brunette who looked…worried. Abigail tugged Birdie back, but her daughter pulled away, obviously engrossed in the frantic pantomiming of the driver.

"Sorry about this, Leif," the driver said as the passenger door opened and a ball of white fluffy tulle emerged. "Marcie made me do it. I was supposed to be her maid of honor. I guess it's, like, an obligation."

Maid of honor?

Abigail glanced at Leif; he looked gobsmacked, blinking his eyes a couple times before repeating, "Maid of honor?"

And that's when the fluffy ball flipped over her veil and sneered. "Yeah, maid of frickin' honor. Today was supposed to be our wedding day, asshole."

LEIF'S MIND WHIRRED, random numbers lining up like on a slot machine. December sixteenth. Today would have been his and Marcie's wedding day.

Oh, shit.

Marcie's veil was pinned to heavily sprayed blond tresses and one side had fallen down to wag against her sweaty face. Mascara ran beneath her eyes, reminding him of something he'd once seen in a horror movie.

"Marcie—" He couldn't even figure out how to ask why his ex-fiancée had put on a wedding dress and tracked him all the way to Magnolia Bend. They'd ended their engagement five months ago, and he hadn't heard a peep from her until now... when his very proper neighbor stood on his front walk, no doubt looking on with disapproval.

This might make the *Magnolia Bend Herald*...or, at the very least, the Facebook hall of fame.

"Ohhh," Marcie slurred, wriggling around the car

in the tight mermaid gown she'd raved about for weeks last summer, nearly tumbling to the ground despite hiking up the dress. "You remember my name. Ain't you sweet?"

"What are you doing here?"

"Didn't think I'd find ya, did ya?" she asked, shoving a finger in his face. "My daddy knows a lot of people in this state. You can't hide, you no-good bastard."

Leif inhaled and exhaled slowly, trying to figure out how a dude handled something like this. He felt caught in some crazy docudrama or a Maury Povich special. "I wasn't trying to hide from you." Much.

"Bullshith." Marcie teetered as she tried to square her shoulders. "You were runnin' like a damn...uh, something I can't think of right now."

He glanced at Marcie's best friend, Rachel, who still sat in the Mustang looking guilty as hell. "How much did she drink, Rach?"

She held up a half-empty bottle of Crown Royal. "She started last night. I'm sorry. I couldn't talk her out of it and I couldn't let her drive herself. She's loaded."

Good Lord. Marcie swayed, her blue eyes still locked on him. Abigail had edged onto the grass and he could only imagine the censure in the woman's eyes. He'd seen her around St. George's, hovering over the school like a blimp or like that character in *Monsters, Inc. Always watching.* Abigail Beauchamp Orgeron seemed to be the perfect mother, business owner and citizen—always going the extra mile. She was the kind of woman who made him twitchy.

"Okay, look, Marcie, this isn't the time or place to talk about what happened between us. Things didn't work out, honey. One day you'll see breaking off the wedding was the right decision for both of us." Leif placed a hand on her elbow, mostly so she wouldn't fall, and turned her toward the car. "Now go back with Rachel. It's crazy to show up here like this. When you sober up, you're going to feel—"

"Don't tell me what I feel. I waited all my life to wear this dress. See what you've done to me," Marcie said, wrenching her arm away and catching sight of Abigail. She dragged her drunken gaze from his neighbor's head to her loafers. "Wait. Who's that?"

"Uh, nobody," Leif answered before Abigail could open her mouth. Somehow it made him sound guilty. Marcie narrowed her glazed eyes.

"Wait, are you sleeping with her? *Her?* She's not your type. She's, like, old. My mom wears shoes like hers."

Abigail looked at her sensible loafers, then at Marcie. It was like watching Courtney Love go toe-to-toe with Katie Couric. "For your information, I'm his neighbor, and every woman should have a good pair of loafers—even rude, inebriated women."

Marcie's brow crinkled. "Inevreated?"

"Drunk," Abigail clarified.

"Well, that's his fault," Marcie said, pointing to

Leif. "But I'm sorry I said that. Still, my mom totally has those shoes. Guess you shop at Talbots, too."

Abigail turned to the waiflike preteen staring at him and Marcie with eyes as big as dinner plates. "Come on, Birdie. We'll do this later. Mr. Lively has his hands full."

Birdie stood agog, not budging. "Okay."

"Wait." Marcie held up a finger. "I got something for you, Leif."

Oh, God. Please don't let it be a shotgun. Surely Rachel didn't let her bring a weapon. But then again, Rachel wasn't the most sensible of girls. She'd brought a drunk, bridal-gown-wearing Marcie from New Orleans.

"Now, Birdie. Come on." Abigail's voice sounded more urgent.

Leif glanced at Abigail, then worriedly at the rump of Marcie. The rest of her had disappeared into the car. "You guys don't have to go. It's fine."

But it was not fine.

The fluffy veil swayed as Marcie wriggled out, lunging toward Leif.

Whew. No shotgun or pistol or machete.

Just a plate. With a huge hunk of cake.

"This is for you," she said, scooping a hunk of white iced cake off the plate. "Thought you might like a piece since you insisted on almond buttercream for the wedding cake."

And then she smashed the entire piece right between his eyes.

He didn't try to stop her because he knew he had it coming. He was the one who'd broken off the engagement. He was the one who'd broken her heart… or at the very least ruined her grand New Orleans wedding, complete with the vows at Saint Louis Cathedral, a carriage ride through the Quarter and a honeymoon in Tahiti.

"There," Marcie crowed, twisting her hand, grinding the cake in good. He felt the icing slip down his face and tasted the sweet buttercream frosting. "Hope you like it."

He swiped the cake from his eyes in time to see Marcie rake her icing-covered hand down her gown and spin on a heel, nearly falling onto the hood of the still purring Mustang. She marched to the open passenger door, spit out some of the netting that had gotten into her mouth and glared at Leif. "And now you can go screw yourself."

Except she didn't say *screw*. She said the other word, making him glance over at Abigail, who had earmuffed Birdie. Too late, of course.

Leif scraped off some cake and flung it to the ground, then swiped a finger through the icing, sliding it into his mouth. "Mmm. Almond buttercream *was* the best choice."

Marcie growled at him before giving him the finger and crawling into the car. "Get me the hell away from him."

And with that last directive, Rachel reversed the car out of the driveway. With a small regretful wave, she aimed the shiny Mustang toward the bricked gate of the subdivision. Leif waved, then took another swipe of icing and sucked it off his finger. The cake really was excellent. He wondered if Marcie had been obligated to pay for the wedding cake she'd hemmed and hawed over for a month. Or maybe she'd picked up a random white cake and played it off as the wedding cake. He wouldn't put it past the pretty drama queen.

He'd loved that about her.

At one time.

Abigail's head wagged between him and Birdie.

Leif shrugged. "You know, it really is good cake."

The too put-together woman's mouth opened slightly and she stared at him as though he'd grown devil horns...rather than having just gotten cake in the face from a drunken woman wearing a bridal gown.

Birdie shimmied down the driveway, craning her neck to catch a final glimpse of the sports car. As the vehicle roared onto the highway, she spun toward them, a fantastical smile invading her face. "That was awesome."

CHAPTER THREE

THIRTY MINUTES LATER, Leif stepped from the shower and shook his hair, causing droplets to fly and speckle the mirror spanning his bathroom wall. No more buttercream frosting, thank God. Only the lavender and mint of the organic shampoo his friend in Colorado made by hand. The scent comforted him, reminding him who he was, where he came from.

Damn, Marcie.

What kind of woman did something like what she'd just done? So over-the-top. Thank goodness he'd realized what his life would be like with the drama queen of Saint Charles Avenue and gotten the hell out of town. Of course, he probably should have broken things off before she had ordered the cake, but by that time Marcie had turned into a locomotive, bearing down on the planned wedding date full force. Once he'd agreed they should get hitched—a proposal extracted in the middle of some raunchy sex—Marcie had taken the reins and dragged him behind her on her way to New Orleans's wedding of the century.

Before he could say "maybe this isn't a good idea," wedding rings were ordered. Looking at the excitement on Marcie's face and checking out the emerging crow's-feet around his eyes, he'd decided marrying the daughter of old New Orleans money wasn't a bad way to spend the rest of his life. She was good in the sack and pretty as a buttercup. So while Marcie spent the next few months booking reception halls, ordering invitations and analyzing bridesmaids' dresses, Leif tried to envision a life of...chains.

Because eventually that's what his impending marriage started to feel like. Prison. His casual proposal spoken in the heat of the moment had turned into a nightmare.

And then his mother passed away, leaving him a cryptic piece of the puzzle to her past, to a life he'd never known existed.

He'd returned to New Orleans a week after the funeral, telling himself that finding out the truth about his past wouldn't change his future with Marcie. But he'd awoken the next morning beside his future wife and couldn't breathe. Not literally, but almost. His heart galloped, a crushing weight sat on his chest and his clammy palms curved around the edge of the bed, holding on for dear life.

He just couldn't do it.

Marcie was a nice girl, but not his soul mate, not the woman he wanted to wake up next to each morning, not the woman he wanted to sit beside in a rocking chair, watching the sun sink over the marshlands of Louisiana. He had never wanted to live in Louisiana. He craved the mountains, thin air and people who appreciated good tofu.

So Leif had broken the engagement three weeks

before the first wedding shower. *This* time he'd not written a Dear John letter and bolted. He'd learned his lesson at the hands of his second former fiancée's brother and found the balls to pull Marcie out of a gown fitting to tell her he wasn't going to marry her.

She'd thrown a trash can at him.

That particular action had scared the hell out of the coffee-shop patrons sitting outside enjoying a sweltering day on Magazine Street. The trash can had spilled nasty old coffee on his new trainers, but he hadn't had time to worry about that. Marcie picked up the nearest plate and hurled it at him, screaming "asshole" over and over. The poor man who didn't get to finish the bagel that rolled into the street didn't shout in outrage—he just slunk in the opposite direction.

Leif couldn't blame him.

He also couldn't make Marcie listen to reason. She was like a wounded rhino—nothing but a tranquilizer dart would calm her down. She had to burn herself out, and Leif didn't intend to stick around for the show. Eventually, Marcie would figure out that his ending their relationship would save her greater heartache down the road.

Guess she hadn't internalized the last words he'd spoken—*someday you'll thank me*.

Unless the cake was a belated thank-you gift.

Immediately after the trash-can throwing, Leif had resigned from the art department at Delgado Community College and packed up the small garage apartment he'd rented in the Garden District. Then he'd left New Orleans much the same way he'd entered it—running from a woman.

Yeah, he'd made a bad habit of getting engaged to girls who, on the surface, seemed perfect but underneath weren't what he needed. The broken engagement prior to Marcie had occurred three weeks before the wedding. He hadn't wanted to hurt Jenna—she was as sweet as the buttercream frosting he'd just washed off. Her father and brother, however, weren't as nice. Leif felt lucky to still be walking after they'd caught up with him in Beaumont.

So Leif had regrets...lots of them. He'd escaped the wedding noose three times and regretted hurting the bystanders. But most of all, he hated that his fear of commitment had dragged three innocent women through the mire with him. Hadn't been fair to them, but he comforted himself with the thought he'd done the right thing.

Leif's feet couldn't be nailed down. He wasn't the kind of guy who stuck...and stayed. Even though he wanted to be someone who belonged somewhere... and to someone.

Arriving in Magnolia Bend had been an accident of fate, but even if he hadn't gotten lucky with the position as art teacher at St. George's, he would have come to the town that held the answer to the biggest mystery in his life.

So the time to uncover his past was here. This

place held the secrets about why his mother had run…and it held the secret of who Leif's father was.

Here he began, and here he would hopefully find the answer to the questions that had pricked at him for years. Then maybe he could stop avoiding the ties that bound and find a good spot to settle down.

The doorbell sounded and he grabbed a linen drying towel and hurriedly scrubbed the remaining moisture from his body. Sliding on the *hatachigi* pants he'd abandoned on the bathroom floor, Leif hurried toward the foyer. The darkening sky had thrown his living area into gloom. Flicking the porch light switch, he opened the door to find Birdie standing on the stoop. Cool air swooshed in, so he grabbed the Patagonia pullover from the nearby hook and tugged it on.

"Birdie," he said, peering out to see Abigail standing once again at the mailbox. Obviously the two had given him some recovery time before resuming whatever mission they were on. Something about drawing. Maybe Abigail wanted her daughter to have private lessons.

"Hey," the girl said, shifting nervously in her Converse high-tops. "Mom made me come back to apologize."

"For…?"

"Uh, two things. First…" She glanced at her mother. Abigail gave her an encouraging nod. "I shouldn't have said that woman smushing cake in your face was awesome."

Leif couldn't stop the laugh. Right after Birdie had declared the awesomeness of Marcie's actions, Abigail had hustled her daughter away with a quick farewell. She'd nearly dragged Birdie toward the adjacent access walk to the Laurel Woods Bed-and-Breakfast. "Well, it wasn't awesome for me, but I can understand from your vantage point."

"Yeah. She was pretty mad at you."

Leif lifted a shoulder. "Eh, I deserved it."

"You did?"

From her post Abigail cleared her throat. Loudly.

Annoyance shadowed Birdie's eyes. "And the second thing I'm sorry for is spying on you."

"Huh?"

Birdie turned and called to her mother. "There. I told him. Are you happy?"

Abigail gave her daughter the "watch it, missy" look mothers had been giving from the beginning of time.

Leif braced his hands on the door frame, drawing Birdie's attention. "You've been spying on me? Why?"

Birdie swallowed, shifting restlessly before tilting herself closer to him. "It was last month. I accidently spied on you when I climbed a tree…for, uh, some sketching." She inclined her head toward her mother and dropped her voice to a whisper. "That's how I get away from her. She stresses me out."

He could see that. His observation of the buttoned-up Abigail had given him the impression someone needed to release a pressure valve inside the woman. Glancing at her now in her navy sweater, her mouth pressed into a serious line, he figured it was tough to have a mom who carried a label maker and a thick accordion binder of forms, calendars and sanitizing wipes. "Okay. Apology accepted."

The girl leaned even closer, so that he could smell the apple scent of her shampoo. Her gaze pleaded with him. "I didn't tell my mom you were naked. Please don't tell her."

Whoa.

Leif sucked in air. Dear God. He'd never considered that while swimming his daily laps, someone would see him clad in his birthday suit. His privacy fence topped out at eight feet and he usually did laps in the cloak of darkness. It had grown colder the past few weeks so he'd started swimming at the rec center, but last month he'd been in his pool. "Jeez, Birdie, that's, uh, not cool."

The girl rocked back on her heels, tears sheening her eyes. "I didn't mean to, okay? I didn't really see anything. Much."

"Okay, don't cry. The human body isn't something to be ashamed of so let's not make this something skeevy."

"You're not mad?"

"No, but you need to tell your mom at some point. Keeping a secret like this isn't a good idea." He nearly choked on the last thought. He'd kept a big secret from everyone in the town. He was the son of

Calliope—a woman they thought murdered someone. He was also the son of some guy who still lived
in Magnolia Bend. He just needed to find out who
that guy was.

"She'll make it into something bad."

Leif looked at Abigail, who had given up the aggravation and now appeared concerned about the
quiet conversation her daughter was having with
him. "Curiosity about the opposite sex is natural,
Birdie. Not bad. It's how we're made. But the deal
is I'm a teacher at your school. Things like this can
get complicated."

Birdie squinted her eyes, obviously seeing it from
his point of view for the first time. But then her expression grew pleading again. "It was an accident.
I won't do it again, and we don't have to tell anyone
you were naked. This is all my fault. Not yours. I'm
the pervert."

"Is everything okay?" Abigail called.

Leif raised a hand and gave her a flashbulb smile
before directing his regard to her child. "Don't say
that. You did what any eleven-year-old would do."

"I'm twelve."

"Okay, but even so, you don't have to be ashamed
of being curious. I accept your apology, and I will
make sure next time I pull on a suit, okay?"

Birdie nodded, diamond teardrops clinging to her
long lashes. "I'm really sorry."

"Okay. We've put this behind us. And you do realize that in some art classes, students sketch un-clothed bodies. Artists see things differently, right?"

"Of course," Birdie said with a nod before easing off his porch. "Thank you, Mr. Lively."

Leif smiled, even while inside his gut clenched. He would have to tell Abigail about the "secret" he now shared with Birdie. But that would be hard. He could envision Abigail overreacting to her daughter acting on natural curiosity. She'd make it something it wasn't. Abigail Orgeron wasn't a helicopter mom—she was a tank who sat on her daughter. Poor kid. Birdie tried to escape someone who wanted control over every aspect of life.

Shove a lump of coal up Abigail's ass and he'd have a diamond in a week.

But, damn, it was a nice ass. He'd noticed as she marched up and down the halls of St. George's, out-lined as it was in slim trousers that hung perfectly, the hem brushing sensible loafers…that he guessed she bought at Talbots. Abigail also had a nice rack and a slim waist. But most striking of all was the shiny black hair that fell just past her shoulders and held a single silver stripe that framed the right side of her face. The whole look was somehow sexy. The artist in him loved the contrast, the eruption of some-thing so unexpected. It made him want to dig deeper, to know her better, to unwrap the fleeting vulner-ability that shaded her eyes.

He could see the sensuality in the curve of her bottom lip, the grace in the way she moved her elegant hands and the passion trapped beneath those ugly-ass sweaters.

Leif had seen a lot of woman who needed a good screwing, but he'd never seen a woman who needed it more than Abigail.

If she weren't such a cactus with a lonely daughter, he would take up the challenge of giving her relief, but after the bad decisions he'd made with the last few women in his life, he would take a rain check.

He'd come to Magnolia Bend for one reason, and one reason only—to clear up the past while finding out who his father was. After that, he would likely be off again. His papa wasn't a rolling stone, but Leif was. When things got tough, he got out.

Birdie jogged down his steps and just before she reached her mother, turned. "I'm going to ask Fancy to give me the art lessons as a Christmas gift."

"Fancy?"

"My grandmother. She hangs my art all over her house."

"Great. Thanks for apologizing, Birdie. Takes a big person to do that."

Abigail gave him a smile then. Not a big one, but one that expressed appreciation for his being gracious.

If only the woman knew.

But not yet. He'd speak to Abigail later because presently he had to get his midterm test typed up and follow up with the Magnolia Bend Chamber of Commerce president about the upcoming Laurel Woods Art Festival. The chairman of the festival, Hilda Brunet, had contacted him weeks ago and asked him to serve on the committee. Being an artist of slight renown had its pros and cons. This wasn't necessarily a pro because he wasn't the committee type. Yet having some of his work featured in a few galleries across the Southwest and being named an up-and-comer in *Objet d'Art* magazine apparently made him desirable as head of judging. The Golden Magnolia art prize once meant a great deal in the Southern artistic community. The town was hoping to resurrect the festival and the prestige of the award. Hilda had beamed at him when she asked him to be part of the team to put the Laurel Woods Art Festival back on the map. What could he say?

Telling Hilda no didn't seem to be an option.

Yeah, he guessed he had a problem with telling women no.

But surely saying yes to being on the committee wouldn't land him a face full of buttercream frosting.

"Good night, Mr. Lively." Abigail waved, placing a hand on Birdie's shoulder, which the girl immediately brushed away.

"Night," he called, turning to the house he'd leased four months ago. The clean lines and blank canvas of the cottage had appealed to him, and the lap pool in the backyard and nice stretch of zoysia grass for practicing tai chi had sold him. He closed the door and entered the living area he'd furnished with an overstuffed sofa and huge beanbag chairs. The soft carpet beneath his feet had come from his mother's last residence. The walls were covered with huge canvases, some done by his mother and others by friends. The incense he'd lit after Marcie's fit in order to clear the bad karma had burned away, leaving a pungent, earthy scent.

He scooped up a crumb that he'd missed during cake cleanup.

Not exactly the way he'd planned to spend Sunday evening, but then again, what in life came when expected?

Certainly not a marauding drunken bride.

Or an attractive neighbor with a disapproving stare.

Or a twelve-year-old voyeur.

Long ago Leif had learned to roll with the punches, a requirement for the son of a renowned artist, for a kid with no father, for a man with no ties.

Yes, he embraced the unexpected as the poetry of life.

CHAPTER FOUR

Six weeks later

ABIGAIL STOOD OUTSIDE the college classroom next to Birdie and read the sign next to the door. Introduction to Drawing. Leif Lively.

What in the hell had she been thinking?

She couldn't draw a straight line. Or a circle. She'd never even mastered one of those stars *everyone* could draw, though she had managed to render the brick wall with Ziggy peeking over it. That image had graced every notebook cover in middle school.

Birdie turned to her, excitement pirouetting in her eyes. "This is going to be perfect."

That, right there, was why.

Birdie looking at her the same way she'd looked at her when she learned to ride her bike—that was the main reason she'd agreed to the mother-daughter art class.

That, and the fact that the classes were a Christmas present from her mother, Fancy. Her mother had given her a talking-to as they took down the Beauchamp family Christmas tree several weeks ago.

"Why the art lessons, Mom?" Abigail had asked.

"Because you need to do something to connect with Birdie. And that means doing something she wants to do, not what you want to do. Organizing her closet with pink bins and polka-dotted shelf paper is not fun for Birdie."

"I can't draw to save my life, Mom," Abigail had complained while nestling antique glass ornaments in bubble wrap. She'd enjoyed organizing Birdie's closet. She'd even downloaded current music for her iPad, docking it so they could rearrange to some new jams. Birdie had given her a look that could peel paint. So, yeah, she guessed it was safe to say her daughter hadn't enjoyed the closet revamp dance party.

"Your life is not in danger. Just the relationship you have with your daughter. Remember the camping trip we took when you were about Birdie's age?"

Abigail thought to when she was in Girl Scouts and her poor mother had tried to start a fire and chipped her recently manicured nails on the flint. "Okay. Point made."

Fancy had given her the "good girl" smile she'd been using to manipulate Abigail all her life, and just like that—snap! Abigail and Birdie were signed up for Leif Lively's introductory art class at the Southeastern Louisiana University Annex.

"Let's get a seat up front," Birdie said now, motioning for Abigail to hurry up.

"I'm more of a middle-of-the-classroom kind of girl." Anyone who had graduated from St. George's with Abigail would know that was the fib of the century. Abigail loved sitting up front and being teacher's pet. But being that close to luscious Leif Lively filled her belly with crickets.

Abigail had no clue why.

The guy was strange.

He smelled like the vegetarian café her friend had taken her to in Baton Rouge. Like herbs and incense. And he paraded around in all states of undress. Once she'd seen him doing some kind of strange dance with swords in his front yard. He also played bongo drums on his front porch, just like Matthew McConaughey.

And he was sexy, just like Matthew McConaughey.

For the past month, Abigail had been having erotic dreams about Leif. In one they'd been twined in silken cords like circus acrobats, clinging to the peach-colored swaths of fabric as they arched and twisted...totally naked. She'd woken up covered in sweat and so turned on that she'd almost reached for the vibrator she kept locked in a box in her bedside table. But if she went there, she knew she'd never go back. All her fantasies from then on would be about the hot blond guy who lived less than a football field away from her.

Yet despite that restraint, she couldn't stop thinking about Leif naked. Her mind was as rebellious as her daughter.

"I want to be up front," Birdie said, petulance surfing her tone.

"Fine," Abigail breathed, finally stepping over

the threshold. She spotted Leif talking to an older woman with big hoop earrings, bright red lipstick and dyed-blond hair piled on top of her head like a haystack. He appeared to be listening attentively.

As she and Birdie wound through the tables, Leif glanced in their direction, his Nordic eyes widening when they stopped at the long table in front.

"Hey, Mr. Lively," Birdie said, brightly.

Oh, God. Ever since the apology last month, Birdie forgot to be brooding each time Leif's name came up in conversation. The child had even tried to invite him to the Beauchamp family Christmas Eve extravaganza. Luckily, Leif hadn't been in town. The last thing Abigail needed was someone picking up on her attraction to him. Her cousin Hilda would have noticed for sure, which was why Abigail had balked when Hilda had approached her about volunteering for the art festival. The Beauchamps were such a tight-knit bunch they might as well have been high-thread-count bedsheets. Hiding anything from family was impossible.

"Hey, Birdie," Leif said, holding up a finger to the older woman he'd been speaking with. She shot Birdie a look of aggravation before pasting a smile on her face.

Birdie set her drawing pad and pencil case on the table. "I brought my mom."

Leif's gaze strayed to Abigail's. "So I see."

"And I have a new drawing pad and pencils. Fancy and Pops got them for me for Christmas."

Abigail hadn't heard Birdie string two sentences together since the girl had decided to go all Joan Jett on her. But in Leif's presence, Birdie was…effervescent. Abigail found it slightly embarrassing. Leif seemed to understand and kept his warm smile on Birdie.

"And what about your mother?"

Birdie glanced at her. "My mother?"

"Does she have a new pad and pencils?"

"Nope," Abigail said, waving a pad half-filled with Birdie's drawings. "I'm starting with a used pad and pencils."

Leif's smile reached his eyes. "I'm surprised to see you here, but I'm glad you came."

If only.

Warmth dripped into Abigail's belly before she could strike the naughtiness from her head. What was wrong with her? Daydreaming about a guy like Leif? He was too different, too earthy and holistic and—

He had the best smile in three parishes. He had a slight dimple in his left cheek and eyes the color of a fall sky. His jaw had a blockish quality, while his lips were sensuous. How Abigail knew they were sensuous, she wasn't sure, but she was certain he could kiss her up one side of a wall and down the other. And make her beg for more.

"I didn't have a choice. My mother gave us the lessons for Christmas." Abigail pulled out a chair next to an older African-American woman who was knitting a baby blanket while watching them with hawk eyes.

Birdie's thunderous expression told Abigail she'd screwed up again.

"So the college wouldn't give you the money back, huh?"

Abigail smiled. "Nope. You're stuck with me."

"Well, your daughter has to have gotten her talent from somewhere."

Birdie bloomed pink. "I get it from my dad. He's a musician. Don't you play guitar, Mr. Lively?"

"In this class, I'm Leif. Save the mister stuff for school. And, yeah, I play guitar, ukulele and—"

"Drums," Abigail added.

His head jerked toward her. "Not too loud, I hope."

Abigail shook her head. "I saw you playing them once when I was passing out flyers."

Leif's eyes twinkled. "Ah…the flyers about the noise ordinance or the zoning issue?"

"Both." Abigail shrugged. "Didn't do much good, but a girl has to try. I owe it to my guests. They come to the B and B for tranquillity."

"And your banana bread."

"That, too."

Leif glanced up as another woman entered the room. "Well, I'm happy to have you both in class… whether you had a choice or not."

He moved to speak to two college girls who had tumbled into the room in shorts…in January, for cripes' sake. They were wearing UGG boots, slouchy tunic shirts and ponytails that swung in tune with their lazy strides. They took a seat at the middle table, the smell of honeysuckle wafting off them.

Leif took his place in front of the classroom and held up his hands. "Welcome, friends, to Introduction to Drawing. I'm Leif Lively, your instructor, and I know something brought each of you here for a good reason."

Oh, please.

Yet the man sounded so sincere, so welcoming.

"I know some of you are here because you need the credit—" he gestured to the coeds behind Abigail "—and some of you are here because you want to progress in your study of art." This time he looked at Birdie.

"And some of you don't know why you signed up for a nighttime class that will teach you the basics, and hopefully the joy of drawing." At this, he looked at Abigail.

She felt the heat in his glance, a small flare of attraction. Her first inclination was to revel in the idea he found her attractive, but she quickly quelled the thought. She'd misread the emotion in those blue eyes. She wasn't the kind of woman Leif pursued. She'd seen Marcie in her tight, gaudy gown and flashy red Mustang. The bodice had dipped to the woman's navel, showcasing enough boobage to smother a small child. Marcie was young, pretty and nubile—three things Abigail was not.

She had no business reflecting her bizarre attraction to her art teacher back on herself. Something was wrong with her—probably the beginning of a midlife crisis. Turning forty pressed down on her. When her ex-husband neared forty, he'd loaded his convertible with his Les Paul guitar, a new wardrobe and Morgan Cost, the waitress/karaoke deejay at the Sugar Shack in Raceland, and headed to California to pursue his dream of becoming a recording artist.

Yeah, midlife crisis.

"So, let's get started," Leif said, clapping his hands together and jolting Abigail from her reverie.

After they'd been drawing for a while, Leif came by her table where she'd flat-out screwed up her attempt at shading an apple. She really sucked at drawing—but if Leif needed his closet organized, she was his gal.

"That's a nice line," he said, leaning over her, flooding her senses with the heady scent of mint mixed with pure male. Dear God, he smelled good. Not like incense at all, but rather clean with a hint of sultry. Like sitting by a fire atop a mountain, crisp air dancing—

What was she doing? Waxing poetic over Leif's shampoo?

But that didn't stop her from swaying toward him, before she caught herself. "I'm not good at this," she said.

"Relax," he said, his voice stroking over her like a hand over velvet. "You've got the basic concept. All you need are—" using his own pencil, he made a few swoops, rounding out the shading "—a few curveballs in your life. You like to live on the straight and narrow, don't you, Abigail. Or is it Abi?"

His question oiled the creaky, unused portion of her heart. No one called her Abi anymore. Except her mother, now and again. She'd once been like those girls at the middle table—young, silly, full of dreams. But as time went by and she struggled to take care of Birdie while her husband drove into the sunset with a mediocre karaoke singer and the funds from the savings account he'd emptied, she'd transformed into Abigail—a woman who didn't moon over sappy movies or embrace being called by a nickname.

"Abi?"

"Oh, sorry. Um, call me Abigail, please."

His hot breath fanned her neck. "Whatever you want."

Cripes, why did everything the man said sound like an invitation to have sweaty marathon sex? She rubbed away the goose bumps rippling up her arm. "That's what I like to hear."

His soft laugh only increased her awareness of him. Something in her longed to lean back and place her head in the crook of his neck. Wait, had she just purred *That's what I like to hear?* Jesus. What had she been—

"Leif?"

The red-lipstick-wearing middle-aged haystack waved her hand. "I need a little help over here."

The woman asked for his help the same way a woman might ask a man to slip off his boxers and mount her.

But maybe Abigail's imagination hadn't punched the time clock. She glanced around, realization dawning on her. The whole class was filled with women. Not a hairy chest in sight.

Right.

She felt as if she'd been sucked into the Leif Lively fan club. Haystack would likely run for secretary. Birdie might go for treasurer. The kid was good with money, and firmly entrenched in the belief that Leif was the sun, moon and stars—all wrapped up with a bow.

But even though Leif looked mighty fine in his worn blue jeans and waffle T-shirt that left little to the imagination, Abigail had to remind herself that he *was* the David Lee Roth of Magnolia Bend. "Just a Gigolo." "The Ice Cream Man." A "love 'em and leave 'em" sort, with his laid-back charm and sexy blue eyes. She had no business wanting to take a lick from Leif's ice-cream cone.

She needed to remember who she was—a mother, a business owner, a crappy art student. A woman who should leave ice cream well enough alone.

She renewed her efforts to draw an apple, as a new Van Halen song became an earworm—"Hot for Teacher."

LEIF CAREFULLY HELPED Peggy Breaux correct the curve of the pear she'd drawn on her page while avoiding the way she intentionally brushed her breast against his biceps.

"You've got the general idea here," he said, breathing through his mouth because her perfume stung his nostrils.

"Oh, I'm not good at it. But I want to be," she said, her words dripping with double entendre.

"That's why you're here," he said neutrally, lifting his head to survey the class. Most of his students were concentrating on their work. Birdie had her tongue caught between her teeth as she carefully controlled the lines she made with her charcoal pencil. Her mother sat with her head bent, mouth twisting this way and that as she focused on her pretty horrible drawing of an apple. The college girls were texting. Not cool. He shot them a look. The older lady who had been knitting earlier had already rendered quite a nice drawing of a pineapple. She'd returned to her knitting and her needles clacked a steady rhythm that didn't seem to bother anyone around her.

He returned his gaze to Abigail.

He didn't understand his fascination with her. She seemed layered to such a degree that no man could unwrap her. Steely one minute, achingly vulnerable the next. Abigail was the Mona Lisa, complicated and mysterious. Her beauty a masterpiece of shadow and illumination, a study in contrast. He found himself wanting to know her better, to break through the shell she'd built around herself.

If only Abigail could let go.

He imagined her clothes pooling on the floor, her lithe body moving in the moonlight, eyes dark and dilated. Moments before she'd swayed toward him and he'd wondered if she felt something, too.

Maybe…

"Is this better?" Peggy asked.

"Huh?"

"Ha, caught the teacher daydreaming." The older woman chortled, a flirtatious smile curving her lips.

Abigail lifted her eyes, catching his gaze on her. A faint pink stained her cheeks as if she could read his thoughts before she lowered her head and resumed drawing. Maybe…

"Daydreaming's good for an artist. I often think a good deal about what I want before I go after it."

Peggy raised her painted-on eyebrows. "Indeed."

Leif caught himself. "I meant artwise, sly lady."

Peggy liked that, giggling like a geisha, her hand pressed to her mouth.

"That's a good point," he said to the class, noting the college girls slipping their phones into their pockets. "Envisioning your subject is very important, which is why I asked you to sketch from memory a particular fruit that spoke to you."

"Fruits can't speak," Abigail said, humor lacing her tone.

"You must never have tripped on LSD," he joked. Everyone laughed. Except Abigail.

"I'm joking," he said. "Whimsical wording amuses me. I'm aware fruit doesn't talk, Mrs. Orgeron."

She shrugged. "Never know with you guys from California."

"Ah, she has a sense of humor," he said with a smile, enjoying the good-natured volley of words. "And it's Colorado, actually."

"Where it's legal, of course," one of the college girls joked.

"Actually, when it comes to art, I don't recommend using drugs or alcohol as a creative aid. My purest ideas come at times when I am open to the universe, not under the influence of any chemicals. I urge you to think about your subjects, delve into why you are attached to that particular image. When you approach your work, a measure of passion is important. You need to feel something for that piece, for art is the transfer of emotion. The best works of art convey the intent of the creator."

Several people nodded, washing away the fear that he would be stuck with a classroom of students who didn't understand the significance of emotion in art.

"When you complete your drawing, place it on my desk. I want to study each one to help me determine your current level of skill. There are no bad drawings, only opportunities for improvement, so please don't be embarrassed if your banana resembles a—"

Peggy opened her mouth.

"Don't say it," he teased.

The rest of the class chuckled good-naturedly. Except for Abigail. She bobbed her head toward Birdie and he got the drift. No quasisexual jokes. Or jokes about LSD for that matter. He had to remember he had a child in his class.

Even if Birdie had likely heard much worse in the halls at school. St. George's might be a religious school, but its students were worldly thanks to Snapchat and YouTube. Not that that justified making off-color jokes.

He gave Abigail a look that said he understood her unstated concerns. She inclined her head as a thank-you.

"Once you've turned in your drawing you may leave. Your homework is to look for opportunity. Where are the subjects you wish to sketch? Why do you feel compelled to draw them? Tie your emotion to the object and examine it."

Five minutes later, only Birdie and Abigail remained in the classroom. Birdie hunkered over her drawing, eraser crumbs scattering the tabletop, her tongue trapped between her teeth. Abigail stood beside her, shifting in an impatient manner.

"She's almost done," Abigail said as he moved closer.

"Let her finish. No big deal." He pushed a chair into place and met Abigail's gaze. "Someone told me you're taking Shannon's place on the Laurel Woods Art Festival committee. Guess having a baby trumps art, huh?"

"Motherhood isn't something you do part-time."

"No, I guess not."

"You're on the committee?"

He knew she knew that he was. What was her game? Did she not want to appear interested in him? And if so, what did that mean? "Yeah, I'm in charge of procuring judges and cataloging the entered artwork."

Abigail sighed. "It's hard to say no to Hilda. She's more like Attila. That's what Jake calls her—uh, Jake's my younger brother."

"We've met. And, yeah, Hilda as Attila the Hun is a pretty good comparison. My arm still hurts," he said, rubbing his biceps.

"Your arm?"

"From the twisting," he said, nodding toward where Birdie still fussed over the teeniest line of her fruit bowl. "Overachiever like her mother?"

Abigail's lips held a ghost of a smile. "She's serious about art."

"She has natural talent," he said, winking at Birdie when she glanced up, gratitude in her eyes. "So, we'll be working together on the committee? That should be fun."

"I've never found committee work fun."

He was certain Abigail found very little in life fun…and what a travesty. Life wasn't always a party, but he always dressed for one, hoping that whatever lay ahead would be good, soaked in bubbly with a decent dance floor. To approach life as if it were anything less didn't make sense to him. "Well, I'll bring some tofu dip and some beer I've brewed. We'll make it fun."

Abigail's eyes widened. "You're going to bring beer to a committee meeting?"

"No?"

"Probably shouldn't. We're meeting at Hilda's."

"Scotch, then?"

"Uh…"

"Well, I'm running out of the fun stuff." He gave her a wolfish smile just because he wanted to. Maybe he wanted her to feel the full effect of his charm or maybe he simply liked putting her out of her comfort zone. Because it was…fun.

"I'm sure you don't have to bring a thing but a willingness to serve."

She sounded like a Sunday schoolteacher. Abigail wasn't just a good girl—she was the girl everyone hated because she didn't screw up, because she gave others "that look" when they did. "You don't like me much, do you?"

Abigail pulled back. "Oh, no, that's not true at all. We're just very different people with different views."

"But different is good. Makes life much more interesting, don't you think?"

Abigail seemed to turn that over in her head—a virtual convenience-store hot-dog rack. "Sure. I guess that's a good way to look at it."

But he could see she was lying. Different likely scared Abigail right out of those loafers. He glanced at her feet and saw that she wore boots. Sensible boots. The woman was as challenging as a blank canvas. What wonder could be brought forth if one bothered to spend the time creating on her page?

But as tantalizing as the thought of pulling out his brushes and tackling the wall she'd erected was, something inside him warned against delving beneath her stoic facade. It was presumptuous of him to think he stood a chance with the obviously damaged woman. Still, he'd seen her gaze linger on him. He'd felt the interest she tried to hide behind her disapproval.

But Leif never went where he wasn't welcome.

Birdie gave a sigh, lifting her drawing, eyeing it critically.

"So I'll see you at the next meeting?" Leif said.

Abigail had been staring at him, her eyes revealing...desire. She quickly looked away.

At that moment he wanted to gather her close to him, push back that intriguing dark hair with the silver streak, cup her face and break through her wall. Whether either of them admitted it, the music had started. There were only two ways to go—leave the dance floor or hold on tight.

Abigail raised her chin—the gesture seemed stubborn to him—and looked at him with eyes the color of emerald gulf waters. "I'll see you on Thursday."

"Yes, you will."

The sound of the door opening and a "Yoo-hoo"

made them all turn. In the doorway was a man Leif had never seen before.

"This the Intro to Drawing class?" he asked, his gaze landing on Birdie and Abigail. He laughed. "Well, well. There're my girls."

Birdie jumped from her chair, sending it screeching back. "Daddy!"

Abigail stiffened, a panicked look on her face. "Hello, baby doll," the man said, catching Birdie in midair as she launched herself at him. "A little birdie told me my little Birdie was taking art lessons."

"Cal?" Abigail said, her voice incredulous. She appeared to vibrate beside him. As if a unicorn had stepped through the door. Or, on second thought, a dragon.

"Hey, babe." The man looked uncertain but determined.

"What are you doing here?" She moved away from Leif, stumbling over the chair Birdie had abandoned.

The man with the broad face and silver-flecked dark hair offered a smile. "Well, no good reason to keep it from you—I'm moving back to Magnolia Bend. To stay."

"What?" Abigail clapped a hand to her chest before dropping it to her side.

"Yay!" Birdie shouted, sliding out of her father's embrace. "You're going to live here again?"

"You're… Wait, what about Morgan? And LA? You haven't been back since—"

"Don't worry, we'll work it out. I'm home now

and ready to be the man I need to be. For Birdie." He chucked the child under the chin. "And for you, too."

Abigail blinked, looked at the scuffed tile floor and then at Leif, her eyes jumbled with emotion. "But why are you here?"

"I told you—"

"No. Here." She jabbed a finger toward the floor. "Why would you come here? We're taking a class. Couldn't you have waited?"

Cal's smile reminded Leif of an alligator. "Well, honey, when you wake up from a trance and see who you've been for the past few years isn't who you really are, you want to get back to where you belong as fast as you can."

Abigail shook her head. "You're crazy."

Cal's smile flickered. "No, I *was* crazy. Now I'm sane. I'm ready to make things up to you and Birdie. When I crossed that city limit sign, I felt like my life started again. Mama told me where y'all were so I came. I couldn't stop myself if I tried."

"Well, you should have. This is just like you. You don't think. You should have called me. You should have—"

"Mom," Birdie cried, shaking her head. "Don't turn this into something bad."

In Birdie's eyes was a soft plea, a child's yearning for her father. Leif could feel Abigail soften. So could Cal. "We'll talk about this later. This is obviously not the time or place." She shot Cal another look.

The man ignored it, directing his attention to Leif instead. "Sorry for interrupting your class. The older lady said y'all were finished and my girls were still inside. Didn't mean to impose."

Leif nodded because he had no other choice. This was Abigail's business. Not his. And even though an emotion he barely recognized as jealousy welled inside him, he knew this was the universe's way of reminding him that Abigail Orgeron was not his... no matter how much he wanted to rip her from her world of schedules, logic and reason to a place where only sensation reigned. "It's fine."

"Good," Cal said, wrapping an arm around Birdie. "Don't be mad, Abigail. I couldn't wait to see Birdie."

"Really? Wish you had felt the same way at Christmas."

Cal's eyes shadowed. "Don't, okay?"

Abigail snatched the two art pads and pencil cases sitting on the table, muttering "surreal" and "bastard" if Leif heard correctly. "Thank you, Mr. Lively, for the interesting class. I'm sorry about this last bit with Cal. Sometimes life hands you—"

"It's not lemons, Mom," Birdie called, impatience mixing with disappointment in her voice. She looked at her father and beamed. "It's lemonade."

Her father tweaked her nose and Leif almost vomited in his mouth. He couldn't picture Abigail with this slimeball with the saccharine smile and slick ways. He wondered what had happened between them. Wondered if Cal had left her and now regretted his choice. Leif understood regret. But he didn't understand a man abandoning his wife and child. He knew what it was like walking life's path without a father. Not easy.

But there was no sense jumping to conclusions.

Abigail rolled her eyes before passing him a sheet of paper. "Here's Birdie's assignment."

"Thanks." He took the sheet and placed it over Abigail's drawing of an apple…or a blob. Either descriptor worked.

Abigail walked toward her ex-husband and daughter. "Let's take this conversation elsewhere."

"Can I ride with Dad?" Birdie asked.

"Sure," Abigail said, following them out the door. Just as her nice derriere disappeared, she stuck her head inside, the dark curtain of her hair swishing. "Hey, at least I don't have to shower."

"What?"

"My blast from the past didn't bring cake."

Leif laughed. "There's that."

"Yeah. See you Thursday?"

"Thursday."

And then she was gone, leaving nothing but eraser crumbs on the table in front of him.

CHAPTER FIVE

ABIGAIL PEEKED IN at Birdie curled beneath her quilt. The girl slept on her back, mouth slightly open, out like Lottie's eye. Abigail had no idea who Lottie was, but her mother had used that expression all her life and it had stuck.

"She down?" Cal said from over her shoulder. The family quarters were on the third floor of Laurel Woods's main house. Abigail had wanted to revamp one of the guest cottages to serve as their home, but money had been tight after the divorce—and Cal hadn't been there to carry out their former vision. Instead, her part-time employee and friend Alice Ann occupied one lone cottage, dividing her time between Laurel Woods and her son's place in town. Abigail nodded, closing the door with a soft click and motioning toward the stairway. She walked down the stairs to the B and B's common area, Cal following.

When she reached the main floor, she saw Mr. and Mrs. Hendricks had returned from their day-long swamp tour aboard the *Creole Princess*.

"Oh, hello, Mrs. Orgeron," Rita called, wiping snickerdoodle crumbs from her mouth. Abigail set hot cocoa and cookies out each evening for her guests, and her great-aunt Vergie's snickerdoodle recipe always garnered rave reviews. "I adore these cookies. You must tell me the recipe."

"Sorry, it's a secret family recipe. My great-aunt would haunt me if I gave it away…and I'm not sure there's room for any more ghosts in this house. Rufus is about all I can handle."

"Rufus, eh?" Mr. Hendricks laughed. "I've not seen hide nor hair of your Confederate ghost."

"Now you've done it," Cal said, smiling at the older couple. They looked questioningly at him, so he extended a hand and his most charming grin. "I'm Cal Orgeron, Abigail's husband."

"Ex-husband," Abigail said smoothly, wiping up the drips of cocoa on the antique sideboard, ignoring the awkward pause.

"Yes, ex-husband," Cal clarified with a laugh. "And now ol' Ruf will have to make an appearance. He doesn't take to doubters."

"Oh, my," Rita said, looking to her husband.

"Don't worry. If Rufus shows, he's harmless. Not a mean bone in his noncorporeal body," Abigail said.

The Hendrickses chatted for a few more minutes, before retiring for the evening.

"How many people are staying here tonight?" Cal asked, snagging a cookie. They had always been his favorite.

"Five," Abigail said, picking up the tray and pushing through the swinging door into the large kitchen. Cal followed.

"That's pretty good for midweek."

"Yeah, an early Mardi Gras piggybacking onto Christmas has me busier this year." She set the tray on the counter, frowning slightly when Cal snagged another cookie. She didn't like the way he made himself at home. Laurel Woods no longer belonged to him. She'd received the house in the divorce settlement, and though she struggled to make ends meet, she was proud of what she'd done on her own.

"I love these things. If I ate these every night, I could play Santa in the Candy Cane Parade." He patted his still trim stomach.

"Well, it's fortunate you don't eat them every night," Abigail said, sealing the leftovers in the plastic storage container and tidying up the kitchen. A last-minute arrival had made her almost late for the art class, but she couldn't turn away a paying customer.

Leif's image flitted across her mind, and she let it gallop past. She had to deal with the man presently in her kitchen.

"I've got some questions, Cal."

He swiped a hand across his mouth, the silver threads in his hair glinting in the pendant lights hanging over the granite-topped island. California had agreed with her ex-husband. His sun-soaked skin gave him a healthy glow and the crinkly lines around his eyes weren't as pronounced. Maybe he'd had some work done. She wasn't sure. She hadn't really looked at him in years. No reason to take stock of the man who'd broken her heart, betrayed their vows and treated their daughter like she didn't matter.

"About me coming home?"

"No, about the playlist on your iPod." She bit off the "dumb ass" she wanted to add. "Of course, that's what I mean. Why are you back?"

"Because one day I woke up and wondered what in the hell I'd been doing."

"Simple as that?"

Cal shrugged, settling his behind against the counter. "Yeah. Look, I know I've been an ass, but I want to make amends for—" he paused, his dark brown eyes staring into the space above the oven hood "—my midlife crisis? I guess that's what most would call it."

Exactly. That's what everyone in Magnolia Bend had called it.

"Yeah, that's what they call it," she said, casting her gaze at the herbs growing in her garden window. The thyme looked a bit yellow. Maybe she'd watered it too much.

"I'm ready to show you how much regret I have. I want to press Rewind, but I can't."

"Where's Morgan?"

Cal flinched. "We're, uh, not together anymore."

"Why not?"

His gaze rested on her, searching her face for any crack of sympathy. She wouldn't give him any and he seemed to sense this. "She's moved on."

"Ah," Abigail said, unable to stop the corners of her mouth from tipping up. "You were forced to 'wake up' because she left you. Another man?"

He nodded. "But even before that, I knew what I'd done was wrong."

Abigail's laugh tasted bitter.

"I know," he said. "I don't expect your forgiveness. I just hope you'll let me back into my daughter's life. I love Birdie and I owe her so much. I don't know where to start, other than being present."

"I would never keep you from your daughter."

"And you?"

"Me?" Abigail's butt hit the opposite countertop, echoing the jarring in her soul. "What are you saying?"

"I'm asking if there is anything left between us." His eyes beseeched her, his strong throat moving as he swallowed nervously.

At one time, her heart would have leaped at the suggestion of Cal wanting her. She'd known him since elementary school. Big solid Cal, football star, wide smile, girl at each elbow. He'd gone to prep school in Tennessee and returned his senior year, more handsome and confident than ever. With his parents' prestige and his classic good looks, he'd been the quintessential Southern boy, a little wild, but mostly grounded. He'd come by the church tailgate party after a district play-off win, his truck idling with beer in the cooler, and crooked his finger at Abigail. Her sophomore heart had cartwheeled and her friends had sighed. Cal Orgeron wanted her. And she'd let him have her—body and soul. For a time, nothing else existed but Cal.

But she wasn't that girl anymore.

"No." She turned away from him. "It's too late."

"Don't say that, Abi. I lost my mind, had some kind of mental breakdown, but I never stopped loving you."

"Don't you dare." She whirled, jabbing a finger at him. "We're over and you know it. Don't try to play me. I'm not some twentysomething-year-old fool with stars in my eyes."

Cal didn't say anything, just watched her, like a hunter assessing his prey. Abigail wanted to retreat from the emotions throbbing in the room. She wanted to slap the devil out of him. She wanted to scream all the outrage she'd sat on night after night, knowing her hurt did no good, knowing her pain only trickled into Birdie. She hadn't wanted Birdie to suffer any more than she already had.

But Abigail didn't lose control. She dropped her hand and shook her head. "We can't go there, Cal. You regret what happened now because you're alone. You were never good at being alone. You think you can slip into our lives like you pressed a pause button and we froze. You want comfort, and I have none to give you."

Cal inhaled. "Okay, fine. I understand how you feel, but I'm not letting you go that easily."

"News flash, Cal. You don't have me anymore. And I suggest you leave well enough alone." She couldn't believe him. He was going to try to win her back? Sorry…not going to happen.

"I'll concede the battle for now, Abi."

"It's Abigail. Wave the flag now and concede the war. The last thing we need is another thing we're at odds over. Focus on Birdie and doing whatever else it is you're going to be doing in Magnolia Bend. I'm guessing you won't be headlining at the Sugar Shack?"

Cal gave a sheepish smile. "I think my music days are over. LA has a way of stomping out dreams and pissing on them. I'm going to work for Dad. He gave me my old job."

She raised her eyebrows, surprised Buster Orgeron would be so quick to accept his son in the family company again. The president of Orgeron Fertilizer hadn't supported his son's dream of bright lights and big titties. As far as Buster was concerned, when Cal left his wife, daughter and job, he'd lost his damn mind.

Buster and Minnie Orgeron had been gracious to Abigail, helping with Birdie and providing some of the financing for the Laurel Woods renovation. Abigail had let them help not because she thought they owed her anything, but because she'd been fighting depression along with creditors.

Their anger at Cal had stayed in place for a good year, but then, as to be expected, it had faded. Well, it had waned for Minnie. Cal was her only child and she convinced herself that his running from his life in Louisiana had been Abigail's fault, that she'd failed to make Cal happy. Minnie believed they'd married too young and never should have bought the Harveys' historic house. It was too much pressure for Cal. Minnie understood his wanting to leave.

Which was utter bullshit.

Buster hadn't been as understanding, however.

"Well, that's good. You staying with them?"

"Until I can find a place. I'm thinking about the subdivision behind here. Nice to be close by in case you or Birdie need me."

Something shrank inside Abigail. She didn't want Cal that close. It was bad enough he'd come home, showing up like a bad penny just when she'd developed an interest in another man.

Wait.

Not a true interest. A potential flirtation. Or maybe just good fantasy fodder for cold, lonely nights. Leif wasn't an actual contender for her affections. That was crazy, premenopausal delusion talking.

Then she recalled the heat in his gaze when she'd caught him looking at her in art class. So maybe Leif was a contender?

She wasn't a big-boobed Marcie, but she wasn't chopped liver, either. She knew how to kick off her loafers. WD-40 might be in order, but the parts still moved.

"Well, once you get settled permanently, let me know. You have my phone number."

He frowned, pushing off from the counter. "Oh, you'll see me before then. I thought I might come over tomorrow night and take you and Birdie to dinner."

"I can't leave the bed-and-breakfast two nights in a row. But Birdie will want to spend some quality time with her father. She didn't see you for Christmas." Abigail tried to not make her statement an accusation, but it stuck anyway.

"I couldn't fly home. Airline prices were crazy and Morgan—" His voice faded. A hurt expression flitted over his face before he regained control. "Things were unsettled."

So he'd been trying to save his relationship with the twenty-six-year-old, while putting his daughter on the back burner once again. Morgan wore her South Louisiana roots well with her olive coloring, big brown eyes and soft bayou accent. Lithe and sexy, her voice had a mesmerizing, otherworldly quality. Abigail knew because she'd been the dumb ass who had suggested she and Cal watch Morgan perform with her local zydeco band six years earlier. No doubt, Morgan had now moved on to bigger fish who could further her career.

"So you said. I suppose the upside to ending your relationship with Morgan is being more present in your daughter's life." Abigail walked toward the kitchen door, hoping Cal would get the hint. His appearance at the art class had pulled the rug out from beneath her. Abigail needed to think. And plan. And think some more. She had to be careful with Cal and Birdie, especially since her daughter had been buzzing with excitement, her eyes sparkling at the news that her father was home. The child had been cut adrift when Cal left five years ago and she'd never really recovered.

"True," Cal said, following her into the formal parlor with its richly colored carpets, marble fireplace and Audubon painting of a crane standing vigil over the bayou. "I should've called you, but I didn't know what to say. I wanted to surprise Birdie. And you."

Again, warning bells sounded. "We'll figure things out. I'll tell Birdie you'll pick her up for dinner tomorrow night. Needs to be early since it's a school night."

"Good," Cal said, stepping closer to Abigail. She moved back. "I appreciate that, Abi. I mean Abigail."

He ducked his head toward her.

Abigail threw up a hand, hitting his chin. "What are you doing?"

"Kissing your cheek. Saying good-night."

"Don't."

Cal scowled. "Jesus, it's just a friendly gesture. We can be civil, can't we?"

"Sure. As long as it's not with your lips."

"Goddamn, you're cold," Cal said in a hurt voice.

"What did you expect? I'd be the same as I once was?" Abigail opened the front door. "I'll treat you cordially, Cal, because of Birdie. But if we didn't have a child, you would have never crossed this threshold."

Cal studied her for a moment, saying nothing, before slipping out the door, leaving behind the scent of Brooks Brothers Gentlemen cologne. She watched the taillights of his truck fade before she stepped out into the chilly night. The porch that ran across the front of the house was deep enough for several sets of rocking chairs perfectly centered on the plantation windows. Her breath puffed white as she shuffled toward the swing at the end of the porch. Her body felt brittle, her soul tormented by tonight's events. Cal was in her life and she had no say about it because they shared Birdie.

Wonderful, temperamental, soulful Birdie.

She released a breath.

"Sounds like you need a drink."

Abigail nearly jumped out of her skin as she spun toward the porch railing. Standing in the moonlight, clad in a down-filled jacket, was Leif. He held a liquor bottle and two glasses.

"You scared me to death."

His teeth flashed in the moonlight. "You look alive to me."

"What are you doing here?"

"Checking on you."

"Checking on me?" She stiffened, grappling with the idea that Leif cared enough to check on her.

"And bringing you a drink."

"A drink?"

He climbed the steps, his shoes quiet on the slats as he moved toward her. "You expected something more herbal from me? I've heard the rumors, but I don't smoke weed. I do, however, like a good Scotch." His blue eyes were sparkling with warmth. He wagged the bottle.

"I could use a drink." She sat on the swing and glanced at the spot beside her. If he were anyone else, she would have expected him to sit in the rocker a few feet away, but she wanted to feel him beside her.

Yeah. She'd gone nuts.

Leif settled beside her, twisted the lid off the bottle and poured two generous fingers of what looked to be Balvenie. He'd brought the good stuff. Handing her one, he clinked his glass to hers. "I'd make a toast but this isn't about futures or well wishes. You just need a drink, hon."

"No shit."

She didn't bothering sipping. Tonight called for a belt.

"Whoa. Slow down there, soldier." Leif leaned back, his shoulder brushing hers.

Abigail did as he bid and took a demure sip. "Why?"

"What?"

"Why are you being nice to me? You don't know me."

He tilted his head. The move made him cuter. "Best way to get to know someone is over a good Scotch."

"But why would—"

He pressed his finger against her lips. "Shh... sometimes it's enough to be still. Just relax."

It was the second time he'd said that to her, and she let the words sink in. She leaned against the swing, folding in on herself like a bouncy castle deflating after a kiddie birthday party. Sweet comfort.

Leif kicked the swing into motion. The clunk of the bottle hitting the porch was the last sound she heard before the night tucked them into quiet contemplation.

After several minutes, Abigail released a sigh.

"Ah, there you go. A good Scotch cures a lot of things."

"Tonight sucked."

"I know. Feels like getting sideswiped," he said, his voice soft.

"Yeah, sideswiped," she breathed, looking out into the inky darkness as if it could provide a solution to Cal showing up...a solution to her wanting to rest her head on Leif's shoulder. "You know, you're a decent guy for a lothario."

"Lothario?"

"I'm sorry. That's not fair. Just because women hurl themselves at you..."

He stuck a finger to his cheek. "It's the dimple."

She felt her lips twitch before she could stop herself. "Magic, huh?"

His eyes grew flirty. "Is it working on you?"

Inside, she stilled much like the darkness around

them. Should she laugh it off or tell him the truth? Roll the dice or hold her cards close? "Eh, kind of."

"Perfect."

He settled back, kicking them into motion again, seeming content to do nothing more than sit beside her, sip liquor and enjoy the intimacy of not having to say a thing.

An owl hooted and the squeak of the swing created a soothing lullaby as the warm liquor made Abigail feel languid and heavy. After they'd been sitting there for about a quarter of an hour, Abigail stopped the swing. "I should go inside."

"It's late," he agreed, rising and extending a hand. She took it, almost sighing at the warmth of his skin against her cold hand. God help her, but she wanted to feel his arms around her, to give him what she'd denied Cal earlier.

"Thank you," she said.

His eyes stayed soft as he whispered, "That's what neighbors are for."

"Neighbors?"

"And friends."

"Oh." She glanced away, trying not to feel crushing disappointment. Stupid woman. Leif had been doing what he did best—charming anything in a skirt. Not that she wore a skirt. Too cold for that. But he probably flirted with grocery store cashiers, phlebotomists and anyone he came in contact with—including lonely, pathetic neighbors.

"And women I want to kiss."

Abigail blinked. "You want to kiss me?"

He brought her hand to his mouth, brushing a kiss on the back of it. His whiskey breath fanned her skin, causing heat to shimmer in her stomach. "Another time, pretty Abigail."

Abigail stared at the hand he released before snapping out of the trance he'd put her in. "Oh."

"Night."

"Good night, Leif. Thank you."

He picked up the bottle and lifted a hand as he walked down the steps. "My pleasure."

Then he left her with a smile…and a hunger she knew would keep her awake long into the night.

CHAPTER SIX

THE NEXT MORNING Leif skirted the woods behind his house. Laurel Woods sprawled in the middle of twenty acres of pine, hardwoods and scrubby brush that harbored deer, raccoons and pesky squirrels who cut pinecones into his lap pool. Technically, he was trespassing, but since he'd taken Abigail a drink last night, he was sure he could get a pass for traipsing through her woods on an early-morning hike.

Of course, his real intent was to poke around the abandoned cabins that sat to the left of the huge white house.

His mother had lived in one of them.

Hell, he may have even been conceived in one of them.

All along he'd intended to get to know the owner of Laurel Woods. But he hadn't realized the owner was the fusspot PTA president, the kind of woman who made a guy's fellows shrink to the size of blueberries. His neighbors had told him that Abigail had petitioned against the subdivision, even going as far as to solicit the aid of the Historical Society. She'd lost. And she hadn't been happy about it, erecting a huge fence to block the development from her sight.

Leif had practiced patience hoping to eventually befriend the woman. And finally opportunity had plopped in his lap by way of Birdie.

He glanced at the large Greek revival house standing proud and rebellious in the face of the elements determined to wear away the centuries-old edifice. It was just like its owner—defiant and guarded.

As he pushed through the bushes that encroached on the trail, he wondered if anything his mother had created remained in the former slave cabins that had been modified forty-five years ago to house traveling artists. He had little hope since the cabins had been shut up for years, but he'd wanted to see where his mother had lived. Perhaps something remained of her, some hint of who she'd been…of whom she'd fallen in love with.

At the coffeehouse where he sometimes played on Friday nights he'd run into Royal Desadier, the grandson of Simeon Harvey's former groundskeeper. Royal lived with his grandfather Cletus, who suffered poor health but whose mind was still sharp. Leif asked to visit Cletus because the man had been around when artists populated the grounds.

Simeon Harvey had brought in artists from all over the world, including Leif's mother, who had journeyed from her Colorado commune to a studio in one of the cabins. She'd left four short months after arriving amidst allegations of murder, taking with her what she called her one true masterpiece—Leif.

On his birth certificate, there was a suspicious blank. His mother had refused to discuss the man who'd fathered him anytime Leif brought up the subject. He'd received the last name Lively from a small Colorado town his mother had once visited. For thirty-four years, Leif had made do without a father.

And for those same thirty-four years, Leif had pretended he didn't need to know the man who had impregnated his mother. It had been easier to pretend there wasn't a void in his life. But underneath the happy-go-lucky hippie veneer was a small boy who longed to know who his father was.

Calliope had died holding fast to his name.

So Leif had no clue who his biological father was.

And no one in the small community of Magnolia Bend knew Leif was the son of a murderess.

Leif emerged into a clearing and saw an older woman pulling weeds in front of the first in a string of cabins.

Quickly, so as not to be seen, he ducked behind the huge magnolia tree blooming on the edge of the woods. He had no idea who the woman was, but he didn't feel like explaining why he trespassed.

Soon he'd have to confide in someone with regard to the search for his roots. Southerners were definitely hospitable but they closed ranks fast if they knew you weren't one of them. And it had been obvious from his first day in Magnolia Bend that he wasn't one of them. Maybe Abigail would be the perfect person to reveal his true purpose for being here to. Her family had lived in this area forever and she could provide him with some history and help locate someone who might remember his mother.

Abigail.

She was the antithesis of overblown and easy. Her willowy frame harkened back to Jane Austen and buttoned-up dresses. That stubborn chin, dark hair and intellect were reasons to move away from her rather than inch closer. Yet he'd shown up at her house last night, liquor in hand.

Oh, he'd argued with himself about going, but reason had lost.

Why?

She intrigued him. Her edges needed rounding out. Like she needed someone to show her how to freakin' relax, to let the woman beneath the field sergeant climb out and play.

He could do that—ply her with pretty words, treat her to a bit of romance and laughter. But why he felt like doing so was as clear as morning on the San Francisco Bay.

Maybe it was because he knew how she felt when her ex-husband had slammed back into her life. Or maybe there was no good reason. Maybe he was an eternal hopeless dumb ass looking for someone to belong to. Maybe it was a really stupid idea.

Doubling back toward his house, he tried to talk himself out of any further romantic interactions with Abigail Beauchamp Orgeron. But by the time he stepped onto his porch, he'd decided to not worry so much about the reasons he shouldn't and embrace the reasons he should.

If there was one thing Leif always did, it was listen to what the universe told him.

And the wind whispered her name.

"JOHN OFFICIALLY PROPOSED to Shelby," Francesca "Fancy" Beauchamp said, handing Abigail the scissors so she could trim the ribbon on the pillow she held.

Abigail looked at her mother, eyeing her handiwork critically. Thankfully, the pillows looked custom-made, something she could no longer afford. "I thought he'd already asked her? When did this happen?"

"Last night. Your brother drove her out to Boots Grocery, got down on a knee in the middle of the bar and told her he was glad he'd gotten drunk and knocked her up in the bathroom. And then he asked her to become his wife. Can you believe it? Our John?"

"No, the way he grieved Rebecca, I didn't think it possible."

Fancy shrugged. "Me neither, but I'm happy for him. Your father's a bit appalled at the proposal locale."

A bar wasn't exactly the kind of place Reverend Dan Beauchamp frequented but it was where her brother had met Shelby...and where they'd made a mistake that set fate on its ear. "Well, it's hard growing up a preacher's kid. We constantly disappoint."

Fancy smacked her hand, making her drop the scissors. "Don't say that. Your father and I worked hard to raise you as regular kids, to be able to make mistakes without being judged by a ridiculous standard."

Abigail picked up the scissors. "I'm not criticizing you and Dad. It's just how it is. We accept it, but sometimes it's hard. Take John. Who could have imagined someone so steady would topple head-over-boots for someone like Shelby? Never in a million years would I have put those two together." She snipped the ragged threads that had not been sewn down. The ribbon made a perfect square in the middle of the flowered fabric. A pretty monogram sat in the center.

Fancy rose from the breakfast table and carried her empty mug to the sink. The large farmhouse sink anchored a generous slab of marble in the bright kitchen. Her mother's kitchen reflected her personality—cheerful, with clean lines and purpose. Yes, it was an optimistic kitchen if there were such a thing.

"I like Shelby, and sometimes a person needs to be balanced out by someone who is their opposite," Fancy said.

"I like Shelby, too. But they don't look like they'd fit."

Fancy returned to tug at a wayward thread, rolling it into a ball. "Can't go on what we see. Scripture tells us man sees what is on the outside, but God sees a man's heart. Perhaps John—"

"Oh, you can bet he was attracted to that outside." Abigail bounced big pretend breasts against her chest.

"Hush," Fancy said, but laughing anyway. "Speaking of not judging a book by its cover, how are the art lessons going?"

Abigail stilled, her mind flipping to the intimacy between her and her instructor the other night. "We've only had one lesson. I suck at drawing."

"Language," her mother warned.

"Oh, please. *Suck* is a perfectly good word. Don't act like you don't use it."

"Me? I'd never use language unsuitable for a preacher's wife," Fancy said, a twinkle in her eye. Abigail knew very well her mother dropped the occasional curse word, but that was what made Fancy Beauchamp one of Magnolia Bend's most-liked women. She could bake a mean pie and dance the tango, and believed a well-placed curse word was effective.

"The class is filled with women."

"He's a good-lookin' man."

"But odd. He wears sandals with pants and has a ponytail."

"So did Jesus."

Abigail rolled her eyes. "Only you would compare Leif Lively to Jesus."

"Why not? Both have magnetic personalities and woman kneeling at their feet."

"Would you be serious?"

Fancy reached out and tweaked Abigail's nose. "Lighten up, Francis."

"You're quoting *Stripes*? Nice." Abigail stacked the three pillows at the end of the scarred wooden table. "So are you going to get around to what you really want to ask me?"

"You mean something besides how your art lessons with Mr. Yummy Yoga Pants have been going?"

Abigail couldn't help herself. She chuckled.

Her mother brushed her wispy red hair from her face. "Now, that's the Abi I love. Big laugh. Fun girl."

Abigail snorted. Yeah, right. Her mother remembered things differently than she did. "I still laugh."

"Not often enough."

"Yeah, well, life *sucks* sometimes."

Fancy sank into the fluffy armchair. "Come sit and tell me about Calhoun."

Abigail took the opposite chair, releasing a huge sigh. "Well, he's back. He says he's home to stay."

Fancy's gaze dissected Abigail's face. "You think he's serious about staying?"

"He says so. Morgan left him, presumably for another man. Quite frankly I'm surprised she lasted five years with him. She saw him as her ticket out of the bayou, but no one could have told Cal that.

He was so certain he'd missed out on the life he was supposed to live."

"What a dumb ass," Fancy said.

Abigail trilled, "Language."

"Yeah, yeah. I grew up a Burnside. My papa could make a sailor blush. Apple, tree and all that. Besides, I say my prayers every night. The Good Lord knows Calhoun is a dumb ass, so forgiveness should be forthcoming."

"True. So Cal's living with his parents and says Buster gave him his old job at the plant. That surprised me—Buster was furious at him for abandoning us to go chasing fame and fortune."

"Time has a way of healing anger for some folks. Buster loves Calhoun and the man isn't getting any younger. He needs someone to take over the business when he retires."

"Buster will never retire."

"Don't be too sure. Diabetes is tough on the body and he's been having issues with his legs." Fancy stared out at the winter-weary branches of the roses she loved to tend. "So what are you going to do?"

"What do you mean?"

"I've known Calhoun Everett Orgeron ever since he drank his first sip of milk. He's the kind of man who leans on people to get what he wants." Her mother looked at her, eyes soft and sympathetic.

"What?"

"He wants you back?"

Abigail clutched the arms of the chair, worry

clawing her insides. "Why would you think he wants me back?"

"I just told you. I know Calhoun. He'll want his old life. He thinks he deserves it because he's an Orgeron…and because he has a pretty smile. He blew through his savings living in California, played footsie on the beach with a veritable child and now he's home. He's not going to sign up for eHarmony, so he'll be over at Laurel Woods sweet-talkin' you."

"Well, he can bark up another tree."

Fancy reached over and patted her hand. "You never could resist Calhoun."

"The hell I can't." Abigail sat up straight. "He broke my heart. I spent years with my self-worth pancaked, so I'm done with Cal. His smile doesn't work on me anymore."

"Good girl. I've been worried. I saw Birdie yesterday and I swear that child could not stop talking about Daddy this and Daddy that. She's going to make it harder to say no to Calhoun. Birdie will want to be a family again."

"We are a family…just not a family who lives together. Birdie understands that. I just need to come up with some guidelines."

"It won't be just Birdie who'll press this. Be prepared, daughter of mine. Be prepared."

Abigail nodded as her cell phone rang. The clanging bells signaled the ringtone for St. George's. "That's the school. Hope Birdie's sore throat hasn't turned into strep again."

Abigail stood, answering her phone. "Hey, Lelah, don't tell me Birdie's running a fever."

Lelah Carter, the most efficient school secretary this side of the Mississippi said, "Oh, no. She's good. Just thought you should know Cal checked her out thirty minutes ago. Said he was taking her to the Dairy Maid. He's on the checkout list so I let her go with him, but after I thought about it, I figured you should know."

Abigail closed her eyes. This was why she needed to clear her head of fluff and attend to Cal and what his return meant for their lives. "Thanks, Lelah. I don't want her to miss any instructional time, so I'll have a word with Cal." She clicked the end button and collapsed into her chair.

"Everything okay with Birdie?" her mother asked.

"Yeah, she's fine. Cal checked her out to take her to lunch. The man didn't even bother to call and tell me. I would have told him no."

Her mother made a face. "Well, he *is* her father. But this confirms what I said earlier. Things are about to get complicated."

"Yeah," Abigail said in monotone, knowing it was important she sit down with Cal to create some rules regarding Birdie. Having Cal in town, something she'd wanted years ago, felt like being shit on by a bird. She didn't want him here, throwing her life into chaos. She didn't need him bribing Birdie with hamburgers and ice cream and suggesting he could make up to her what he'd destroyed so long ago.

She was tempted to call Morgan and beg her to take Cal back…for the good of everyone.

"I've been praying for a little excitement in your life, but I don't think you want Calhoun Orgeron to give it to you," Fancy said.

"Lord, no," Abigail said. "It's like he's trying to rattle me. Provoke me. That's not the excitement I need."

"Calhoun's a man obsessed with himself, so don't make this about you. He wanted to spend some time with his daughter today and didn't think about how it might affect anyone else. He's all about treats and giggles. Always has been."

"Maybe he didn't mean to ruffle my feathers, but it was irresponsible of him. And what is he teaching Birdie? That it's okay to shirk school for a root-beer float?"

Fancy chuckled. "Oh, come on, Abigail. You're mad because you didn't give your permission. I've sat by for several years watching you exercise such firm control over your life that wiggle room is non-existent."

"Oh, God, Mom. Please don't start this now. Not when I have to go deal with Cal and Birdie."

Fancy crossed her legs Buddha-style and shrugged. "Maybe that's why I mentioned it. Yes, you and Cal need to lay some ground rules, but he hasn't seen his daughter since last summer. Missing a few hours of school won't hurt her. Birdie needs you to give her a break every now and then."

Abigail looked at her mother, at the woman who *never* let her or her brothers miss school unless vomit or a high fever were involved. As a former teacher, Fancy had declared that personal days were for other people. Beauchamps didn't miss school for no reason. "Who *are* you?"

"A woman who has stared cancer in the face and known fear. A woman who realizes that doing the right thing is not always the best thing. A woman who has been watching her daughter hold on tighter and tighter to life, thinking she can control every aspect. Birdie needs breathing room, honey."

"Why do our conversations always turn to my mothering skills?" Abigail shoved her phone into her purse and gathered up the pillows.

"I'm not trying to be critical."

"Yeah, you are," Abigail said, attempting to stuff the damn pillow into the bag it fit in moments before but was now refusing to go in. "Get in."

"Calm down," her mother said in that voice that made Abigail feel anything but calm.

Aggravation exploded inside her. Screw everyone. She was doing the best she could to raise Birdie. So she liked schedules and rules. People functioned better when they had them. And one of the rules she had was her ex-husband wasn't allowed to check their daughter out of school for a cheeseburger. "I know I'm not perfect, but I try really hard to give Birdie parameters. That's my job. To keep her safe and help her make good decisions."

"Sure, but—"

"No. No *buts*, Mother. I have to go. Thanks for the pillows." Abigail didn't give her mother the opportunity to say anything further. She headed for the front of the house. Her mother called out to her, but she ignored her.

Fancy had become increasingly meddlesome when it came to Birdie, constantly bringing up the way Abigail parented. Her mother's well-placed suggestions wore on Abigail. She loved Fancy and certainly valued her mother's opinion, but that didn't mean she agreed with her.

"Birdie needs some breathing room," Abigail mimicked under her breath. "Breathing room, my ass. She needs to straighten the hell up is what she needs to do. And Cal needs to learn there are parameters."

Abigail tossed the bag with the pillows in the back of her Volvo wagon and climbed inside, aware she'd been muttering to herself like an old woman. As she put the key in the ignition, she glanced at her loafers.

The ones she'd picked up at Talbots.

The ones that were like Marcie's mother's.

She pulled down the visor and clicked open the mirror. Her brow had knitted into four lines so that when she relaxed, her forehead remained wrinkled. She rubbed at the lines, noticing the dark circles under her eyes and the ever-present swoop of silver that fell over the right side of her hair. The stripe had appeared almost overnight five years ago—a month after Cal left her.

She wore her life on her face and the look wasn't becoming. She stared at her hands that gripped the steering wheel. Slowly, she unfurled her fingers, wondering why she held on so tightly. Her insides felt just as tense. As if she might snap any moment.

She glanced into her own green eyes and sighed.

Who had she become?

If she stood back and observed herself, what would she see? A thin woman who wore buttoned-up cardigans with old-lady shoes. A woman who drove the safest car available. A woman who organized her calendar with colored tabs. Who wore dark colors. Who didn't date because it was too much of a hassle. A woman who hadn't had sex in one year, four months and a handful of days…with another person, that is. And even going to the trouble of picking up her vibrator had become too big a commitment. She didn't have the energy for invoking fantasies that turned her on enough to go there.

Pathetic, really.

No. Really pathetic.

What was she so afraid of? That she would be humiliated once again? That love would beat her up and leave her bleeding on the ground?

Who lived like that?

She glanced at herself in the mirror again before shifting into Reverse.

CHAPTER SEVEN

Hilda Brunet wasn't a woman to be messed with. She had severe features, a biting wit and shoes that would make a prostitute jealous.

And any project she undertook succeeded.

Because if there were even a small chance for failure, she never touched the project.

So it was expected that each member of the Laurel Woods Art Festival committee pull his or her weight. That meant everyone on the committee would be present in Hilda's parlor on Thursday night to report on what they'd accomplished since October.

Yes, parlor. And said parlor was very pink. Leif sank onto a velvet settee—at least he thought that was the right word for the tufted monstrosity.

"Would you care for tea, Mr. Lively?" Hilda asked. She wore satin pants that looked like pajamas and backless, pointy-toed shoes.

"I brought Scotch." He lifted the cylinder containing the fifteen-year-old Highland Park.

Hilda raised her perfectly waxed eyebrows. "You do know the Baptist preacher's wife is on the committee?"

"She can have some, too," he said, giving her his most charming smile.

Hilda's lips twitched. "You're a naughty boy. I like

you." She set down the teacup and walked across the parlor to pull two whiskey glasses from the cabinet.

No one else had arrived yet. Leif had come early, hoping to find out a little background on the festival and Simeon Harvey. "Thank you," he said, accepting the glass and pouring for himself. "I like you, too."

Hilda folded herself into a chair. "Really? Most people dislike me upon meeting, but I rather like that about myself. Approval is given too easily these days."

Leif crooked an eyebrow. "Maybe so, or perhaps some of us are simply born less intriguing."

"I gather you consider yourself to be not as intriguing? Ha."

"I'm an open book," Leif said, sipping the Scotch and looking around at the virulent pink parlor. The decor didn't fit the sleek, droll Hilda in the least.

"It's interesting you see yourself as such when no one in this town knows anything about you."

He lifted a shoulder. "No one asks much about me. They just look at me like I'm an alien. The little green kind. Not the 'in the US illegally' kind."

"You're easy to look at, alien or otherwise. So why are you here?"

He pointed down and lifted a questioning eyebrow.

"Not my parlor. Magnolia Bend."

"I needed a job."

"Hogwash. A man like you taking a job like the one at St. George's? Don't get me wrong, it's a fine school but it's a small school. Feels to me as though you're hiding." Hilda crossed her thoroughbred legs. "Are you?"

A frisson of alarm slithered up his spine. "Of course not."

"Then you're seeking."

Damn sneaky woman. He'd been wrong about her. He would get nothing from her until she got something from him. "I suppose that's part of it. I am looking for something."

"Ooh," she drawled, her dark eyes brightening. "Do tell."

"You know, perhaps there's something to this intriguing business. I might want you to work a little harder to get my secrets. As you said, things are so readily given these days." He smiled so she knew he teased, but he could see Hilda had found a thread to tug. She'd pull until she unwound his story…or rather his mother's story.

Calliope.

His beautiful, tragic mother.

What reaction would Hilda have if he mentioned his mother's name?

Hilda would have known of Calliope. Of that he felt sure. But something held him back from bringing up the artist who'd once lived on the grounds of Laurel Woods. Even as a small child, he'd sensed that his mother held on to some sort of sadness from her past. And on the day she died, a mere hour before she took her last breath, Calliope had whispered to him, "Baby?"

"Right here, Mother."

"I never told you. Never did," she said between shallow breaths. "He doesn't know about you. I should have told him but I couldn't."

"Wait, who doesn't know about me? My father? You never told him he had a son?" He'd tried not to sound accusing but the emotion was there. He took her hand and stroked it, tried to calm himself. "Who is he?"

"I'm scared. They think I murdered a man. He made me leave. He said no one would believe me. You have to understand. I couldn't let anyone hurt you. You were—" Her words faded and she gasped for air, shuddering.

"It's okay, it's okay," he said, his heart thumping against his rib cage, his mouth dry as sand.

Her words were likely jumbled by the drugs the nurses had given her to make her passing more comfortable. His mother's emaciated, cancer-ridden body was already reminiscent of a corpse, awaiting relief. Her dark eyes reflected madness.

"I didn't do it. Fi-fin—" She opened her mouth as if tasting the air before refocusing on him. "I didn't say goodbye. Can't you see? I didn't tell him I loved him."

"Who? Who are you talking about? My father?"

"I'm afraid, Leif. I should have told him. He needed to know about you. Will you tell him for me?" she whispered before closing her eyes, her breath falling away.

"Wait is he still alive? Where is he, Mother?"

"Mag…Magnolia. Ben…" she managed to say before squeezing his hand as she faded into unconsciousness. She never woke. He left the room not knowing what she meant about murder, his father or her past. He'd gone home, done some research and hit upon Magnolia Bend. He'd made plans to land in town some way and, just like that, the job at St. George's had landed in his lap.

For the past five months he'd imagined his father in every man in the town, but he hadn't made much progress. He told himself it was because he needed the townspeople to trust him first before he started asking questions, but something else held him back—the fear of rejection, the idea that the truth of who his father was might be worse than not knowing.

So even though he could use Hilda's help, he wasn't ready to tell her what he truly sought.

"Oh, a tease to boot," Hilda said, jarring him into the present and the meeting that would take place in ten minutes.

"So tell me about the festival. Why resurrect it?" he asked, picking up a piece of celery from the silver platter holding snacks.

"Well, the festival never should have been canceled, but when the town council decided to do away with it, I was living in New Orleans. I've been here

for a few years now and I petitioned for its revival.
And voilà!"

"Hilda gets what she wants," he said, chewing the
celery, which did little to complement the whiskey.

"Of course," she said.

"When did the festival first begin?"

"Back in the early seventies. Simeon Harvey
was the driving force behind it. His father owned
Tri-State Drilling, which meant the Harvey family
had as much money as Louisiana has mosquitoes.
Simeon was the last of the Harveys and the boy was
an odd duck. He wore the strangest clothes and—"

Leif looked at his fair-trade hoodie, drawstring
pants and rope sandals.

Hilda paused, assessing Leif. "Not like you, dear
boy. Simeon liked frothy clothing, carried a pocket
watch and collected butterflies. He even wore a mon-
ocle. Perfectly nice man, but odd. You understand?"

"I like odd."

Hilda fanned herself, looking slightly uncomfortable. "Simeon came to live at Laurel Woods shortly
after he graduated from a prep school on the East
Coast. His parents left him the estate and we rarely
saw him around town. But one day he showed up at
the city council meeting wearing a pair of silk slip-
pers, a long trench coat and a bad toupee."

Leif lifted his eyebrows.

"I know. Why on earth would a man with so much
money buy a bad toupee? But anyhow, he submitted a proposal calling for a springtime art festival

to celebrate local artists. Since Simeon volunteered to fund the first festival on his own, even offering a top prize of one thousand dollars for the winner of an art competition, the council chaired by my late husband couldn't think of a good reason why we shouldn't give the festival the green light. All Simeon asked was that we name it after his historic home, so the Laurel Woods Art Festival was born in 1973. The top prize in each artistic category was named the Golden Magnolia."

"So this guy loved art."

Hilda made a face. "Well, of course. His mother had piddled in ceramics and collected paintings. For a while, the Harveys owned a Monet, a Rembrandt and a sculpture by Degas, all of it sold when oil took a downturn. The family recovered financially, but Simeon got hooked on art. At one point he even tried to create a commune on the grounds of Laurel Woods."

Leif already knew most of this from his internet search, but feigned interest anyway. "A commune, huh?"

"He converted the old cabins on his land into studios were artists could live and work. He even brought in artists from Europe. Made Magnolia Bend a more interesting place, I'll tell you. Artists are—" she paused, her gaze lifting to meet his as she searched for the right word "—a colorful bunch."

Leif chuckled. "Nice save."

"Oh, pish, I forget myself sometimes. That's what happens when you get old."

"How would you know? You're not old."

Hilda looked him straight in the eye. "I love a man who lies to make an old woman feel better."

"So what kind of artists came to Laurel Woods? I live right behind the place and I'm fascinated that an artistic community once thrived there."

"Well, *thrived* is a relative term, but there were all sorts of creative types—weavers, painters, some guy who made sculptures out of old tires. Some were older, many were young. All were interesting."

He still had no insight into his mother. He'd hoped Hilda would mention Calliope in some manner, but then why would she? As she'd stated, all kinds of artists flocked to Magnolia Bend on the whim of a rich man with a bad toupee.

"Of course when Simeon died, his nephew did away with all those crazy artists—his nephew's words, not mine. None of us were surprised by Bart's refusal to continue housing the artists since Simeon's death came under suspicious circumstances. It was—"

The doorbell rang.

Damn.

Hilda rose and pressed her hands against her pants, a habit her cousin Abigail shared with her. "Right on time. I had worried people might be late." She headed toward the foyer, leaving Leif to wish she'd finished her sentence.

Was his mother involved in Simeon Harvey's death? Was that why she was so terrified?

He couldn't bring it up to Hilda again without her growing suspicious, but an internet search could net him more info, and if that failed, the parish library no doubt had copies of the *Magnolia Bend Herald* in their database.

"Come right on in, Mr. Godchaux. You, too, Violet. Oh, and here comes Abigail," Hilda said, stepping back so a man with silver hair and a woman with a ginormous cross necklace could enter. Leif would bet his Taylor guitar the woman was the Baptist preacher's wife.

He rose and shook hands with the other committee members. Mr. Godchaux settled on the far end of the settee and eyed the Scotch like a dog eyeing a bone. Violet eyed it like it was a porno mag.

Abigail entered, looking a little softer around the edges in a fluffy sweater. The peach color didn't necessarily flatter her, but it did make her appear more approachable. Hilda eyed the sweater much the same way Violet eyed the booze.

"Hello, everyone," Abigail said, perching on the edge of a straight-backed chair Hilda must have brought from the dining room to accommodate the meeting. "Does everyone know Leif? He's the art department head at St. George's."

Leif smiled, first at Abigail and then at the two others. "I missed the meeting in October. Nice to meet you. It'll be cool working on this committee."

Mr. Godchaux said, "Yes, cool. You can call me Ed."

Hilda clapped her hands. "Now all we're waiting on is—"

The doorbell rang.

Hilda spun toward the door and Leif took the moment to look at Abigail. "Hello, neighbor. Thanks for introducing me."

Abigail crossed her legs. She wore a pair of not so sensible heels and a skirt that looked a bit shorter than normal. Being that the temperature had dropped in the past couple of days, he wondered why she'd elected to show off those very nice legs.

For him?

God, he hoped so.

"Hello," Abigail said with a tight smile. "I see you brought some refreshment after all, Leif."

He shrugged. "I know you said it wasn't necessary but I'm indulgent."

The preacher's wife frowned and studied her cuticles. Ed reached for the bottle.

"Nothing like a little toddy on a cold day," Leif said, looking pointedly at Abigail's bared legs. She tucked the sides of her skirt under her thighs.

"Indeed," Ed said as the sound of masculine voices filled the foyer. A second later Abigail's ex-husband and a tall man with a thinning hairline entered the room.

Hilda gestured to the other chairs set up near Abigail. "Cal, Bart, have a seat. We need to get started."

"Hello, everyone," Cal said. Abigail closed her eyes as if she were sending up a prayer. Heck, maybe she was. Her ex popped up like a weed, unwanted, but impervious to the fact. The only silver lining to having charming Cal show up and surprise Abigail was the recognition that her high heels and skirt hadn't been for her ex's benefit. The thought warmed him as much as the Scotch did. "Mother decided the best way for me to reaffirm myself as a good citizen of Magnolia Bend was to take the family's place on the committee. Looks like you guys are stuck with me."

Abigail looked as if Medusa had glanced her way—completely stone-faced.

The other man who'd come in with Cal appeared bored, tugging at his shirt, which looked a size too small.

"And some of you know Bartholomew Harvey. His family started the art festival and he's agreed to serve as an adviser."

Bartholomew inclined his head and offered a faint smile. "Call me Bart, please."

Leif felt as though pieces were dropping into place. He needed access to Bart and here the man stood.

"Now." Hilda clapped her hands again and picked up a stack of colored folders. "I have prepared these folders for you. Please put them in the binders I gave you at the first meeting. This is the schedule of events, mock-ups of the posters that will go out next week and the press release."

For the next forty-five minutes, Hilda led the meeting, and Leif spoke when it was appropriate, trying like the devil not to stare at the woman across from him. He did manage a peek at Abigail's smooth legs and that niggle of concern that was a permanent fixture between her pretty eyes. It made him want to ruffle her feathers, mess her up a little bit, make her laugh. Slide his lips—

Hilda snapped her binder closed. "You all have work to do and I would like a report by next week. Leif, as soon as you've confirmed the final judges, I'd like a bio for each to place on the website. Please include Bart as an honorary judge."

Leif looked at Bart, the man who had once owned the land his house sat on, the man who might be able to help him in his quest for the truth about his parentage. "Would you mind if I stopped by to pick your brain about the judging criteria?"

Bart startled. "Me? I don't know a lot about art, but I suppose I could look it over."

Violet was the first to stand. "I'll get back with you after I speak to Patty Ann about the catering menu. Nice to meet you, Leif."

"You, too," he said, knowing the minister's wife didn't mean what she said. No skin off his nose. Ed was the next to make his exit after saying his good-byes.

Abigail remained in her chair, scribbling notes.

She was in charge of the parade grounds and facilities, including security and ticketing. A big job but probably not for Abigail. He waited because he wanted to walk her out, but it was obvious Cal had the same idea.

Finally, she stood. "Thanks, Hilda. I'll do some checking around with the organizers of The Revel up in Shreveport. I think they have an auction every year for seed money and we might plan something similar for next year, especially if we can get some interest from galleries in New Orleans."

Hilda studied the two men standing beside her cousin. "Sounds like you know what you're doing."

Veiled words.

Cal placed his arm on Abigail's elbow. "Can I grab you for a sec, Abi? I'll walk you out to your car."

Abigail tugged her elbow free, shifting her gaze to Leif. "Later, Cal. I need to talk to Leif."

Inside, Leif gave a fist pump. Score. Then he chastised himself. Abigail was probably only using him as an excuse to get away from Cal.

"Okay, then I'll stop by later. I wanted to continue the conversation we had earlier." Cal dogged her footsteps as she moved into the foyer.

Abigail shook her head. "Not tonight, Cal. I'm tired."

Leif didn't want to look as if he were eavesdropping so he turned to Hilda, who held out the Scotch bottle.

"No, keep it," he said.

Hilda shifted her gaze from the back of Cal's head. "You obviously know what a lady needs."

The way she said it was more thoughtful than flirtatious.

Then she leaned closer. "You're a laid-back, generous man, but there are some things worth going after. Know what I mean?"

Leif refused to look toward where Abigail stood with Cal. "You're barking up the wrong tree, Hilda."

"I don't think so. I haven't seen her wear heels in over a year."

"And you assume it's because of me? That's a huge jump. Her ex just showed up in town. Maybe she wants him to know what he's missing."

"Maybe, but I don't think so." Hilda smiled like a cat with feathers caught in her whiskers. "There's one thing I know and that's human nature. Abigail needs someone who can pop her buttons. And she's interested in you. Make no mistake. So the question is, Leif…"

He crooked an eyebrow.

"Are you a good button-popper?"

Leif laughed. "Oh, Hilda, if there's one thing I do know…"

This time she crooked the eyebrow.

"It's that Abigail's not going to let me touch her buttons."

"Come now, Mr. Lively. I have faith in you. Bet you could unbutton things with that delightful smile alone."

"Use my teeth, eh?" He snapped his pearly whites and grinned.

"Jesus, go practice double entendres with Abigail, you devil. She needs some romance in her life…and some 'curl her toes' sex."

Leif stilled as Cal's angry "Later" signaled the end of Abigail's conversation with her ex-husband. "Her life is pretty complicated at present."

Hilda's tilted her head, darting a glance at Abigail. "True. But never let complicated stand in your way. She was once full of laughter. I miss that about her."

Her words pummeled his resolve. That was the first thing he'd noticed about Abigail. Okay, the second. The first thing had been her frown at the custodian's failure to fill the ice chests for back-to-school night, which she'd tempered with a pat on the shoulder and an offer to help him. Then he'd noticed the absence of something in her smile. Such a pretty woman who looked so… He didn't really have the words.

Joyless?

So what would it hurt if he flirted with her? Gave her a little attention? Or a lot? It wasn't charity. Abigail was an attractive, single woman who he suspected hid her sensuality beneath a cloak of PTA-attending, Volvo-driving, committee-organizing responsibility. Question was—could she let go enough to let him in?

Just because she put on a skirt and heels didn't

mean she wanted to straddle him...or even share a cup of coffee with him.

There was only one way to find out.

He picked up Hilda's hand and kissed it.

Hilda sighed. "If I were thirty years younger and fifty percent more flexible, I'd lock you in my bedroom."

Leif chuckled. "And I'd let you."

He turned toward where Abigail stood looking half aggravated, half uncertain. "Coming, Abigail."

"Let's hope so," Hilda drawled before waving to her cousin.

"You're a bad girl, Hilda Brunet," he whispered.

"Yes. And let's see how bad a boy you can be for my Abigail. I'm putting money on you."

Leif shook his head before heading toward Abigail. "You needed to talk to me?"

Abigail blinked. "Huh?"

"You told Cal you—"

"Oh, yeah. I wanted to talk to you about Birdie."

Leif opened the door, tucking his folder under his arm. He stood aside to let her pass. "So what about Birdie?"

"Why didn't you tell me you were naked when she spied on you?"

CHAPTER EIGHT

THE CRISP NIGHT air met Abigail as she stepped out her cousin's door. She'd been stupid to wear the short skirt. Her knees probably looked wrinkly and it was too cold for her legs to be bare. And the ridiculous high-heeled pumps pinched her toes. Vanity, thou art a bitch.

All because of that damned Marcie.

No.

All because Abigail wanted Leif to see her as something other than Birdie Orgeron's staid mother.

And then she'd gone and extinguished the flirty look in Leif's eyes by bringing up that little nugget—her daughter spying on him when he was naked.

It was like farting in an elevator.

"Uh, Birdie told you that?" Leif asked, walking down the steps slightly behind her.

"No. Shelby did."

"Shelby Mackey? The substitute at St. George's?"

"Yeah. She's about to marry my brother John. We were talking the other day and your name came up."

"Oh?"

"She brought up the whole spying thing. I don't think Shelby meant to let it slip. But she caught Birdie doing it."

Leif fell silent, no doubt trying to figure out how to handle the situation. Abigail still didn't know how to handle it. She'd thought about asking Cal but felt he'd overreact, especially since the naked guy had been Leif Lively. If anything, Cal knew who his competition was. Her ex-husband had grown accustomed to being the best-looking man in a room, accustomed to being the golden boy of Magnolia Bend. His shine had worn off, though, and it didn't take long to realize half the women in Magnolia Bend fluttered when Leif passed by.

"So Birdie didn't confess?"

"No, why?"

"Well, she told me the naked part. And I wanted to tell you when the time was right, but I had hoped Birdie would do it herself. Secrets are never a good idea." Something flitted over his face…as if he knew all too well that secrets led to heartache. Maybe that's what had destroyed his relationship with Marcie.

"So why have neither of you mentioned it to me? It's an important issue."

"It is…and it isn't."

"No, it *is*. It's one thing to spy on someone. It's quite another to spy on a naked man, Leif."

"Why? Do you really think your daughter is attracted to me?" Leif said as they walked toward her car. His own small Mazda was parked across the street. "Really?"

"I don't think Birdie knows what she is. She hasn't gone through puberty yet."

"But she's a normal kid. Curious. Besides she doesn't have a father."

"She has a father."

"I meant at home. Cal hasn't lived there in a while, right? So the male physique is not something she sees much of. I didn't make a big deal because she was embarrassed…and the human body shouldn't be treated as something to be ashamed of."

The thought of his wanting to protect Birdie warmed her. But still, she was annoyed both he and Birdie had kept this from her. "I don't know… ugh. I'm handling this all wrong. I'm just going to apologize for my daughter. I'm not sure why you were naked, but she had no business spying on you. Makes me feel like a bad parent."

Leif took her elbow, turning her toward him. "Why would you feel like a bad parent? Kids do those things. It's normal. Didn't you ever do a little looky-loo as a kid?"

Abigail felt her cheeks heat. "I had brothers."

"So the answer's yes."

Abigail looked at him. He'd gathered his hair into a low ponytail bound with leather and wore a hoodie that broadened his shoulders somehow. In the glow of the moon he became a Nordic warrior. Except for that smile. No fierce warrior had a charming smile that dropped panties.

Abigail squeezed her knees together just in case.

"You're just being nice," she said, noting her mood had shifted. Something in the way he talked smoothed the wrinkles in her thoughts. Relaxed her.

"You think this is me being nice to you?" His eyes dropped from hers to her mouth.

Without thinking about what she was doing, she slid her tongue over her lips. Something pinged. Or was it a buzz? Whatever it was made her girl parts zing. Zag. Awaken. "You're nice to everyone."

"You need someone to be nice to you, Abi."

His words slithered over her like silk, making her lean in slightly. What would it be like to taste him? To take just a little piece of Leif for her very own, for fodder on those cold nights. But what then? How would she ever be able to attend his art class or see him in the halls at Birdie's school knowing she'd been so desperate as to rise up on her toes and—

"I have plenty of niceness in my life," she said, moving back, latching onto common sense as a drowning sailor might a flotation device. She felt overcome with desire, as if she'd drunk love punch rather than water during the meeting.

"Then maybe it's not nice that you need," he said, stepping forward. He wasn't letting her retreat. "Maybe you need something else."

Desire beat down common sense. Common sense was so overrated anyway. Hadn't she done the commonsense thing for a long time? And what had it gotten her?

Lonely nights, an empty bed, no fulfillment.

So maybe…

Abigail darted a glance to her left and then to her right. No one was around.

"What do you think I need?" she asked, lifting her gaze to his.

Those eyes. She could dive into the blue depths. They were full of teasing, warmth and crazy sexiness. Those eyes made her want to forget about propriety. To forget he was too cool, too young, too different from her. Those eyes made her want to sin.

"I think you need a little naughty in your life, Abi."

She gave a short laugh. "So a guy who just last month got cake in the face from a woman wearing a Vera Wang wedding dress is giving me advice about being…irresponsible? Okay."

"I didn't say irresponsible," he said, his hand grasping her hip and tugging her toward him. "I said naughty."

At his touch her body lit like a match on sandpaper. Full-on blaze. She put her hand on his chest, noting the firmness. This guy worked out. Had muscles. Even had one of those six-packs that models sported. Yeah, she'd noticed that when she saw him doing his crazy sword dance outside.

"Maybe you should show me the difference."

"I should," he said, his gaze on her lips as his head lowered.

Yes. He was going to kiss her and she was going to let him. Because deep down underneath all her reservations was a wild need to have him touch her.

And why should she not kiss him?

No good reason.

She grabbed the front of Leif's shirt, slid a hand around his neck, tugged his head down and kissed him hard. Like she meant it. Like she had control of her own damn life.

But the moment her lips touched his, everything changed.

The world widened, then narrowed.

Abigail softened, hyperaware of her fingers pulling his hair out of the leather strap. Aware of his scent, a clean yet sultry smell. And his lips so warm. He tasted like whiskey.

Leif Lively tasted like pleasure.

Abigail pulled back, breaking the kiss.

"Well, all right," Leif said, giving her a little smile.

She blinked, scrabbling with the fact she'd kissed Leif. She hadn't waited on him. She'd taken what she wanted and it was good.

A horn blew.

Abigail jumped as headlight beams swept over where she and Leif stood, her hand still on his chest, his hand still on her hip. She stepped away. "Good Lord, we're in the middle of town."

Leif ignored the headlights moving toward them. "You weren't thinking and maybe that's something you need to do more often."

"You sure like to hand out advice, don't you?" She stepped out of the headlights realizing she didn't know what on God's green earth she needed.

A psychiatrist, probably.

Leif merely lifted an eyebrow. A very sexy eyebrow.

Damn it. Why did he have to be so good-looking? And so nice? And so eager to make her do naughty things? And why had they been interrupted? She had wanted that kiss to go on and on, so she could take the memory home.

The horn sounded again.

"Crap on a cracker. Stop honking at me," Abigail called out, flipping the driver—whom she assumed was Cal—the bird. And that's when Violet Joyner's head popped out of the driver's-side window.

"Abigail Orgeron, you ought to be ashamed of yourself!"

"Oh, my God!" Abigail slapped a hand over her mouth.

The Baptist preacher's wife jabbed a finger toward her. "I waited all this time to tell you the Milners' cat climbed inside your open car window. And that's how I'm repaid?"

Violet pulled away with a small screech of her tires.

Leif started laughing. "You just flipped off the Baptist preacher's wife."

"Oh, my God," Abigail repeated, dread sinking inside her. What had she just done? Violet was a huge gossip. What if she'd seen Abigail kiss Leif?

"Come on. That was funny," Leif said, laughter still in his voice.

"That was not funny. That was horrible. I can't believe I just up and—"

"Flipped someone off? Kissed a man? Took a chance?" Leif lifted her chin. "Come on. It was a little funny."

Abigail felt her lips twitch. She shouldn't smile. It was wrong, but even so, laughter bubbled inside her. "It was a little funny."

And then the laughter escaped. "The look on her face. That was…so… Oh, God. I wonder if anyone has ever flipped her off before?"

"Probably not to her face, but trust me. Yes, they have." Leif tucked a piece of hair behind her ear. "You're pretty when you laugh. You should laugh every second of every day."

Abigail stopped laughing.

"Let me take you out," he said, shoving his hands into the pockets of his pants. "I want to drink wine, make you laugh and make up for that awful kiss we just had."

Awful kiss?

If that was awful, what was his definition of spectacular?

"That's probably not a good idea. You're my child's teacher. Heck, you're *my* teacher. Things are complicated in my life right now. Cal is—" She didn't really know what to say about the way her exhusband had waltzed into her life, ready to pick up where he'd left everything. Ready to be the family man he'd forgotten to be.

"Just a date. We don't even have to kiss. Unless you want to. I personally like the kissing thing, but I can restrain myself. But the laughter thing has to stay."

Abigail stood there, the moonlight making Leif look so…yummy. "I don't think it's a good idea."

"It's not a good idea—it's a great idea. I'm thinking about a picnic."

"It's the end of January."

"I know. We'll have it in front of the fire pit. Marshmallows, hot cocoa and my famous tofu hot dogs."

She made a face.

"Okay, screw the tofu dogs. I'll think of something else."

"So when?" She was actually entertaining the notion. And why not? She was an adult who could spend time with another adult…and maybe share a few kisses.

"Saturday?"

"Can't. I have a full house."

"Monday, then."

Four days away.

Leif stepped close to pick a piece of lint off her sweater. She inhaled his scent, hoping like hell she didn't resemble her mother's dog, who took every opportunity to shove his nose in everyone's crotches. "If you say yes, you can type up an agenda."

"For a date?" She snorted, trying to stop her stomach from flipping at his nearness. "That *is* tempting."

"Fine. Throw in the label maker."

"Why would we need that?"

"I'll let you label my body parts," he drawled, his voice still teasing as he stepped even closer. Her breasts almost brushed against his chest.

"Sounds perverted."

"I like perverted."

"You would," she said, her mouth twitching into a smile for the second time. Smiling was becoming a habit around him.

"So?"

"If you let me bring my label maker, I'll do it."

"I knew you were kinky."

Abigail laughed and this time he was the one to stop her...with his lips. It was a nice kiss, sweet and full of promise.

He kept it rated PG, and when he pulled back he said, "The only requirement is you wear something with buttons."

"Beg your pardon?"

"A blouse or dress with buttons."

"Why?" She'd never had a man request that she wear something particular. "I need to practice something." He dropped his hands from her waist and picked up her right hand, bussing a kiss on it just like an old-fashioned suitor. Then he shoved his hands in his pockets and strolled toward his car, whistling "That's Amore."

Abigail shook her head and climbed into her car, wondering how he'd bamboozled her into going on a date, wondering if she had time to get a pedicure, a new pair of jeans and a bikini wax.

No, strike the bikini wax.

Not going to happen.

Besides, an earthy guy like Leif would probably prefer her au naturel.

Oh, dear Gussy. She was thinking about her pubic hair. Had she lost her ever-lovin' mind? She wasn't going to have sex with him. They were going to eat tofu dogs.

But still, she might want to get a new bra. One with lace and pretty satin bows.

As she pulled away from the curb, she heard a meow.

Oh, right. The Milners' cat.

ABIGAIL GLANCED AT BIRDIE, who had finished up the supper dishes before pulling out her binder to work on math. It was Friday night, but Birdie had always been the kind of student who couldn't rest until her weekend assignments were complete. Friday had gone smoothly for Abigail, even after a sleepless night pondering the previous night's events.

Yeah, the woman who was rarely indecisive waffled about following through with the date. This strange thing they had between them had her spinning…and unable to rest. She kept flipping toward going, then flopping toward calling it off.

The whole thing boiled down to her fear of getting hurt again. Leif could call it "just a date" but she'd never felt pulled toward a guy the way she felt pulled toward Leif. At least not since Cal.

It made her feel naked.

But she'd never been a chicken, running away from difficult things. So maybe—

"Mom," Birdie said. Abigail banked her indecision and looked up from the praline scones she'd been placing on the cooling rack.

"Yeah?"

"Do you still love Daddy?"

Oh, God. She knew this would come, but she couldn't lie to Birdie.

"No, I don't. Well, at least not in the way a woman loves a man. I do care for him because he was my first love and he gave me you." Good answer.

"Can you fall in love again?" Birdie examined the nub of her pencil, not making eye contact. "Cassidy's mom and dad got divorced and then they got remarried. So I guess it can happen."

"Sure," Abigail said, walking to the drawer to grab the plastic wrap, reminding herself this was natural. Birdie wanted a family. Every kid wanted an intact family. "But it's unlikely. When people fall out of love and divorce, there's usually something wrong…or something between them that can't be mended."

"Oh," her daughter said with a frown. "But it could happen, right?"

Abigail shrugged. "It could."

"Okay," Birdie said, biting her tongue and tackling the fractions scattered across her work sheet.

Crap.

Abigail understood why her daughter wanted Cal at Laurel Woods. They'd been happy here once, but that was long ago. Before Cal went dog-assed crazy and drove away leaving both her and Birdie crying and confused. Abigail had hurt for a long time and Cal's setting her aside for another woman, a woman who was only three years out of being a girl, had done irreparable damage to her esteem. Even though five years had passed, she still doubted herself when it came to relationships. Was she pretty enough? Smart enough? Talented enough in bed? On the outside she was strong, an ox pushing and pulling against life. On the inside, she was a naked baby bird content to stay in her nest.

Which was why Leif scared her to death. Whatever it was they had between them had tentacles. As soon as she pulled one loose, another latched on. Part of her wanted to let go and succumb, part of her wanted to punch desire in the face and run from it.

But one thing was certain—Cal had no place in her life other than being Birdie's father.

Abigail went to the fridge and pulled out the milk. Pouring a glass, she sat next to Birdie.

"Hey," Abigail said, snitching a cookie and taking a big slug of milk before sliding the glass toward her daughter. "You want some?"

Birdie shook her head. "I'm trying to do my homework."

That meant *don't talk to me.*

"Hey," Abigail said again.

"What?"

"Your dad and I are over. You know that, right?"

"Whatever. I'm busy, Mom."

Abigail sighed. "It's great your father is in your life again, but he won't be coming home to Laurel Woods."

"Why not? He didn't leave me. He left you." Birdie lifted her gaze, anger reflected in her green eyes. Same old story. Birdie had implied many times that Cal's leaving was her mother's fault. It was how Birdie dealt with the fact Cal actually left both of them. If Birdie had mattered enough, if Cal hadn't been such a selfish bastard, then he wouldn't have left…not even if it meant missing his last shot at fame.

"Okay," Abigail said with a measured breath. "There's something else I want to talk to you about."

"What?"

"Don't take that tone with me."

Birdie gave her a flat stare.

"It's about Mr. Lively."

"What about him?"

"You didn't quite tell me the truth about spying on him, did you?"

Her daughter's face paled, green eyes widening.

'Look, I know you're curious about the opposite sex."

"Oh, my God, Mom."

"We haven't really had the talk we need to have about, uh, sex," Abigail said, stumbling over that word. She wasn't ready, but Birdie spying on Leif took away any options. "Being nude isn't bad, but it's private. It's not something you put on display. Just like we talked about girls at school wearing short skirts or tops that show their cleavage."

"Please stop, Mom. Please."

"You need to know what is right and what is wrong. Mr. Lively thought he was alone and you violated his privacy without his consent."

"I didn't mean to. Not at first, and I already know this. So just stop. I said I was sorry and that was humiliating enough."

Abigail opened her mouth to respond but a knock sounded at the kitchen door. Abigail prayed it wasn't Cal. This conversation was the wrong one for him to interrupt.

The door opened and her brother Jake stuck his head in. "I smell scones."

"You have a good nose," Abigail said, trying not to look aggravated. She rarely saw her baby brother anymore. "What are you doing here? It's Friday night. No hot date?"

Jake stepped inside and shut the door. "What? Two sexy women like you all alone and I'm supposed to go elsewhere?"

Birdie gave him a relieved look. "Thank God you're here."

Jake cast Abigail an amused look. "Let me guess, you were about to drop down and give her twenty?"

Abigail gave them both a frosty look. "How did you know I was making scones?"

"A little birdie told me."

Birdie snorted. "He called earlier."

Abigail looked at Jake, who wore tight faded jeans, cowboy boots and, if her nose were to be believed, a little too much cologne. He had a sleek smile, compact body and overt charm that drove the ladies of Magnolia Bend and its surrounding parishes wild. He looked like a walking ad for sex, something she could see even if she'd once changed his diaper. "You know, if you could find a woman to cook for you, you could settle down."

He'd already scooped up a scone and devoured it in three bites. "Mfff."

Abigail retrieved the milk and a glass, shoving them toward him.

"Thanks," he said after he'd washed down the scone. "Delicious. Can I have another?"

Abigail nodded. "I have only two couples staying tonight so you can take a few with you."

"Aw, you're my favorite sister."

"I'm your only sister."

He grinned. "Exactly."

Abigail never minded her brothers dropping by. Of course, John worked so hard in the sugarcane fields, it was rare to see him, but maybe with Shelby in his life, Abigail would see him more. Her older brother, Matt, was the principal of St. George's so she saw him at school. He'd recently separated from his wife and Abigail worried about him. That was a sister's job, wasn't it? Or maybe it was just her. Worrying could easily become a career.

"So how are things at the station?" she asked, wiping the counters. Jake popped up on the island. Abigail gave him the evil eye so he slid off, pulling out a chair across from Birdie, who had gone back to her work sheet.

"Good. An opening for captain is coming up. The only competition I have is Eva."

Jake had spent four years at Louisiana State University studying prelaw, but after a car accident involving his best friend, he changed his direction and went to school to become a firefighter. He'd been certified to be an EMT last year, though he remained full-time at the fire station. The man had become intensely committed to saving lives…and becoming a honky-tonk legend.

"Great opportunity, but don't discount Eva. She looks gentle but she's like a praying mantis. You may wake up without a head."

Jake made a face. "They only kill their mates, not the person up for a promotion against them."

Eva Monroe was the only female firefighter in the parish and also one of Jake's closest friends. "Speaking of which, is she still dating that guy? Uh—"

"That's over," Jake said, dabbing up crumbs with his pinky finger and popping them into his mouth. "I'm not here for idle chitchat."

Abigail glanced up and Jake jerked a thumb toward Birdie.

"Oh." Abigail dropped the dishcloth. "Hey, Birdie, I need to talk to Uncle Jake for a minute. Can you go finish your homework in your room?"

Birdie's lips flatlined. "Why do you treat me like a baby? I can carry on a conversation with Uncle Jake. I'm not a kid anymore."

"It's not that," Jake said, pulling a hank of Birdie's hair. "I need to discuss something private with your mom, 'kay?"

"Is it about sex? 'Cause I know you have sex with a bunch of women."

"Birdie!" Abigail shouted.

"What? I know about sex, Mom, so you don't have to have your little talk with me. Geesh."

Abigail opened her mouth, then snapped it closed. How much did Birdie really know about sex? Yeah that "talk" thing breathed down her neck. She'd bought a few books to help her discuss the birds and the bees with her daughter, but until Birdie had forced her hand, she'd been too chicken to broach the subject.

Another parenting fail.

Jake laughed. "Man, I love coming by here."

"What?" Birdie said, with a lift of her shoulder. "Maddie Free told me all about sex last year. She brought one of her brother's *Hustler* magazines to a slumber party. The pictures were really perverted, but then we read about sex and stuff in her mother's *Cosmopolitan* so I know how it works."

"Hustler?" Abigail said weakly. She looked around for the stool she'd shoved out of the way earlier and sank onto it.

Jake popped up, grabbed the wine Abigail had opened and poured a glass. Setting it in front of her, he said, "Drink."

Abigail lifted the wine, seeing her brother distorted though the glass. He looked like a wicked jack-o'-lantern. She took a long draw and caught Birdie with a gleam of triumph in her eyes. The little shit. After two more gulps, Abigail set down the glass. "Birdie, Uncle Jake isn't here to talk about his sex life, and I'm disappointed you took your lessons about sexual intercourse from a disgusting magazine. We'll talk about this later. Gather your things and get upstairs."

Birdie glared at her. "I didn't like the disgusting pictures in case you're worried. Man, you have some crazy sex hang-ups. You should really start subscribing to *Cosmo*. They have all kinds of articles on things like the G-spot and how to—"

"Birdie!" Abigail could feel the heat in her cheeks. Birdie smirked, knowing exactly what she'd done. "Upstairs now, missy."

Her daughter slammed her book shut and stalked toward the door.

"'Bye, Birdie," Jake called.

"I'm going by Brigitte now. 'Bye," she said, pushing out the door with a swish of dark hair.

"Holy shit," Jake said, his shoulders shaking with mirth.

"Oh, shut up." Abigail ran a hand over her face, grappling with the fact that she now had to correct the information her daughter had gleaned from a porno mag. She drained her glass, almost wishing it had been Cal who'd dropped in rather than her brother. Birdie would never have dropped that bomb on her dad.

"So what's up with her...besides now knowing what the G-spot is?" Jake asked.

"Oh, God," Abigail said, shaking her head.

"It's okay, Abi. Don't you remember your *National Geographic* collection and finding that copy of *The Joy of Sex*? It's natural."

"Maybe so, but Birdie's mad at me because I told her that I wouldn't entertain the thought of her father living with us. That was her way to get back at me."

"Does Cal want to reconcile?"

Abigail shrugged. "Probably. He hinted about making things up to me."

Jake's eyebrows lifted.

"Yeah, but that ship sailed...to California with Morgan. He's not coming home. At least not to me."

"Cal's an ass."

"Understatement of the year," Abigail said, pouring another glass of wine. "You want some?"

"No. I'm meeting Kate over at Ray Ray's in thirty minutes."

"Is she the stripper?"

"No. She's a librarian."

"Oh, sorry. So what's up?"

"Well, it's ironic you already mentioned it, but I came by to warn you about Cal. I overheard him talking to Merv at the general store and he said something about finishing the work on the cabins."

"My cabins?"

"I'm assuming. It was so strange. Like going back five years. To hear him tell it, he was already living here. He even made a nagging wife joke about you."

"He what?"

"He said, 'Better get going on this before the wife calls a contractor.'"

Abigail didn't have the words. The nerve of that man, thinking he could step into his old life and no one would say boo about it, much less her. "He's lost his marbles."

"Or is just being Cal. The man's so full of bullshit, I have to wipe my boots after standing next to him."

"I thought he'd get the message the night he turned up like a bad penny."

"He doesn't operate that way." Jake strolled over to the scones. "I just thought you ought to know. He's going to push this. Be prepared."

"First, I find out my child got her sexual education from *Hustler* and now Cal's going around town acting like he's still my husband. The hits just keep on coming." She might have to open a new bottle of wine.

"You have a lot going on. I'm sorry." Jake shoved his hands into his pockets.

"Thanks. I'll talk to Cal. And Birdie. And if there's anyone else who needs some counseling, send them on over."

"I may need some counseling on finding the G-spot…but I can ask Birdie about that."

"You are evil," Abigail said, throwing a dish towel at him.

"Of course." Jake caught it and wiggled his eyebrows before tossing the dish towel toward the sink. "Oh, I'm bringing Kate to John and Shelby's wedding. Kinda had to with them choosing to have it on Valentine's Day."

"They're getting married in three weeks?"

"Wait, you didn't know? You mean, I know something before you?" He performed a victory dance.

Abigail rolled her eyes. "Jeez, Jake. You'd think you won a gold medal."

"I did. The gold medal of one-upping my sister." Jake moved toward the door, scooping up a few scones to take with him.

"So, are they getting married at the church? I can host the reception. Let me grab my reservation book and—"

"Relax, Mom said she's hosting a small reception at her house."

"But I have all this—"

"Don't," he said, his hand on the doorknob.

"What?"

"Don't run roughshod over everyone. Mom can give a reception without you taking over. Handle Birdie. Handle Cal. Take a bubble bath. Go to a movie. But don't try and take over every aspect of every person's life."

"I don't."

Jake snorted. "You don't know how to relax. Your picture's next to the antonym for *chill* in the dictionary."

Abigail picked up a second bottle of wine, annoyed that Jake knew her so well. She waggled it. "I can chill."

"That's a start but don't use getting wasted as a replacement for relaxing. One drink's good for you, five will land you passed out in the kitchen with burned scones." Jake pointed to the oven as he waltzed out the door.

"Oh, crap," Abigail said, grabbing an oven mitt and rescuing the scones from getting burned. She huffed out a breath, suddenly feeling messy and out of control. The thought of Cal acting like he was still her husband made her stomach hurt. Stubborn man.

Well, it was time to put things in order. Do as she'd always done when faced with unmade beds, unbalanced checkbooks and people who didn't fall into line.

If she could just make everything…

She tossed the mitt onto the counter. She didn't

deal well with feeling out of control. She wore a girdle on her life, holding in the bad stuff even though it pinched. It was just easier that way…and the same reason why she couldn't complicate her life by seeing Leif on a personal level.

Leif felt messy, like something that couldn't be pinned down. He laughed too loudly, smiled too much and didn't care what anyone in Magnolia Bend thought about him. He couldn't be cinched into her world even if he made her feel something she never thought she would again.

Not desire. This was more than her girl parts going zing. Leif brought light into the dark places inside her, into the places that had long gone dead. He made her wonder…what if?

And that was dangerous.

Not that she hadn't gone on dates before. She'd even managed a three-month relationship with a home builder who lived in Baton Rouge. He'd been her rebound relationship, scratching an itch, until they decided the distance was too hard, code for things were getting boring. So it wasn't as though she hadn't had some kind of a life as a single woman. Just nothing worth bragging about.

But Leif was bragworthy with his disarming smile, hard body and oozing sex appeal.

So why was he interested in her?

She'd never won any beauty prizes, although she knew she wasn't homely. Her eyes were her best feature, her stubborn silver swath of hair her most dramatic and thanks to good DNA she had remained slim and athletic. But other than those things, she was a normal forty-year-old woman fighting crow's-feet and sagging boobs and contemplating reading glasses. She wasn't like the other single moms who haunted the halls of St. George's carrying cupcakes, splashing around smiles, wiggling in tight jeans and sending unstated invitations over top gravity-defiant breasts. Those women knew what to say, how to seduce and play those games that Leif was no doubt very good at playing.

Abigail didn't play games, especially footsie. Not when she'd spent the past few years being the referee, keeping order between the lines.

She had no business letting herself go with Leif Lively.

No business at all.

CHAPTER NINE

LEIF WALKED BESIDE Hilda and her French bulldog, who wore an absurd striped pink sweater.

"Come on, Clyde. Do your business so I can take Leif over to the mercantile," Hilda said to the dog, who merely looked up with an adoring grin and promptly lifted his leg on the tire of Leif's car. "That's a boy."

Leif frowned at the dog, but he supposed he'd had worse on his tire than dog pee so he kept walking. "Isn't it closed?"

"Of course it is, dear. It's Sunday and everything closes in Magnolia Bend on Sunday. Except the Short Stop. People still need gas."

Leif remained silent as they walked toward the middle of downtown. Surrounding them were yards tired of winter, some clinging to ragged pansies and the occasional snapdragon. The large houses on Hilda's street gave way to smaller Arts and Crafts– style houses. Magnolia Bend was a pretty town with a white gazebo in the main square and an imposing courthouse with a history that included an infamous hanging judge. Quintessential small-town USA with Creole zest.

"Now over there is where they strung up a poor man before civil rights." She pointed to a huge oak tree. "Such violent history here in Louisiana. Seems so long ago but it wasn't all that many years really."

Leif inhaled, letting his breath go slowly as he stopped at the tree of twisted darkness, sunshine streaking through, dappling the rich soil where the roots fought to emerge. "I never knew Magnolia Bend had that sort of past."

"Oh, yes. All up and down this river. Started with the Native Americans. That's what they call them these days. When I was young, we called them Indians. Took away their land. Many of them hid in the bayous with the pirates and runaway slaves. We've endured slave revolts, the War of Northern Aggression." She laughed. "People still think of it that way. Can you imagine? But along this river, such hardship and such beauty. I hate that past, but I love this land. Thought about moving back to New Orleans, but my people have lived and loved here for so long. It's in my blood, you know?"

"I can't imagine feeling that way. I feel like I'm from nowhere, yet everywhere."

Hilda stopped. "Why are you here, Leif?"

"Is that why you asked me to brunch? To get at my secrets," he teased, even as fear nattered away at his gut. The Harveys were still part of this community and Southerners seemed to hold grudges.

"That or have my wicked way with you. Of course, my sciatica has been terrible and the arthritis just as bad, so I'd say you're safe…though I must say, your loss."

Leif choked down a laugh. "Indeed."

Hilda started walking again. "Over there is where my husband's grandmother lived. Eloisa Rigaud Burnside. She was quite a lady. Some even suspected her of voodoo."

"Voodoo?"

"Heavens, yes. Her family came from Saint-Domingue after the slave revolt and settled in New Orleans. Her mother had been a slave, her father a soldier in the French military. Her *grand-mère* was a mambo—that's a priestess—and it's said Eloisa inherited her knowledge from her."

"Wow." Leif enjoyed the sun on his shoulders as much as Hilda's tour of Magnolia Bend. She prattled on about her kinfolk, all of whom had owned land—including one who'd had a brothel outside of New Orleans—and he listened because it was required of a guest.

He supposed he was a guest. He'd been surprised by her phone call that morning, which had woken him from a dead sleep. When he'd arrived at her house, still longing for the comfort of his bed but not willing to miss an opportunity to ask about his mother, she'd suggested a walk before they dined.

"So, have you made progress with the button-popping? I'm not one to look out windows or anything, but I'm sensing a promising direction."

"You sneak," he said, nearly tripping over uneven pavement. "So this is about Abigail?"

"Of course it's about Abigail. She's my cousin."

"Why are you so vested in my screwing your cousin? Not that I have or am. It's odd."

"Oh, hush. Sex is sex. Nothing odd about it." Hilda jerked Clyde's leash a bit too hard and the dog stumbled over a large rock he'd been sniffing on the edge of a driveway. "But that hound dog Calhoun Orgeron is sniffing around, trying to stake his territory."

"And you think I can dissuade him?"

"Yes, and give Abigail a good time in the process."

"You know I'm a person, not a tool."

Hilda stopped and patted his cheek. "Of course you are. I didn't mean to imply otherwise, but the timing is so good. And I could see plain as day that you made her uncomfortable. And you watched her like a hungry man."

"So?"

"So, no one makes Abi uncomfortable. I could see she thinks you're a hottie."

Leif snorted.

"That's what the kids call a man who heats up the blood."

"I knew what you meant, I merely—" He paused. "Never mind. You were saying?"

"Did you make progress?"

"None of your business," he said, as they reached the park in the center of town. The area was deserted, probably because most people were in church…or at home sleeping.

"Ah, I see. You are going to be a hard nut to crack…and I mean *nut* in the most complimentary of ways."

"It's fine. I've been called a nut most my life. Probably because of what I wear." He indicated his linen trousers and rugged hemp shirt. He'd elected to wear sneakers, which had been providential, since they'd walked over a mile.

"Very impolite of them. I, personally, would dress you in Hugo Boss or Calvin Klein, but if you prefer to look homeless, so be it. I would never take away your right to be fashion challenged." She sashayed toward the square in her lululemon yoga pants and matching hoodie. Her fluorescent Asics completed the bold look. Hilda Brunet was a Magnolia Bend fashion plate.

"Thank you, Hilda," he said with a smile. "If I hired on to be your kept boy, I'd let you dress me in a suit woven by eight-year-old children in Taiwan, but since your sciatica is acting up…"

Hilda pulled her designer sunglasses down her nose to look at him. "Damn, I do like you."

"So you've said."

"Such power you have in that smile." She patted his cheek again. "Employ it on my cousin, will you?"

"*Heil*, Hilda," he said, falling into step with her as they crossed the street and headed toward an old-fashioned general store owned by the Burnsides.

"And a sense of humor, too. Lucky Abi," Hilda

said, stopping before the large plate-glass window. "There."

In the center of the window stood a bronze sculpture of a young boy holding a small bird in his hand. He knew right away that it was his mother's work. He glanced at Hilda. "You know."

"That your mother's Calliope? Yes."

Leif turned, studying the beauty of the sculpture. "How?"

"You look like her."

Leif turned away from the display, which showcased the upcoming art festival with the poster Hilda had designed and several other pieces of art the owners of the store must have collected over the years. He walked away to lean against a cast-iron parking meter. "You knew her?"

"Yes. I was on the committee then and Simeon was most insistent that your mother's work be in the showcase tent. He was enamored of her."

"Simeon Harvey was in love with my mother?" Leif shook his head as the possibility Simeon was his father poured over him like the hot wax his mother had used in her castings.

"Oh, not the way you think. Simeon was gay, but he loved things of beauty, and your mother was one of the loveliest creatures I've even seen. He wanted her like he wanted a Monet. Had nothing to do with romantic love or sex."

Leif stared at the storefronts across from them. "I don't understand."

If Simeon had been gay, he couldn't be Leif's father. Or could he? If Simeon was attracted to beauty, maybe it didn't matter. Maybe the man played both ways.

"Simeon loved your mother as a friend. He loved her work, loved her very nature. Calli possessed a quality not many others do—she was a free spirit, very ethereal but at the same time earthy. When she wasn't creating, her head stayed in the clouds."

Leif gave a hard laugh. "Yeah, you knew her all right."

Hilda nodded, jerking her head toward the way they'd come. They fell into step together.

"So what really happened to Simeon? I heard that—"

"Your mother killed him?"

"Pretty much," he said with a shrug, trying to distance his emotions from the facts. This was why he'd come to Magnolia Bend. He needed to know what happened when his mother lived here, needed to know who his father was. The key to his future lay in his mother's past.

"Are you here to clear your mother's name? And if so, what took you so long?"

"I didn't know anything about her life in Louisiana until she passed away several months ago."

"I'm sorry. She passed at a young age."

"Cancer."

"Mmm." Hilda's expression was somber and respectful. "And your father?"

He stayed quiet for a few minutes. Hilda watched him.

Finally he bit the bullet. "That's the thing. I don't know my past and that keeps me from my future. Not knowing my father didn't really bother me before. As a child, if I thought at all about him, it was in the context of some fairy godfather who might swoop in and save me from being normal. Beyond that, what did I care? As I grew into a man, I put away thoughts of who my father was or what had happened between him and my mother."

Hilda stopped. "So now we reach your real reason for being in Magnolia Bend. It's not about a job or even clearing your mother's name."

"I guess."

"You seem embarrassed. Why? Everyone wants to know who they are. Everyone needs to belong to someone."

Leif stiffened. "No. I don't need a relationship with him. I just want to know who he is. Calliope admitted he didn't know about me and she wanted me to right that wrong. To fix it for her."

"That's a little selfish of her."

"How?"

"She left the dirty work to you…and obviously gave you no idea of where to start. Why didn't she reveal his name?"

"She was dying. It wasn't a good death."

Hilda started walking again, her gaze fastened on the houses they approached. "Well, if you can forgive her, I certainly have no business criticizing. I'll do what I can to help you discover the truth."

"I don't want people knowing, especially since most think my mother's a murderer."

Hilda shook her head. "I never thought Calli could do something so heinous. Some people were willing to believe because money was involved."

"My mother didn't care about money."

Hilda sighed. "Yes, but people are foolish. They like to believe the worst, and money always seems to be motive. Besides, half the women in town disliked your mother solely because she was beautiful. They didn't like their farmers' attention on another woman. Rumors ran rampant that spring and summer. Some implied your mother was more than a free spirit, more like a free woman."

"So she was painted a whore before she was painted a murderer?"

"Only by some small-minded people. Calli didn't like conventions and some people are scared of letting go of their godforsaken morals about what is right and wrong. For them, it was easier to cast your mother as some loose woman who sculpted naked people and nosed around after Harvey money."

They walked a little farther, nearing the two-story Victorian Hilda called home. "I'll try to remember who Calli ran around with. I'm sure Simeon kept some kind of record of the artists who were there. A few local boys chased her a bit, but I can't remember who tickled her fancy. I'll look through my old albums. I have pictures from the festival that year since I was the historian for the Laurel Woods Art Foundation. Maybe something will ring a bell. You can also talk to Carla Stanton. She now lives south of Baton Rouge but she worked for Simeon back then."

"Thank you. I figured I would talk to Mr. Desadier and see if he remembers my mother...or anything from the night Simeon died."

"Good plan. The person who would have the most knowledge is Bartholomew. He was there that night, but be careful. Bart gained a lot the night his great-uncle died and he might not be willing to tell the whole truth. Know what I mean?"

Leif jerked his head around. "Do you think he's covering up something?"

"I'm not saying that. Just reminding you this is a small town and the Harvey family is still influential in this state. What Bart said, no matter that he was likely half-drunk with strong motivation to run your mama out of town, carried weight then...and still does now."

"I'm not afraid of the truth, Hilda. I'm willing to bet my next paycheck that my mother had nothing to do with Simeon's death. She might have been there that night, but being responsible? No." He climbed the front steps.

Hilda pulled her keys from her pocket and inserted one in the lock. "Just a friendly reminder because you're an outsider and, though Magnolia Bend is filled with hospitable people, they can close ranks pretty fast. Doesn't mean there's not a place for the truth, but you might not get much help."

He nodded. "I'd appreciate your discretion in regard to my father."

Hilda smiled. "Oh, honey, I'm the soul of discretion, and I won't tell anyone about any potential button-popping because, Lord Almighty, that woman needs a good screwing."

"I never said I would," Leif said, entering the overly warm house, inhaling the cinnamon smell wafting from the kitchen.

"But I'd bet my next paycheck you will."

"Do you get a paycheck?" he asked.

"No, but if I did, I'd bet it," Hilda said, sweeping a hand toward the dining room shining with crystal and silver. "Let's eat, darling. I'm starved."

ABIGAIL WASHED THE DISHES, handing them over to Shelby to dry. Sunday dinner at her parents' house had been almost comforting in its normalness. Abigail, her brothers and their families gathered after church every Sunday to dine on Cajun ham, gumbo, rump roast or some other equally delicious fare while catching up with each other. Another Beauchamp tradition.

"So are you excited about the art festival in March? John told me you're on the committee," Shelby said as she brushed by Abigail to set the dried platter on the counter. They'd drawn cleanup duty after playing Rock, Paper, Scissors with Abigail's brothers, but she didn't mind. Standing at the sink of her child-hood home always made her feel normal.

"It'll be good for Magnolia Bend."

Shelby chuckled. "You sound like you work for the tourism department. This family is so funny that way."

"Well, it's our town, you know. Magnolia Bend is important to us from the rusted old jungle gym at Meyer Park to the almost dried-up Hunter Mill Pond. This art festival will bring in tourists and help local businesses. So I'm all over helping the town and myself."

"I wasn't being critical, just teasing. John gave me the old soft-shoe sell on staying here every time I spun around. I actually like how much this family loves their community."

Abigail sighed and shut off the hot water, hand-ing over the last serving bowl. Outside she could see her brothers helping their father move a huge barbecue he was planning to clean up and use to smoke chickens during the festival in order to raise money for the church's youth program. "I'm sorry. Just prickly today."

"Because of Cal? Or Leif?"

"What?"

Shelby started putting away dishes. "Well, Jake told John that your ex-husband's been going around acting like you never got divorced."

Abigail frowned. "I can see you're going to fit right in with this family."

"What?"

"Nosy people."

Shelby immediately looked contrite. "I'm sorry. I wasn't gossiping. You're almost my sister-in-law and I care about you."

Now Abigail felt like crap. That's how Shelby made people feel—as if they should apologize. She was too damn nice. "It's okay. I guess I never stopped being prickly about Cal."

"His leaving was hard." It was a statement, not a question.

Every time Abigail thought about the day Cal left, her stomach cramped. She knew—hell, everyone knew—that the reason she was so careful with herself was because she'd essentially made a complete and utter ass of herself that night.

People didn't forget a woman begging a man to stay…and then passing out in the driveway.

Five years ago Cal had chosen the annual Fourth of July family-and-friends picnic for his big getaway. Abigail had pleaded to host the festivity at Laurel Woods instead of having it at her parents' house. She and Cal had worked so hard getting the grand old house ready to open as a bed-and-breakfast. Fresh paint, new doors and windows and all the trim complete on the new house had Abigail itching to show the place off several months before they were to open for guests. The day had been perfect—low humidity, plenty of good Louisiana food, old-fashioned games on the lawn and, outside of Speedy Wilson losing his best hound dog somewhere in the fields, incident free.

Until Morgan arrived.

Cal had been going to Houma to play some sets at a local club. Abigail had chalked it up to something he needed to do to blow off steam and make the extra money they needed for the new cabinet hardware. So she hadn't said boo about his disappearing a few times a week to do something he loved. But as soon as Morgan arrived, walking down the long driveway carrying a suitcase and with her guitar slung over her back, Abigail had gotten a weird feeling. She'd rushed out to greet the singer even though she'd met her only twice. Cal had introduced her to all their friends, telling them they'd been playing together for the past two months. Abigail had had no clue Morgan had been playing gigs with Cal.

Just before dark, Abigail headed to the detached garage to grab some bricks to anchor the cylinders Jake had brought for launching the fireworks being set up in the field. And that's when she'd seen Morgan loading her suitcase into Cal's convertible— the one he'd bought only months before. He'd come around the corner carrying the red Samsonite luggage—the same set they'd taken on their cruise a few years ago—walking quickly, smiling at Morgan.

When Cal spied Abigail, he froze, his smile turning into an expression of panic. "Abi."

"What are you doing?" she asked.

Cal looked at Morgan, who dropped her gaze and

studied the cute sandals Abigail had complimented her on earlier.

"Well, I left a note, but you might as well know," Cal said, walking to the car and placing his suitcase next to Morgan's.

"Know what?"

"I'm leaving."

Her brain couldn't seem to process. "Leaving? To go where? Everyone's waiting on the fireworks to start."

"No, I'm leaving for good."

Abigail struggled to make sense of the words coming out of her husband's mouth.

"Morgan's coming with me. We're going to California. There's a guy out there who thinks he can get us on a label. Until then we're going to play some shows and get some exposure."

"Wait, what?"

"I'm sorry, Abi. This—" he turned to the house and spread out his hands "—isn't what I want anymore. Maybe I never wanted it."

"You're the one who bought this house. I don't understand. What's happening?"

Cal shook his head. "I can't stay here anymore. I don't love you and I can't be who you want me to be."

A baseball bat smacked her in the face. Not literally, of course, but it might as well have been. Felt the same. "You're leaving me? Like right now?"

"We have to be there by Thursday, so we need to go tonight." Cal sounded matter-of-fact. Like he was settling a bill or discussing the likelihood the Saints would make it to the Super Bowl.

"Don't do this," Abigail said, dropping the keys to the storage shed and stepping toward Cal. "We're about to open the bed-and-breakfast. We're married. We have a child. You can't do this."

"Everything will be fine," Cal said, his voice soothing, the way he calmed Birdie when she had a nightmare. "You're strong and Birdie will understand. I have to do this. I have to try." He nodded at Morgan, who slipped into the car.

"Try what?"

"Try to be something more than what I am here. Being with Morgan has helped me realize I gave up on my dreams too early. I have to do this. I have to try."

Abigail looked at Morgan's bowed head. "With her? Wait, you're *with* her?"

He looked away quickly and took a breath. "We fell in love. Real love."

"You've been sleeping with her? This is insane. Cal, you can't do this." Abigail placed her hand on his arm. "Don't do this. You have a family. I love you."

Cal patted her hand and pulled out his car keys. "I'm sorry, Abi. I know you don't understand. I wanted to get out of here and save you from a big scene. Just go on back with your family. Let's make it easy on both of us." He removed her hand from his arm and opened the car door.

"Cal. Stop. You can't. This is crazy," Abigail cried, trying to hold the door. He tugged it from her grasp.

"Don't do this. You're making this hard." He made it seem like she was the one in the wrong.

"Making this hard?" she screeched, finally losing it as he cranked the engine. "You're leaving me in the middle of a party we're hosting, and you think I'm making this hard? You've lost your goddamned mind, Calhoun."

"Let's just go," Morgan said, her voice rising in a panic.

Cal put the car in Reverse and gave it gas, not saying another word. His handsome face was set in stone, his dark eyes refusing to make eye contact as he applied the brakes and then put the car into Drive.

"Cal, don't do this. Please stop. You can't leave us," Abigail said, feeling the tears on her face, her heart shattering in her chest at the realization her husband was walking—no, driving—out on her.

The car leaped forward, kicking up gravel, and rolled down the side driveway of the house. Abigail jogged behind him, slapping the rear fender. "Stop. Cal, please stop!"

But he looked straight ahead, moving fast toward the front of the house, toward where everyone they knew and loved milled about eating watermelon, drinking bourbon and lighting sparklers for the kids. Abigail had strung red, white and blue paper lanterns around the perimeter in order to bring some festive light to the celebration. When Cal's car rounded the house, half the people turned and watched with puzzlement at the sight of Calhoun Orgeron sitting beside the young Morgan, driving away without a backward glance.

Abigail ignored the guests, focusing singularly on her husband racing out of her life.

"Cal! Please come back. Don't do this!" She ran behind him, certain she could change his mind. Make him see what he was doing. Make him understand that she loved him and couldn't live without him. She had to stop him. For Birdie.

For herself.

"Cal!" she screamed as he passed the entrance to the circular drive and picked up speed. "Please don't leave us. Stop!"

But he wasn't stopping.

Abigail jogged halfway down the drive, watching the taillights bounce toward the highway. Finally bending over with her hands on her knees, she gasped for air…and for her sanity.

What had just happened?

It didn't seem possible that the man who had massaged her shoulders that afternoon after she'd rinsed out all the drink tubs had loaded up his car with his guitar and a barely legal karaoke singer.

And left her and Birdie.

Jake reached her first. "What in the hell is going on?"

Matt screeched to a halt seconds behind his

younger brother, not even winded by the run. "Did Cal just drive off with that singer?"

"He left me," Abigail said, wrapping her arms around her waist, suddenly chilled despite the heat of the July night. "He's gone."

"That motherfu—"

But Abigail didn't hear the rest of Jake's oath. The ground had come up to meet her, and the last thing she saw before the sweet gift of darkness enveloped her was the sight of two taillights turning west onto the highway.

Shelby dropped a serving spoon and jarred Abigail from the horror of that night.

"Sorry," Shelby said, her ponytail swinging as she shelved the bowls in the built-in china hutch, her rounded belly brushing the ceramic tiled counter. "I know you don't want to talk about Cal. I shouldn't have brought it up."

"It's okay. Truly. It happened long ago and I'm mostly over it." In her mind she still smelled the acrid fireworks, still felt the nausea when she'd opened her eyes to her friends and family looking at her with pity.

Absolute pity.

"So if it's not Cal making you prickly, is it Leif?"

Abigail turned away, pretending to wipe up soap suds. "Why would my daughter's art teacher be on my mind?"

"He's really cute. And nice. And he asked me about you the other day."

"Wait, he asked about me?"

"He wanted to know if you were seeing anyone. He seemed interested." Shelby's eyes danced with excitement. Typical of someone who had just fallen in love. They thought everyone should be as happy as they were.

"He's not," Abigail lied, wishing she had the guts to nod and say, "Damn right he is."

"Yeah, he is. And though not many people could see you with someone like him, I think you'd be good together."

"That's crazy. We have nothing in common."

"Neither did me and John."

"Well, I'm different."

"How?" Shelby cocked her head like a little bunny…a little bunny Abigail wanted to punch. She didn't want to talk about Leif. Or Cal. She'd made up her mind to tell Leif she wasn't interested. That was a rational move. She couldn't take watching him walk away from her. She been there, done that, barely recovered from it. Better to keep him where he was—her daughter's art teacher.

"I'm not you."

"No, duh. But you're still pretty, young, available. You don't have to let it get serious. Just have some fun with him. Cal won't be so presumptive if you're dating someone else, right?"

Shelby had a point.

But Abigail couldn't use Leif for fun…or to dissuade Cal. That would be selfish.

"No. That's silly." But her voice cracked.

And Shelby heard it. "Is this upsetting you? Bad memories or are you really that put off by Leif?"

Abigail had no clue why she was close to tears. This wasn't what she did. She was strong, resolute, didn't cry except in the privacy of her own bedroom. But at that moment she felt so weak. Maybe it was because Birdie had sat with Cal and his parents during church that morning, leaving her alone on the pew. Or maybe it was because she'd just immersed herself in the memory of Cal leaving her. Or maybe because, despite all the roadblocks she'd tossed up, she really wanted to do what Shelby suggested— have some fun with Leif.

"Everyone says I need to get laid."

Shelby's baby blues grew as wide as Aunt Lucy's backside. "Well, that's obvious. Your butt's been working button holes for as long as I can remember. You actually scared me when I first met you. John called you the colonel."

"So I'm a little tightly wound." Abigail lifted a shoulder. Wasn't like she could help it. She was who she was. "And where did you learn the saying 'your butt's working button holes'?"

"I'm very interested in Southernisms. I've been keeping a little list of the ones I like in my purse." Shelby smiled triumphantly, as if she thought she had a leg up on the imaginary Southern citizenship test.

Abigail stared at her for a full six seconds before she said, "I think I was born this way."

"Well, you are who you are, but sometimes it's nice to have our edges smoothed. Leif seems like a guy who could do a bang-up job for you. No pun intended, of course."

Abigail thought about that. "Yeah, he probably could."

"What's stopping you? Uh, is it the church thing? Or is it because Leif's, well, different? I'm from Washington State and we're used to his vibe, but people here aren't so…accepting."

"No. Not that." Abigail felt strange about talking this over with Shelby. "I guess I don't want to be that woman again."

"What woman?"

"The one a man never stays for."

Shelby looked as if she wanted to say Abigail was crazy, but she remained silent, waiting.

Abigail swallowed. "I know it sounds weak. I try to be strong, but underneath all my—" She sucked in air and blinked away the emotion.

Shelby grabbed her hand and squeezed. "Ah, honey, I know. Love is scary when you've been burned."

"It's stupid to be so scared, though."

"No, it's not. Everyone is scared of being hurt."

Abigail looked at their hands. "I wish I was stronger."

"You don't have to be strong. You have to be willing to take a chance."

Abigail sniffed. "I know. But it's easier said than done. Thing is, Leif's the wrong guy. He's not going to stay in Magnolia Bend, and even if he were, he's commitmentphobic."

"And you know this how?"

"I saw his ex-fiancée cream him in the face with their wedding cake. Someone at the school told me he said he's been engaged three times. Three! Who does that? Clearly, he gets cold feet and runs every time things get serious."

"So why do they have to be serious?"

Abigail stared at Shelby. How could she not understand something so obvious? "Because I can't carry on a love affair in public."

"Why not?"

"Because my daddy is a preacher. I'm the PTA president. My family—"

"So this is about what other people think about you?"

"Yeah. I mean, no." Abigail shut her mouth. All the reasons and rationales, the rules and regulations that guided her every move and that seemed so sound in her head, had vanished. "I can't just sleep around with Leif like it's no big deal," she said finally.

"Jesus, Abigail, people date all the time. We're not living in the 1920s and I'm fairly sure you won't be painted a fallen woman if you date someone. What you actually do on your dates is your business."

Abigail blinked several times, not because she hadn't thought about that, but because Shelby made it sound so damn reasonable. "But—"

"You're so much like your brother. Parameters. I'm surprised you don't have rules painted on every wall," Shelby said before making a face when she saw the Grandmother's Rules placard attached to the wall behind Abigail. "Don't you know, Abigail, that there are no rules, no absolutes and no guarantees when it comes to falling in love? But do it anyway, sister."

Abigail turned to the sink, pulling the plug on the dirty dishwater. "I'll think about it. It was good to have someone to talk to."

At this Shelby grew still. Her blue eyes became suspiciously damp. "It really is, isn't it?"

The moment sat between them, sweet and achy like listening to an old hymn.

"Better grab John now. I need a nap in the worst way," Shelby said, tugging off her apron and folding it. "I'll see you soon."

"Like on your wedding day?"

"Right." Shelby turned to leave, then paused. "Oh, and, Abigail—you really shouldn't think in this situation. Just go with it. Give yourself permission to do something for yourself."

CHAPTER TEN

MONDAY NIGHT, LEIF rang Abigail's doorbell, but there was no answer.

He'd told her he'd pick her up for their date at five-thirty on the dot. He didn't wear a watch but the clock in his car said five thirty-two so she should be ready to roll.

The door swung open to reveal an older lady who was definitely not Abigail.

"Hey," he said.

"Oh, hello," the lady said, brushing her hands on a spotless apron. "You must be Mr. Marshall. Welcome to Laurel Woods. I'm Alice Ann. I help out the inn's owner. Come inside and we'll get you checked in."

"Uh, thanks, but I'm not Mr. Marshall."

She looked confused, glancing at the clutch of flowers he held in his hand. "Oh, we were expecting Mr. Marshall sometime this evening. Can I help you with something?"

"I'm Leif," he said.

She extended a hand. "The art instructor?"

"Yes."

"Uh, well, Birdie's dining with her father tonight. Did y'all have a lesson or something?"

"No."

"Oh."

For a good ten seconds they stood contemplating each other.

Leif cleared his throat. "I believe Mrs. Orgeron is expecting me."

"She is?" Alice Ann stepped aside. "Well, she's out working in the flower beds. You can go on back."

Leif wondered why Abigail hadn't mentioned their date to Alice Ann and why she was working in the flower beds. Maybe she'd lost track of time?

He made his way through the pristine lower floor of Laurel Woods with its polished dark woods, shiny crystal chandeliers and impressive art. Even though many of the furnishings and the house itself were centuries old, the place had a fresh feel. He stepped out into a square patio surrounded by thorny roses, some pruned, others still leggy and bare. Abigail stood in the middle of a bed working feverishly to hack a sturdy branch.

Her ponytail flipped as she threw her head back. "Damn it to hell."

"Does your father know you use those words?"

Abigail spun, accidently dropping the loppers. "Leif."

"Yeah," he said, dropping his eyes to the tight, stained T-shirt she wore with a pair of faded yoga pants. The ensemble left little to the imagination— something he could appreciate—but between her hair falling in her face and the camouflage Crocs, he was fairly certain she'd forgotten about their plans.

And that hurt.

He'd thought…well, maybe he'd been totally off on how she felt. The kiss they'd shared Thursday night had advertised an interested woman. But maybe not.

He lowered the clutch of amaryllis he'd bound with red ribbon. "So I guess you forgot about our date."

She shook her head, looking guilty. "No, but I'm guessing you didn't get my message."

"My internet has been out and I didn't check my phone this afternoon. I was busy getting the backyard ready for our date."

"Oh," she said, pink flooding her cheeks, the cuteness edging out some of the disappointment in his gut. "I'm sorry. I, uh, well, I had said something about not feeling like, uh—"

"You blew me off?"

"No. Not blowing you. I just— I didn't mean to say *blowing you*. I meant I didn't blow you off. Ah, basically it's just… Here's the thing. I don't think I need a new relationship right now." Abigail had grown even redder over her mix-up of words and her eyes had dipped to take in his worn jeans and tight long-sleeved T-shirt. He'd finger-combed his hair, letting it dry naturally, a softer look thanks to the Louisiana humidity. Her eyes were appreciative.

So what was the deal? Was she still throwing up roadblocks because she was scared? Or maybe he made her feel too reckless?

Yes. Whatever sparked between them was a little out of control, a little wild, and that scared her.

Abigail needed a slight push.

"In case you don't realize, a date is when two people who might like each other go out to dinner or some other activity to get to know each other better. It's not a huge commitment. No ring, no prenup, no guaranteed sex. Just some food and conversation. It's not a relationship."

"I know what a date is," she said, stooping to pick up the shears she'd dropped. "But I'm not at a good place for—"

"Pasta?"

"What?"

"I made pasta salad. I don't even have condoms in the house. You're totally safe."

"Wait, you don't have—" Abigail snapped her mouth closed, before squeezing her eyes shut. She opened them, doing that forehead wrinkle thing she did pretty much all the time. "I'm sorry, I just can't do this."

"Sure you can."

"I have too much to do. Look at these roses. If I don't prune them now, they won't have blooms this spring."

"Yeah, they will. Double Knock Outs bloom even if not pruned."

"You know what Knock Out roses are?"

"I know a lot of things. I know how many cups are in a gallon, I know how many pixels are on a sixty-inch TV and I know why clown fish can live safely inside sea anemones." He walked toward her, lifting the bouquet of flowers. He stopped in front of her. "I also know it takes the average woman seven-point-five minutes to take a shower, but since you, Abigail, are so very efficient, I bet you can do it in less than five minutes."

"You want me to take a shower?" she asked, staring at his mouth.

"I'd take one with you, but, as previously stated, this is just a date. No big deal."

She swallowed, ripping her gaze away from his mouth. "But—"

"Uh, uh, uh. No buts. You're a woman who fritters her time away doing everything that must be done. It's time someone stepped in and demanded you fritter some time away doing something you never knew needed to be done."

"What?" she asked, her eyes confused.

"Essentially, you need a little bit of nothing in your life."

"Nothing?"

"Yes, you need to let go of what has to be done and hold on to nothing. Or me. Either one."

He set the flowers atop one of the spindly bushes, picked up her gloved hands and set them on his shoulders. He grinned at her, placing his hands about her waist, bringing her to him. She smelled earthy... and a bit like bubble gum.

"Oh," she breathed as their bodies melded together.

Leif took her left hand in his and swung her about in a waltz.

She actually giggled as they took five steps around the small stacks of thorny branches that littered the patio. "You're crazy."

"Yes." He spun her faster, loving the tinkle in her laughter. He started counting. "One, two, three. One, two, three."

"Oh, my gosh, stop. What are people going to think?"

"That we're dancing," he said, hopping over a branch that had separated from the others, but not stopping as he waltzed her toward the door. "And who gives a damn what anyone thinks? We're having fun. You need a prescription for fun and I'm writing out the orders."

Abigail laughed as they continued dancing to the very step that would take her inside the house.

Leif halted, looking at the woman whose cheeks were now pink from exertion. He felt a strange tenderness flood him. Because everything that had happened in the past minute verified his conclusion about Abigail. She needed help. She needed romance and spontaneity. She needed laughter and silliness. "Let's get these gloves off you. It will be hard to shower with them on."

She watched as he unbuttoned the right glove, peeling the leather from her hand. He did it slowly, almost sensuously, dropping a small kiss on her wrist before unfurling her palm and grazing it with his lips. He performed the same on the left hand. When he glanced up, her eyes were filled with a mixture of disbelief and desire.

For several seconds she said nothing. Just stared at him.

"Okay, off you go. The shower awaits."

She glanced at the patio. "But what about the roses? They're half-done and debris is scattered all over."

He turned and surveyed the mess. "The other roses can wait, and I'll take these gloves and deal with those stacks. You shower and—" he ducked his head, brushing a soft kiss against her lips "—don't bother with makeup. I like you just the way God made you. Beautiful."

She sucked in her breath. "Is your vision working?"

"Wait," he said, squinting his eyes, moving his head closer and then away. "You're not Karen Franklin? I'm… Oh, my gosh, I'm so sorry. I got the wrong woman."

Abigail punched him in the shoulder.

Leif laughed. "Seriously, go shower. I have a fun night planned for us."

"Fun?"

"Baby oil and Twister."

Her laughter was sweet reward. "Oh, my Lord. You could talk me into anything."

"That's what I'm banking on."

ABIGAIL DRIED HER hair with a round brush, begging the Louisiana humidity to lay off for this one night. Her skin glistened from the shower, her eyes sparkled and her thumb harbored a small thorn she couldn't quite dig out.

But who cared?

She was going on a date with Leif.

Inside she thrilled at the thought, relieved she'd tossed away her reservations. Last night she'd flipped on the TV and caught a reality show about fortysomething-year-old women relaunching themselves into the dating scene and it had killed the bolstering Shelby had delivered. She'd left Leif a halfhearted message on his voice mail.

But Shelby was right—Abigail needed to stop thinking and start living on the edge a little more.

And the man waiting downstairs made her feel not so much herself.

Or maybe more like herself, like the girl she used to be. Maybe in the face of dealing with Cal's renewed interest and Birdie's impudence she needed to remember the girl who'd taken chances, banked on her dreams and didn't let anyone put her in a box…or a corner.

"What were you so worried about?" she asked her reflection, switching off the dryer. When her reflection didn't respond, she grinned at being so silly. And that felt good. Surprisingly good.

Monday nights weren't for dates. They were for organizing the kitchen junk drawer, getting caught up on the ironing or watching a rerun of some police procedural. It was a very odd night to be gussying herself up and taking time for herself. But Monday felt right. Leif wasn't an ordinary guy.

Despite Leif's no-makeup request, she dabbed a bit of concealer under her eyes and powdered her nose, rubbing a bit of rouge on her cheekbones and swiping her mouth with a light lip gloss. Still very natural, but it hid some of her flaws.

Abigail dropped her towel and eyed her nude body in the half mirror. Not bad. Not good, but not bad. Her breasts weren't full but they'd not been tackled by gravity. Her stomach bore a thin C-section scar and her hips and legs were still firm and varicose vein–free. She picked up her favorite perfume and misted her body with it before tugging on her prettiest bra and panties, ones she'd gotten on a trip to New Orleans with her sister-in-law, Mary Jane. It had been a wasted purchase until now.

Wait.

Just because she wore Belgian lace didn't mean she was going to sleep with Leif.

Her cell phone buzzed on the nightstand. Scooping it up, she hit the answer button.

"Hey, Mom. Dad and I are on our way home. Since I finished my homework early, we're going to watch Netflix. We're getting candy and stuff at the Short Stop. What do you want?" Birdie sounded happy. Not like the sullen girl who'd slunk away from the kitchen table Friday night after embarrassing Abigail in front of her brother.

"Nothing for me," Abigail said, walking to her closet, thumbing through the depths looking for a shirt with buttons. Why? No clue. But she wanted to please Leif after trying to ditch him and their date.

"Jeez, it's not going to make you fat," Birdie said. Abigail could hear some muffled conversation before her daughter said, "Dad says he likes you with a little meat on your bones."

Abigail twitched in irritation and wanted to say, "I don't care what he likes," but she didn't. Instead she said, "I won't be here."

"Why not?"

"I have a date." Abigail pulled out a plain white shirt with snaps. Would snaps work? She looked at the other meager offerings. Snaps would have to work. She snagged a pair of jeans, and after a flicker of indecision, the nude pumps with the gold nailhead studs around the heel.

"With who?" Birdie sounded shocked.

"Your art teacher," Abigail said matter-of-factly.

"Mr. Lively? You're going on a date with him?"

"Don't act so shocked. I'm not dead, Birdie."

The phone was absolutely silent. Abigail held it between her head and shoulder as she slipped the shirt off the hanger. A few more seconds ticked by.

"I need to go, honey. Have fun with your father," Abigail said.

"Mom!" Birdie squealed, not hiding the outrage

in her voice. "You can't go out with him. Dad's coming over. And—"

"Why not? He's a nice guy. Plus, he asked me."

"Why? You're all wrong for him."

Hurt zinged straight to her heart at her daughter's statement. "How?"

"You just are, Mom. I don't mean you're not pretty or anything, but you're just, uh, just not like him."

"I know that. It would be weird if I were."

Birdie sighed. "Look, I'm not trying to be mean, but you're older and you're nerdy. You don't fit with him."

"Eva Brigitte, you ought to be ashamed. I may not be cool, but I'm not a nerd."

"Have you seen your jeans lately? Or the music you listen to? You're dangerously skirting lamedom, Mom. And Leif's, like, hot. I don't understand why he would want to take you on a date."

"Maybe it's because I put out," Abigail said, punching the end button, her breath coming faster, her fists knotting at her side. "That little—"

And then she realized what she'd said…to her twelve-year-old daughter.

Crap.

Who said something like that?

She picked the phone up, dialed Birdie, but got no answer.

So she texted Birdie:

That last comment was a joke, but you hurt my feelings. Have fun with your dad. Don't wait up.

Then she backspaced over Don't wait up.

'Cause that sounded as if she might possibly put out for Leif. Birdie might not even know what *put out* meant. But she probably did because she read extensively…and she had gotten much of her sexual education from *Cosmopolitan* magazine.

She pressed Send and tossed the phone on the bed, her flirty mood diminished by her daughter's hurtful words.

You don't fit with him.

Like Abigail didn't know that. She'd examined their suitability seven ways to Sunday and still had no answer. But that hadn't stopped her from wanting Leif to fit her, if only a little bit. Besides, he seemed just as interested as she tried to pretend she wasn't. That said something, didn't it?

She picked up the jeans, the same fit she'd worn forever. They were comfortable and didn't sag at the waist and show the everyday panties that she bought at the wholesale club. What was wrong with covering your butt? Maybe that was nerdy, but she didn't have a back-door draft going all day long.

Abigail didn't have any other jeans to wear to an outdoor picnic in the middle of winter, so she pulled them on with the white shirt and put on some pretty gold hoop earrings and a coin necklace bearing her initial. Grabbing a jacket and her phone, she headed downstairs.

Leif sat with Alice Ann, who leafed through a huge photo book that showed the renovations of Laurel Woods.

"There you are," he said, lifting those gorgeous eyes, taking in her nerdy jeans and snap-button shirt with amusement. "Alice Ann was showing me all the work you did on this place. Amazing."

Alice Ann looked up. "Yes, our Abigail is an amazing woman."

"The flattery is getting thick in here," Abigail joked, pulling a sweater off the hook beside the door. "Do you have everything under control, Alice? Leif and I are going to be only a short walk away so if you need me, just holler."

"Literally? Or on the phone?" Alice Ann asked, quite seriously.

"On the phone. I'm pretty sure our guests won't appreciate a bunch of caterwauling out the back door," Abigail said, softening her rebuke with a grin. "That's a little too much realism."

"Can I take this book with me?" Leif said, lifting the book from Alice Ann's lap. "I'd love to examine the process a bit more."

"Oh, sure," Abigail said, surprised he'd be interested in the renovations, but after thinking about it, realizing the artist in him likely appreciated the grueling transformation. "Are you ready?"

He rose. "I was ready forty-five minutes ago. Good thing tofu dogs are easy to cook."

Alice Ann smiled like a fool, no doubt thrilled Abigail was going on a date. She'd been pushing Abigail to date her youngest son, Neil, who had a gambling problem and lived with Alice Ann's grandmother. But he was a sweet boy…or so Alice Ann liked to say. Abigail hadn't taken the bait.

"Oh, goodie, fake meat on a stick. Do you do this for all your dates?" Abigail cracked.

"Only for the ones who are late. On-timers get the added bonus of Tofutti."

"What's that? Oh, wait, that weird ice cream? If that's true, I'm going to be late every time." As soon as she said it, she knew it was presumptive. This date might be a one-and-done for her. Leif may wake up and realize he'd asked out a nerd, replete with high-waist jeans and a label maker. Appalling.

"I'll mark it off my grocery list," Leif said, winking at Alice Ann. "Thanks for showing me the pictures."

A quick stroll through Abigail's backyard later, they stepped into Leif's house. The living room was austere with a simple overstuffed twill couch and some not very grown-up beanbag chairs. But the art covering the walls was breathtaking.

"Wow," Abigail said, setting down the banana bread she'd grabbed off the counter on the way out the door and strolling around the room. Some pieces were abstract, strong in color and form. Others were landscapes and still lifes. There was even a sculpture masquerading as a painting. "Did you do these?"

"None of those. I surround myself with the work of others. Feels less indulgent, and it's inspiring to be wrapped in other artists' visions. Like I have a little piece of them with me."

"Most are by friends?" she asked.

"The one you're studying so closely was done by my mother."

"It's incredible."

And it was. The huge piece of art was unusual in that it was half painting and half sculpture, molded out of some sort of plaster. The piece possessed sensual movement even as colors drenched the sweeping form with vibrancy. "I didn't know your mother was an artist, too. Does she still—"

"She's no longer living."

"Oh, I'm so sorry." Abigail sensed Leif's mood fading to reflective. Mentioning his mother had saddened him and though she wanted to know more about the artist who'd created something so stirring, she'd much rather re-create the flirty mood he'd had earlier, when he'd danced around her patio, eyes teasing as his touch promised untold delights. "So where are these tofu dogs of which you speak?"

He snapped out of his reverie and flashed a grin. "Follow me."

He walked through an equally austere kitchen featuring only one piece of art—a bright chrysanthemum done in the spirit of van Gogh. Sliding the back door open, he waved his arm with flourish.

Abigail walked through the door into something out of a fairy tale.

"Oh, you're joking," she murmured as she took in the swaths of shimmering blue silks and Moroccan-style lanterns hung on hooks around the pergola-style patio. Fire pots scattered the perimeter, lending a nice glow to the darkening day. A good-size fire pit sat in the center with plump square cushions scattered on the jute rug. No traditional patio furniture could be seen, but large tropical plants and sago palms created a lush getaway steps outside the door.

Abigail inhaled, noting the scent of jasmine and spices in the air. "I feel like I'm in Sri Lanka or Morocco."

Leif looked pleased with her response.

There were even lotus-flower candle things floating in the lap pool just beyond the patio, their flickering lights heightening the romantic theme. "I can't believe a man did this."

"Plenty of guys get in touch with their feminine side when it comes to creating a cool vibe for a date with a lovely lady."

"Sure, but their date usually has an Adam's apple and the same equipment south of the border."

"Are you implying only gay men have good taste and a flair for decorating? Way to stereotype," he teased.

"I'm sorry, it's just that most of the guys I know

decorate with antlers, milk crates and beer signs. They wouldn't know a lotus flower from a ceiling fan," Abigail said, walking over to the unlit fire pit.

Leif laughed. "Well, maybe my standards are a bit higher because I grew up believing animals were our brothers and sisters here on this good earth. I was taught to enjoy the colors of the sunset and see potential in every element. Making the world more aesthetically pleasing was encouraged."

Abigail turned to him. "That's not a bad way to be raised."

"I always thought so." Leif gestured to the cushions. "Slip off your shoes and make yourself at home while I start the fire and get the appetizers from the fridge."

A few minutes later a nice warm fire crackled in the pit, and a slate tray containing cheeses, hummus and figs sat between them. Leif handed her a glass of wine, clinking his against hers. "To what lies beneath."

Abigail crinkled her nose. "Wasn't that a horror film?"

He tilted his head, a soft smile gracing his pretty mouth. "Still, I like that toast for you."

She crooked an eyebrow.

"Because beneath the layers you cover yourself in lies your true spirit. And I'm looking forward to knowing the real Abigail."

"Oh," she said, nodding at the buttery apple of the

chardonnay, trying to ignore the sudden fluttering of nerves. "Good wine."

"From one of my friends, as is the goat cheese."

"So tell me about where you grew up," Abigail said, snagging some cheese and nodding again to indicate her enjoyment.

"In Sawyer's Peak, Colorado. My mother lived in the Seaton commune there as did many other artists."

"A commune?"

"Yeah, but it wasn't like what most people think. Sure, we were self-sufficient, sharing the work, creating things to sell in the farmers' market. It was a gentle way to live. Simple, much like what the early transcendentalists embraced."

Abigail couldn't imagine living any other way than how she lived. She knew very few vegetarians. Louisianans' cultural dishes and overall outlook reflected a different way of life. So a life without modern conveniences like bug spray and air-conditioning sounded miserable. "I can't imagine growing up that way, but obviously you embrace that lifestyle."

"Not always. You saw how complex things were with Marcie. I'm not always good at being...calm."

Abigail smiled. "Difficult situation. So you said your mother was an artist and I saw her work, but what about your father. What did he do?"

"I don't know."

Abigail lifted her eyebrows. "What do you mean?"

"I don't know who my father is."

CHAPTER ELEVEN

LEIF WATCHED ABIGAIL'S reaction to his statement. Revealing his father was someone still living in Magnolia Bend was a risk. But a calculated one. He needed help and knew he could trust Abigail.

"Oh, well, that's, uh, a hard thing, I guess." She shifted her gaze, embarrassed, looking endearing in her mom jeans and the white shirt with the snaps. With her hair down and slightly messy and bare feet peeking out at the hem, she looked much more approachable.

"It was, but I had plenty of role models in the elders of our community so I never really lacked for male influence."

"Oh," she said, her forehead crinkling. Several seconds ticked by. "So your mother…"

"Oh, she knew. She just wasn't forthcoming."

"But isn't it important from a medical history standpoint? Or didn't you wonder?"

"Sure, I'm normal. Mostly."

She picked at a bit of cheese before tossing it in her mouth. Silence descended.

"Actually, searching for my father is what brought me to Magnolia Bend."

Her head snapped up. "Wait…you think your father lives here?" She sounded incredulous, as if Magnolia Bend were way too small or dull to harbor an unknown father. He almost laughed at her caricature of shocked righteousness.

"When my mother died, she told me my father was still alive. Growing up, she never spoke of him no matter how much I pestered her. But near the end, she told me that she'd never told him about me and begged me to find him. She wanted to make things right, but she also told me people thought she killed someone. Or something like that."

"Wait, what?"

"Her exact words were 'They think I murdered a man.'"

"But she said you father was still alive? That doesn't make sense."

He crossed his legs, sipping the wine as he stared into the flames. "I know, but she was in a lot of pain and not very lucid. Bone cancer. The last few weeks were very hard. They gave her a lot of drugs."

"So she implied he lived in Magnolia Bend?"

"She lived here for half a year. She was one of the last artists who lived at—"

"Oh, my God, your mother was Calliope?" Abigail's mouth dropped open.

Leif felt part dread and part relief. "Yeah."

"Oh, my God."

"So you said."

She snapped her mouth closed, the furrow on her forehead growing deeper. "She killed Simeon Harvey."

"I suspected that's what many thought when I

learned the circumstances around Simeon's death, but Hilda said—"

"Hilda?"

"She invited me to brunch yesterday and hit me with the fact she knew I was Calliope's son."

Abigail laughed. "My cousin is a sharp lady, but even so, how did she know?"

"I look like my mother. If I looked like my father, it would be easier to find him. Hilda said she'd help, but I wanted you to know, too, though I hope you'll keep it on the down low."

"Of course. You need to talk to Bart. His uncle was a quirky Southerner with odd habits. Very Faulkner-esque. Though I was a toddler when he died, I heard about it. Anytime a man worth millions plunges to his death, it becomes local folklore. Everyone knows the story."

"What version do you know?"

"That nothing was proven. Bart found her with his uncle's body and said your mother had convinced Simeon to change his will, leaving everything to her. Frankly, Bart painted your mother as some sort of trickster. He said Simeon could no longer walk so your mother rolled his chair to the second-floor landing and pushed him down the stairs. He broke his neck."

"Why would she do that?"

"Because Simeon had called her on trying to swindle him. He said he was calling the police."

Leif pushed the breath he'd been holding from his

lungs. He hated hearing his mother cast in that light. "None of that makes any sense."

"Why?"

"First, my mother wouldn't allow me to kill a scorpion in our house. If she wouldn't kill an insect, she damn sure wouldn't kill a crippled man. Besides she said they *thought* she killed him, not that she *had* killed him."

"Bart said he found his uncle at the bottom of the stairs and Calliope panicked and ran when she saw him. Supposedly he heard them screaming at each other just before he heard the crash of his uncle coming down the stairs. Maybe there was some sort of a struggle."

"Maybe so but my mother wouldn't fight over something like money."

"Money motivates a lot of people to do things they normally wouldn't. I'm not saying she meant—"

"Money never motivated my mother. She ran away from a wealthy East Coast family in the late sixties. Mother wanted to live in Haight-Ashbury, free love and all that. She ended up in the commune with an old boyfriend who smoked peyote and did a lot of woodworking. An old Pueblo woman taught her how to make pottery, so she stayed and started working in clay before getting into bronze. Calliope's real name was Martha Jane Weiner and her father was a real estate broker on Long Island. She had a trust fund and didn't need money."

"Well, only Bart knows the truth. Or maybe he

doesn't. Maybe he saw what he thought was guilt, heard something he thought was an argument. Simeon could have tripped."

"Not if he was in a wheelchair."

Abigail stared out at the night. She shifted and curved her arms around her knees, her light blue toenail polish incongruent with the serious woman he encountered in the halls of the school. The firelight softened the angles of her face, making her green eyes glow. "Maybe you'll never know, but that doesn't mean you can't find your father."

Leif shrugged. "I've gone my whole life not knowing, so I'll survive if I don't find him. Still, something inside me feels restless, like I need to know the truth. Maybe knowing what happened to my mother here would—" He clamped down on his thoughts. How could he say it would give him a different life? Knowing his father could give him grounding, an idea of why he was on this planet. Maybe discovering how love had ended so badly could help him set his own love life to rights. Leif wanted to stick somewhere…someday. "I don't know. I wonder if it's a bad idea. Maybe knowing about me would make his life worse. Maybe it would make mine worse."

A few more seconds ticked by. "And you don't have a clue as to who he is?"

"The only possible clue is a tattoo my mom had. She had a story for every tattoo on her body, but there was a small tattoo of a bird between her thumb and index finger she'd never speak of. Often I'd catch her tracing the outline, her eyes clouded. I always thought the bird reminded her of my father. But I could be wrong."

"Good thing she didn't say he lived in Dallas or Houston. That would be much harder," Abigail said with a small smile. "So I'm guessing that's why you wanted the book from Laurel Woods…and maybe that's the reason you wanted to go out with me?"

"No," Leif said, seeing very plainly that Abigail thought this was about his mining for information. "Sure, I thought visiting Laurel Woods might give me a sense of where my mother lived and loved, but I don't think there's anything left from her time there."

"There might be. Bart had tons of junk packed away into huge storage containers in the cabins. When we bought the place, he washed his hands of the stuff. I opened a few boxes and it's mostly things like hot plates, old dishes and art supplies. I haven't gone through the rest of them because I haven't had time. My plan was to renovate the cabins as guest-houses, expanding the inn's business. You're welcome to go through the stuff if you think it would help, but your best bet is to talk to some of the folks who were around then."

"That's the plan."

"Well, you've been here for six months. What have you been doing?"

"Uh, moving in, teaching, giving the town time to trust me a little before giving up secrets."

"You think there are secrets?" Abigail's forehead did that little wrinkle thing again.

"There are always secrets in small Southern towns."

Abigail laughed. "You've seen too many movies. We're no different than any other people in any other city."

"You're joking, right?" Leif said, lifting the cheese tray so he could move closer to Abigail. She sucked in her breath a little, her hands pressing against her jeans.

"So we're a little closed off and even backward."

"That's not what I meant. This a cool little town with some interesting characters, but everyone has secrets. Human nature."

"I guess," she said, jumping a bit when he lifted her hand.

"And, Abigail..."

Her gaze rose to his. "Huh?"

"You have nothing to do with searching for my father. You're a delicious side benefit." He lowered his lips to skim across the sensitive flesh of her wrist.

"Why do you do that?" she asked.

"What? Kiss your hand?"

"Yeah, like you stepped out of the nineteenth century. Do you carry a handkerchief, too?"

Leif tugged her to him. She lost her balance and toppled into his lap.

"I don't carry one, but I do like the turn of your wrist," he said, running a finger over the delicate skin. She shivered, which shot satisfaction into his belly. "So very elegant."

Abigail looked at his finger trailing over her pulse. "I never thought my wrist was elegant."

He flipped her hand and bestowed a kiss on the back of it. "All of you is very elegant. Like a Degas. You remind me of one of his dancers."

Abigail swallowed. "I was a dancer once."

Leif brushed a strand of hair behind her ear, marveling at the dramatic streak of white amid the darkness. Abigail's breath came faster and he felt her body amp. Her forearm rested on his thigh, her knees bumping his shins. He loved the way she smelled— light and floral and clean like a meadow or some other poetic thing. "I could tell when we danced earlier. You move so easily, so sweetly against me."

Abigail watched his mouth as he murmured tender things to her. "You sure know how to make a woman feel good about herself."

"You're a woman who should never feel bad about herself," he said, curving a hand behind her neck, bringing her mouth to his. "Never, ever."

Slowly he covered her mouth with his, savoring the fullness of her lips for a second. She leaned into him, surrendering.

"So sweet," he murmured before lightly touching his tongue to her lower lip. She inhaled deeply and moved her hand to his jaw as he tilted his head to deepen the kiss, teasing her with his tongue.

Carefully, he wound his other arm about her waist, anchoring her to him.

And then he merely enjoyed kissing Abigail.

She tasted delicious—like passion and goodness rolled into one. She was pretty talented at kissing, so he enjoyed the feel of her body against his, the promise in her tongue meeting his. Their dance had begun long ago, but Abigail had just now settled into the rhythm, allowing the passionate creature beneath the buttoned-up cardigan to peek its head out.

After a few seconds he broke the kiss.

"What did you do that for?" Abigail murmured, brushing his jaw with that elegant hand he so liked. "Not complaining. I really enjoy kissing you."

"Oh, babe, I liked it, too, but we can't have dessert before we've eaten." He dropped a kiss on her nose and sprang to his feet.

She fell against the cushion. "What?"

"I'm going to get those dogs. You fill our glasses." He indicated the chill bucket behind her before giving her an impudent wink and stepping inside.

Yes, romancing Abigail was better than he expected.

ABIGAIL TURNED TOWARD the silver bucket and lifted the bottle from the icy depths, filling both their glasses. She could feel the wine warm her stomach, giving her that wooziness she needed.

Or maybe she was woozy from Leif's kiss.

Briefly she touched her lips.

Dang, he was a good kisser. Her pulse had galloped with that whole wrist-kissing thing, and by the time his lips touched hers, she could have combusted into flames right there on the man's patio.

You're just horny.

Yeah. Okay. So her inner voice wasn't wrong. It had been a long time since a man had kissed her, since a man had touched her so tenderly. A hot pink vibrator was no substitute for the feel of a man beneath her hands. She'd missed that human touch— the smell of man, the abrasion of five-o'clock shadow against her cheek, the mingling of breaths.

So what if she did let herself indulge in Leif?

She was a grown-ass woman with needs.

Hadn't she sacrificed everything to raise a daughter, keep a roof over their heads, struggling to make ends meet? Hadn't she spent late nights sewing Renaissance-faire costumes and early mornings hauling Birdie to the soccer field? Hadn't she been on the pew every Sunday to hear her daddy preach and spent countless nights in the hospital while her mother recovered from breast cancer? Heck, she'd even helped to plan Cal's parents' fiftieth wedding anniversary party…one her ex didn't bother to attend.

So why not take a little something for herself?

A little lust-slaking with the tight-assed, lickable Leif could be just what she needed.

Didn't she deserve a taste of Leif?

Don't think.

"Here we are," he said, coming through the sliding glass door holding a tray. "I brought mustard but I couldn't find ketchup."

She chuckled at the thought of having him with either of those condiments, and then tried to rip her mind from a naked Leif and her doing naughty things to him.

Hot-dog wieners.

Right.

"I love mustard."

Leif sat the tray between them, lifting the cheese plate to make room. "And look, marshmallows for dessert."

"Vegan marshmallows?"

"We like good things, too." He grinned, lifting a whole-grain bun. "I made the hot-dog buns."

Abigail looked at the bun. "I can't believe you. You're like the perfect man, aren't you? Except I don't think a woman can really catch hold of you."

He cocked his head, a curious smile on his face. "What do you mean?"

"Well, poor Marcie didn't catch you. How many women have you outrun? Someone told me three." she said it flippantly but inside her stomach knotted. "Love 'em and leave 'em" Leif. She'd bet twenty dollars that could be his moniker.

"Ah, back to the whole lothario thing."

"I was teasing. Sort of."

He looked thoughtful for a moment. "Maybe I'm not so good at staying put. Relationships make me itchy no matter how much I want to be the guy who stays forever."

Abigail's stomach pitched, the knot growing heavier. This was exactly what she'd told Shelby.

But wasn't that the point?

Leif was for funsies, not forever. He'd probably leave Magnolia Bend once he found out who his father was.

Parameters were good.

Parameters would keep her heart safe.

She could date Leif, even sleep with him if it happened, but a serious relationship was off the table.

"I can see how being an artist, a sort of wandering soul, might make it hard to settle down."

Leif placed an odd-looking wiener on a long metal stick and handed it to her. He did the same, placing his stick over the fire pit. Abigail followed suit, wondering if a tofu dog would even roast. "Maybe. The thing is, I don't want to spend my life like some gypsy. Growing up, I liked being part of the commune community. It felt safe. But as I hit my late teens, I got this urge to see something beyond the hills of Colorado. I got some oat-sowing out of my system, but even after living it up, underneath the surface I had an unsettled feeling. It wasn't until after my mother uttered those words about my father that I knew what was wrong, what was missing inside me."

"So what happens if you find this man?"

Leif shrugged. "I don't know. There are too many

what-ifs. All I know is I have to try. For my mother. For me."

"I guess you'll deal with the what-ifs as they come," Abigail said, squirting enough mustard on her bun to mask what she was certain would be a horrid gastronomic failure in grilling. She balanced the hot dog over the flames, turning it, noting that it was darkening. Abigail withdrew her wiener and slid it onto the mustardy bun. She took a halfhearted nibble.

"Not bad, right?" he said, taking a bite.

"It's actually good," Abigail said, grabbing her wine and washing down the bite.

For a few minutes, they ate in companionable silence, the firelight flickering in the intimate darkness, casting patterns onto the patio. The smell of the incense, now burned out, still lingered, lending an exotic flavor to a Louisiana winter night.

"Tell me about being a dancer," he said when they'd shoved aside their empty plates.

Abigail wiped her hands on a napkin. "Well, I majored in theater and dance in college. Such a silly major but I had dreams of being onstage—I wanted to do Broadway."

"But you didn't make it there...or anywhere?"

"You're not going to sing the song, are you?"

Leif chuckled. "I'm a horrible singer, so no."

"I didn't quite make it there. Right after graduation as I contemplated what to pack for the Big Apple, Cal proposed to me."

"Wasn't letting you get away, was he?"

She stilled as Leif's comment sunk in. She'd never thought about Cal using a big diamond and a boyish smile to convince her she belonged beside him... not waiting tables in Manhattan, praying for a part in the chorus of some off-Broadway musical. Cal had strategically prevented her from living out her dream. Jesus, she'd never realized that until now. "I guess that's true. Still, it wasn't a practical career choice. I stayed here and opened up a dance studio."

"Oh, working with kids?"

"I loved it. Sharing my love of dance was really rewarding."

"So how come you now run a bed-and-breakfast?"

"'Cause it worked out that way," she murmured. "You know, I don't want to talk about me and my failures. Too many to discuss tonight."

"Want another hot dog?"

"No."

"Marshmallow?"

"Maybe later," she said, finishing off her wine as she stared out at the lotus flowers glowing along the lap pool. "I can't believe you swim naked out here."

As soon as her private musing became a public proclamation, she regretted opening her mouth.

"You want to try it?"

She snapped her gaze to his. "What?"

"Skinny-dipping."

"It's fifty-one degrees and the end of January."

Leif shrugged. "Swimming weather in Colorado."

"It's not in Louisiana."

"The pool is heated. I've stopped swimming since the mornings are cold, but it's not bad tonight. We can go in and then get warm by the fire."

"No," Abigail said, shaking her head. "I don't have a suit."

Leif's eyes danced with delight. "I said skinny-dipping. Haven't you ever been skinny-dipping?"

No.

"Uh, I don't think—"

"Yeah, I know what you don't think. Keep your undies on if you're modest, but don't skip the opportunity to have a little—"

"Fun?" she finished for him. "Don't tell me you think swimming in January is fun."

Leif stood and pulled off his shirt.

Damn.

Abigail tried to look away but couldn't. Mostly because his hands were now at the buttons of his jeans. Oh, good gravy. He was doing it. He was sliding those jeans down pretty spectacular-looking thighs. Denim pooled at his feet.

"Come on, Abi. We'll make out in the pool after our swim." He winked at her, kicked his jeans free and stood before her clad only in thin boxer briefs that molded to—

Abigail sucked in a deep breath, blowing it out her mouth as she watched him walk toward the pool.

She looked at his crumpled jeans and then at his retreating form. His blond hair brushed the tops of those wide, tanned shoulders. A lean waist introduced a spectacular ass. So spectacular that he should model underwear. His legs were muscled and only lightly sprinkled with golden hair that caught in the flickering lanterns.

An aching hunger bloomed in her belly.

Delicious.

Abigail reached for her collar, wrenching apart the two halves of her shirt.

Pop, pop, pop, pop.

One by one the snaps gave way. She shimmied out of her shirt, tossed it onto Leif's jeans, stood and shucked out of her jeans. The chill caused her to break out in goose bumps and her nipples to pucker through the pretty lace.

Wait.

She wore expensive underwear that chlorine could damage. She'd worn them only one other time and hated to damage the silk.

"Oh, yeah," Leif called, a slight splash sounding behind her. "The water is warm. Come on, chicken."

Chicken?

Chicken, her ass.

She reached behind and unhooked the clasp of her bra, glad that her breasts were taut with the cold. Then she hooked her fingers under the waistband, sliding her panties down. She hadn't had time for a bikini wax, but she hadn't let herself go, either.

Slowly she let the silk fall from her fingers and stepped out of the last vestige of protection.

Then she turned and tried to saunter toward the lap pool, but it was hard because it was cold. Walking slinky like a sexy siren probably worked best in warmer weather.

Leif stood at one end, lotus candles doused, his gaze stuck to her.

"Wow," he breathed, his gaze eating her up as she made her way to the handrail and started down the steps toward him. Her fingers trembled and she couldn't believe she'd shucked her duds…in a guy's backyard…on a first date.

Who in the hell was she?

"Like Venus," Leif said, extending his hand, desire aflame in his blue eyes. "But, sweet lady, I promised this was only a date. How am I going to keep my hands off you?"

Abigail laughed and to her ears she sounded like the sexy siren who would have sauntered had it been summer. "Who said you had to keep your hands off?"

She stepped into his embrace, immediately noting the erection brushing her stomach.

Liquid fire poured into her as she lifted her arms around his neck.

"Damn," he breathed. "You really are something, Abigail."

She smiled at him before she kissed him senseless.

Tonight this was how she rolled.

CHAPTER TWELVE

LEIF LOOKED AT the naked woman in his arms and couldn't believe his damn conscience had taken this particular moment to kick in.

He couldn't give Ms. Already Popped My Buttons what she wanted without violating the promise he'd made hours ago on the patio of Laurel Woods. He'd promised a date with romance. That meant a little flirting, a little kissing and maybe a popped button or two in order to get to that lovely neck.

Yet here she stood in her birthday suit, driving his resolve into the gutter…along with his mind.

Because she was so effin' sexy he wanted to do bad things to her.

"So?" She looked at him with an expression so vulnerable it made his heart ping. "Are you going to show me how big boys skinny-dip?"

Leif smiled. "I'm not sure you really want to do this, Abi."

"I thought you wanted to have fun. Didn't you tell me earlier to let go of all the things I had to do? To do nothing…or to do you?"

Yeah, but he hadn't thought she'd take him so literally. When Abigail let go, she meant business. He should have expected as much. He'd watched her over the past few months and knew that anything Abigail did, she gave it her all. And now she had finally let her guard down. She'd taken a risk to strip out of her clothes and join him in the pool. Though he'd teased and cajoled her, he hadn't thought she'd actually do it. He'd thought she'd watch and maybe get a little turned on. Or at the very least, keep her underwear on, but Abigail was balls-out. She'd surprised him. "Yeah, I wanted you to have fun, but I'm afraid you might regret this in the light of day."

Abigail snorted. "I'm friends with regret. Such good friends that we sometimes braid each other's hair and compare horror stories. Regret is not something I'm afraid of."

"But I couldn't stand it if you hated me for pushing you to be naughty. I get the feeling you—"

Abigail trailed a hand over his shoulder, her gaze on the scar from a dirt-biking accident in his teens. "I'm a big girl, Leif. I know what I'm doing…unless you don't want me…"

He pulled her tighter to him, intentionally letting her feel how hard her slick, gorgeous body had made him. "As you can feel, wanting is not the problem. I just—"

"You won't hurt me. This is about sex, not love. For the next few hours I want to forget about all the crap in my life and just be the woman you make love to. Is that so wrong? To want to be wanted?"

Leif kissed her softly. "Nothing wrong with that."

"So?"

He lifted her slightly and twirled her around. The stars spun and he allowed himself to lay his reservations aside. Abigail had ordered up what she needed. He wasn't about to hurt her by throwing it in her face. Besides, he'd wanted inside her pants ever since she'd spun that haughty ass around on his sidewalk over a month ago. And now he held her…very much out of those pants.

He could be stubborn, obtuse and ignorant at times, but he wasn't stupid.

"Okay, if we're going to do this, let's do this right," he said, dropping a kiss on her nose while grabbing her ass and lifting her. She immediately wrapped her legs around his waist. "First we do a little swimming, a little foreplay."

And so he sank beneath the water, holding her tight. He came up and she sputtered, pushing hair plastered to her face from her eyes.

"That was a dirty trick," she said, her teeth chattering though the water was warm.

"That wasn't dirty, but you're about to find out what is," he said, lowering his head and nipping her lower lip as he tweaked one taut nipple on a breast he couldn't wait to taste.

"Ouch," she said, splashing him.

"Oh, so that's how it is?" he teased, splashing water against those breasts he craved. They were the absolute perfect size, tipped with dark pink nipples that beaded in the night air.

He curved an arm around her waist and brought her to him so he could kiss her neck right where her pulsed raced.

"Ah," she groaned, her head falling back. He took a moment to enjoy the salty warmth of her neck before releasing her and kicking off toward the opposite end.

"Hey, where are you going?" she called out, putting her hands on her hips.

He turned and floated on his back, his cotton underwear dragging a little as he stared at the round full moon. "I'm swimming."

"We have better things to do."

He stood and grinned at her while sliding his boxers off and tossing them onto the cement surrounding the pool. The impact made a slap. "Swim over and we'll play a game of Marco Polo."

"Marco Polo?" She snorted but started his way.

"Yeah, I'll close my eyes and try and catch you. When I do, I'll have to try to identify you, right?"

"I'm the only other person playing, silly." She bumped into him, her eyes glinting. He cupped her rump, giving it a squeeze.

"Aw, come on. I want to feel around and try to guess…the feeling-around bit being the key part," he said, sliding his other hand down her belly, fingering the strip of neatly trimmed hair he'd glimpsed earlier when she'd entered the pool.

She sighed and so he dipped his finger lower, thrilling at the slickness as he slid a finger inside her, withdrawing it teasingly. "Marco."

"Oh, dear Bessie," she panted.

"Wrong. You're supposed to say 'Polo.'"

Abigail wrapped her arms around him and kissed him. Pulling back she looked at him. "In case you haven't noticed, I've been having a wonderful time. Can we skip the games? I've laughed and now I want to—"

"Scream?" he asked, running his hands over her bottom up to her waist and to her rib cage, where the curve of her breast began. She sighed and leaned into him.

Eyes half-lidded, Abigail smiled. "Is that a guarantee? I mean, are you really that good?"

He bent his head, caught her nipple in his mouth and bit down with just enough pressure to torment. Lifting his head, he said, "I can't speak for how good I am. I never worry about it. I simply pursue pleasure. Unrelentingly."

He wrapped her in his arms, lifting her again. This time when she wrapped her legs around his waist, there was no barrier. Hard, warm flesh met soft, yielding Abigail.

"Oh," she said, wriggling against him, closing her eyes and leaning against his looped arms. "That's nice."

Leif leaned forward and licked the droplets from her collarbone, sucking in her flesh, nipping lightly up the column of her throat. When he reached her mouth, he fisted a hand in her wet hair, tugging her hair, willingly covering her parted lips with his.

She tasted good—a bit like marshmallow—and she didn't hold back. Her tongue dueled with his as they indulged in increasing each other's arousal with wandering hands.

Her hands fluttered down his back, and she raked her nails gently against his ass. He returned the favor by cupping her bottom, using his fingers to slide down to the slick heat of her, ringing her entrance with one finger. She was wet and ready…but he didn't want to go this fast.

Breaking the kiss, he leaned away, sliding his hands to her waist. "Hey, hey, let's slow things down."

Abigail stilled her hands, her mouth bruised from his kisses, her eyes dilated with passion. At that moment, he knew he'd never seen anything as primitive as a turned-on Abigail. She was sheer beauty with breasts swelling above the water, moonlight highlighting her incredible bone structure, that silver streak glowing against the midnight of her dark hair. "No, let's not slow down. Later we'll slow down. Right now I want—" she slid a hand down between their bodies to grasp the erection jutting against her "—this inside me. Please. We'll play later."

Leif lifted her, blindly wanting to serve her, to give her what she needed. What they both needed.

But then his brain kicked in.

"I need a condom…and I don't have a frickin' condom."

ABIGAIL FELT LIKE she was on fire. Yes, water surrounded her, but inside a need so encompassing had built up to the extent she felt half-crazy.

Maybe she should have used that damn vibrator more, because if she didn't get off soon, she might come undone.

Never had she felt like this.

Maybe this was what all those magazines had meant about a woman's peak sexual arousal happening in her late thirties/early forties. 'Cause she was aroused all right. A damned nitroglycerin plant awaiting the stroke of a match.

"We don't need one," she panted, pulling his head down so he could kiss her and take her to that realm of molten mindlessness.

"Are you sure?"

"I haven't slept with a man in a year and a half. I'm disease-free, on the pill," she said, sliding her hands over his chest. He really was amazing. So damn beautiful. How was a guy so manly and beautiful at the same time? It didn't compute, but she loved the way his nipples puckered and that six-pack was like icing on the cake. "What about you?"

"Uh, I haven't slept with anyone in seven months and I've never had sex without a condom so I'm pretty sure—"

"Perfect," Abigail said, lifting herself slightly, allowing all the parts to align correctly and then sinking down on his length. "Ohhh. That's, oh, wow."

He filled her, stretching her tight, hitting that perfect spot. The air hissed out of his lungs and she peeked as he closed his eyes, pleasure slacking his face. "Oh, you're tight and so wet...so good. I've never felt this. Condoms suck."

She pulled him to her, head falling on his shoulder as she nodded. Her feet sagged around his thighs as he walked toward the edge of the pool. Her bottom hit the side and then she didn't feel anything except Leif moving inside her.

His body thrusting within hers sent her to a new place of pleasure. She leaned away, arching her back, laying her head against the cold cement. Opening her eyes, she watched the universe sparkle above as the passion within her gathered into a colossal storm.

Leif cupped her breast with one hand, his breath ragged, as he anchored her hips with his other hand, tilting her so he could plunge deeper inside her. And then his head lowered and he sucked her breast into the heat of his mouth.

"Yes," she hissed, closing her eyes, the pattern of the night sky seared into her brain. She moved faster against him as the sensations grew, rising, building into something that consumed her.

"Come for me, baby," he murmured against her damp, chilled skin.

So she did.

The wave crashed over her, sheer pleasure radiating from her center to every fiber in her body. She rode the wave and a mewling sound ripped from her as sweet joy pulsated in her body.

Her eyes flew open and she saw the glittering stars again and then she saw Leif, his blue eyes triumphant before he closed them. He kept moving, not allowing her body to rest, taking her yet again to another crest. She stretched her body, much as she did when dancing, reaching up, up, up.

Then she took hold of elusive pleasure again as another orgasm ripped through her body. This time she kept her eyes open, her gaze meeting his. Two becoming one, and with a guttural groan and a slight shudder of his body, Leif joined her, finding his release.

Breathing hard, she wrapped her arms around him, holding him to her as he jerked slightly, emptying himself. She silently thanked those stars above for the awesome experience she'd just had.

It had been a long time since she'd felt the awe of a knee-weakening, effervescent orgasm like that.

Leif fell against her, his breath puffing warm against her shoulder.

"Whoa," he muttered, dropping small kisses atop her breast.

"Incredible," she whispered, stroking his damp hair, still arched uncomfortably on the cement, stars winking at her from above. *We know what you just did, sister.*

Abigail smiled at the stars.

Leif lifted his head. "That got out of control. I had wanted to go slower, to give you something better than—"

"Seriously? How was that not good?" She pushed against him because her back hurt like hell. Nothing like pain to jar her into the here and now. She rubbed the indention from the concrete. "Ow."

He straightened, lifting her with him and walked to the steps of the pool. "And, God, your back has to be killing you. Sorry about that, too."

And then he walked up the stairs, still carrying her, still inside her.

"Uh—" He looked down, as if trying to explain. "Well, since there's no condom."

Abigail smiled. "Yeah, a little messy."

"But worth it," he said, bussing her mouth with a kiss before loosening his hold on her.

She dropped her legs as they reached the patio, praying like hell Birdie hadn't climbed a tree and watched. She wouldn't do that. Not at night. Not when her father—

Hell. Cal and Birdie were yards away and here she'd gone at it like a deranged rabbit with her neighbor in the pool. *Great role model, Abi.*

Leif handed her a napkin from the tray and silently they both did their postcoital cleanup. As she slid on her panties, shivering in the night, she reminded herself that she was not going to regret or be ashamed of what she'd done. She was a normal woman. Normal women had sex when the opportunity arose. And according to the *Cosmopolitan* she'd picked up at the store yesterday in order to see precisely what Birdie had learned, they hooked up with guys who were their friends quite often. Booty calls.

Ugh. Horrible name for what she and Leif had

shared, but she wasn't going to be embarrassed about climbing him like a monkey.

"Hey, you okay?" His voice sounded soft...and knowing. "You said you wouldn't hate me."

Abigail snapped her head up after hooking her bra closed. "I don't hate you. Don't be silly."

"But you're feeling guilty. I can see it on you."

"I'm not—" Abigail shimmied into her jeans. "It's cold out here."

"Come over by the fire." He already wore his jeans and shirt and held a folded blanket she'd seen earlier. "We'll snuggle and get warm."

Except she didn't want to snuggle. She wanted to go home and wrestle with what she'd done. But that was silly. And rude. And would make Leif think she had regrets.

She didn't.

Or at least she didn't want to have regrets. Because she needed this. Okay, maybe shucking her clothes and having sex on the first date was drastic, but her life was stale. Each day she ate the same cereal for breakfast because it was easy.

And then a big stack of bananas Foster pancakes came into her life. She'd eyed them for a while. Then they landed on her plate. She had a fork in her hand. She needed ooey, gooey goodness. Those pancakes were her reward for plastering a smile on her face every morning and pretending life was good.

She looked at her pancakes. He watched her, the fire casting flickering shadows over his face.

The blanket hung suspended between them. Abigail tugged on her shirt, leaving it unsnapped, and stepped into Leif's arms. He enfolded her, tucking her head beneath his chin.

"It's okay, Abi," he whispered, dropping a kiss on her head. Slowly he pulled her down to the pillows, tucking the blanket around them. And like that moment when Cal had come traipsing back into her life, Leif remained quiet, merely holding her. Absently, he stroked her still damp hair, his torso warm against her.

Minutes ticked by as they lay there, lost in thought.

Abigail had no clue how Leif felt but she drew on everything she knew about relationships and realized she might not be prepared to handle being a modern woman who answered a booty call. No. Wait. She'd been the asker. Leif had answered.

Great.

It was as though the shocking things she'd read in *Cosmo*—about threesomes and "How to Go Down on Him…and Make him Beg for More"—had influenced her psyche. All those articles that made it seem as though sleeping around, or "hooking up" as they called it, was no big deal. So why did it feel like a big deal?

Probably because she'd slept with only three guys in her lifetime. One of whom was Leif.

Maybe she was too old-fashioned to play this game.

Then again, maybe she had to be different than

what she was. If she wanted to spend time with Leif, she had to accept it would be as part of an affair. Wait. Was that even the right term?

Maybe it was casual fling.

But she knew one thing—she didn't want everyone knowing she and Leif were doing whatever it was they were doing. Her parents were pillars of the community, running the First Presbyterian Church and serving on boards for the local food pantry and pregnancy crisis center. Abigail couldn't throw her indiscretion with Leif in their faces. Plus, Leif was an instructor at the school where her brother was the principal. Jake would be tossing his hat in the ring for fire captain. She couldn't burden them by acting like a fool the way Cal had a few years ago.

So it was either hide what she had with Leif…or end it. Friends on the outside, something more on the inside.

Was that too selfish? Or maybe it was crazy.

"Hey," he whispered. "Are you asleep?"

"No, just thinking."

"About?"

"How we're going to do this."

She felt his body stiffen…and not in the good way it had earlier. "Do what?"

"Well, I guess I shouldn't presume you'll want to see me again."

"Of course I do."

Abigail closed her eyes, briefly savoring the

thought. "I'm the PTA president, you're the art department head and my father is a preacher."

"So?" he said, relaxing a bit.

"I can't conduct an affair. It's a small town and people still talk."

"About your sex life?"

"That and more. I have a daughter and there are other people who could be hurt if I tossed all my good sense out the window and started, well, having sex in swimming pools in the middle of the winter."

He didn't say anything for a while. She waited because she knew she'd tossed the ball in his court. What would he do with it?

"So you don't want to see me?"

Easy lob.

"It will be hard not to see you. I'm taking your class and we're serving on the Laurel Woods Art Festival committee together."

"You know what I mean."

"I want to always stay friends."

"No problem with that."

Abigail blew out her breath. "Thing is, I don't jump my friends' bones like I jumped yours."

She felt him smile. "How about we not define this? We can see each other as friends in public, but in private, as long as we're both feeling it, we become a little bit more than friends."

"In *Cosmo*, they call this FWB…and another term I won't say because it sounds really crass."

"And friends with benefits sounds…genteel?"

"Compared to that, yes." She turned so she could see his face. His chiseled jaw tensed and his eyes looked serious for once. No teasing or boyish charm. "So what do you think?"

"I think you're not like most women. Most want some sort of commitment. You don't want one and you don't want anyone to know about us. I don't know how to feel about that."

"It's easier to know what to expect."

"You like rules, don't you?"

"Why does everyone say that?"

"Because you do."

As warm, comfy and sated as her body was, her emotions were turning as fast as spokes in a wheel. "Of course I like parameters. They make things easier. I'm not running away from you and what we've started. I just want to have it straight in my mind so I don't misstep and screw things up."

"Did you bring the label maker, too?"

She laughed. "I didn't have time. I wasn't planning on you, Leif."

Turning her in his arms, he gave her a soft kiss. "Unexpected things can be really awesome. I'm going to have a hell of a good time being your FWB."

Abigail kissed him, hoping like hell she could keep this man within those parameters, but knowing how hard it would be. She wasn't like the women in *Cosmopolitan* who made relationships seem so simple. Your Terms: Making Dating Work.

Still, this relationship with Leif was on her terms.

Friends with benefits. Hot sex with no strings. Hanging out. Wasn't permanent. No need for the heart to get involved.

"I need to get home," she said.

"A few more kisses, okay?" he said, doing just that, sweeping her into that place where reason seemed silly. *Don't think. Just feel.*

So for a few more minutes Abigail fell victim to the man who'd helped her let go…if only for a little while.

CHAPTER THIRTEEN

ABIGAIL TALKED LEIF into staying put and letting her walk home alone. The fire pit couldn't be left burning unattended.

And she needed space.

The night air was crisp, making her breath fog. The bared trees framed both the path and the full moon hovering above. The night was hard—cold edges with silver gilding. Such a contrast from the warmth of the man she'd left behind.

Good gravy, she'd entered into a FWB relationship like she was a twenty-five-year-old Manhattan salesgirl and not a forty-year-old divorcée soccer mom. And to think last week she hadn't even known what a FWB was. She'd be proud of herself if she weren't so nervous about keeping her heart out of the mix. Somehow what she'd shared with Leif seemed not so run-of-the-mill. So how did modern girls keep from growing attached? How did they keep sex and love two separate things?

Stepping onto her hibernating Saint Augustine lawn, still mulling over the situation, she felt a movement beside her.

"Oh, crap" she yelped, jumping back and raising her fist in self-defense.

"Whoa, whoa. It's just me," Cal said, throwing both hands up in a nonthreatening posture.

"Oh, good gravy, you scared me to death." Her heart sounded in her ears. "Jesus, Cal, is your mouth broken? Next time say something."

"Sorry," he said, showing her the glow of a cigarette. "I was having a smoke. Birdie fell asleep during some animated movie she sang all the words to."

"Yeah, once she likes something…" Abigail started moving toward the house. Her hair still felt damp and the cold weather made her chilled. "When did you start smoking? Thought California inspired healthy lifestyles."

He fell into step beside her. "Not when you're working in clubs. Kept me awake and focused when I was playing a set. I don't smoke much. Just when stress eats at me."

She didn't want to engage Cal but she was curious. "And you're stressed?"

"Try living with your parents, relearning a job that's changed and getting a divorce."

"Try being a single parent, remodeling a plantation house and having everyone feel sorry for you. No picnic. Wait, you married Morgan?"

Hurt flashed across his craggy face. "Last year. A justice-of-the-peace thing."

"You never told me. Or Birdie."

Cal raised his shoulders in a semishrug. "Didn't figure you'd want to know. But I shouldn't have married her. Thought it would keep her with me. Pathetic, huh?" He gave an embarrassed smile far removed from the Calhoun Orgeron who dunked the football through the goalposts after winning the LHSAA-Class 2-A championship his senior year.

Abigail started toward the porch. "Who you date or marry is none of my business."

Cal grabbed her arm and at the same time flicked the cigarette to the ground, putting it out with his boot heel. Abigail frowned at the butt and he wisely stooped to pick it up. "Can I have a sec?"

"I'm tired," she said, removing her arm from his grasp. "And it's cold out here."

"Your hair's wet."

She raised a hand to the tangled mess. "Yeah."

He waited as though expecting her to explain it, but she didn't owe Cal anything, especially not an explanation of what she'd done with Leif tonight.

"Fine." She jerked her head toward the house, moving quickly. The porch light glowed, promising warmth within. "Did Alice Ann go home?"

"Yeah, she set the cookies out, but the guests were already in their rooms. One dude came to the library and borrowed a book."

Abigail entered the warmth of Laurel Woods, inhaling the scent of the cookies and shivering against the warmth. "Getting cold."

"Yeah, look, I know things aren't good between us, but we need to try harder to be on the same team."

"Just exactly what are you talking about?"

"Birdie's not happy about how we've been treating each other."

"For one thing Birdie is a twelve-year-old girl experiencing her first surge of hormones. She's not happy about much. Second of all, you forfeited your right to play on my team when you left. Understand?" She looked hard at her ex-husband. He'd covered the silver in his hair with dye that was too dark, and he wore a shirt that looked as if it belonged on a twenty-year-old. The rest of him was the same old Cal. She'd once loved him more than she loved herself, but he was unequivocally an asshole of the fifth degree. "Look, for Birdie's sake, I'm happy you're back. She's needed you—"

"I know. I screwed up. I wasn't fair to you or her."

"You have a chance to make some of that up to her."

"But not you?" His voice was soft, almost silky. Warning lights flashed in her head.

"I'm not part of the equation."

He smiled at her. "I get it. You're playing the ice queen and dating other men to make me jealous. You want me to suffer."

"Make you *jealous*?" Suddenly the chill was replaced by hot anger. "You think I'm playing a game? Dating Leif as part of some way to—"

"Everyone can see he's not your type. What else am I to think?"

Abigail curled her fist and thought about smacking Cal. It would feel so good to finally vent the rage she'd harbored toward him for these past few years. Giving him a smack for every pitying glance she'd received, for every smart-mouthed comment from her daughter, for every time she'd cried herself to sleep wondering what was wrong with her that her husband didn't love her. That would feel so damn good...for a few measly seconds. Then she'd be angry she'd lost control.

So she steadied herself inside. "Leif and I are friends," she said, withholding exactly what kind of friends.

"He doesn't seem to be the kind of guy a woman's just friends with."

"I'm no longer your concern."

Cal looked as if he might argue but eventually he nodded. "You're right. Let's just try to get along better. Not because of Birdie, but because we're two grown people who can act decently to one another."

So now he was going to be a grown-up? He hadn't worried about doing the responsible thing five years ago. "I've been a grown person for a long time, Cal. I was the one pulling the weight of parenthood while you were screwing Morgan on a beach somewhere and masquerading as a musician. You do not get to come home and pretend to be reasonable. You don't get to play superdad. And you damn sure don't get to tell me what to do."

Cal turned red. "I shouldn't have suggested anything to you. You like holding on to anger and playing the victim. So don't put yourself out, Abigail." He jerked open the door and the cold rushed in, a reminder of what sat between them.

For a fleeting moment, her heart twisted, the old pain bubbling up and, along with it, the urge to apologize, to smooth things between them. She squashed it all down. Some habits were hard to break. Abigail wasn't used to hurting people. She liked to please. She'd been easy for Cal to manipulate. "I'll try to... temper myself. Because as you said, we're adults."

He paused, his gaze taking her in, dropping to her wrinkled shirt. In his expression, she could see the recognition of what she'd been doing earlier. In her anger with Cal, she'd almost forgotten.

Were her lips swollen from Leif's kisses? Were her cheeks flushed? Did she look like a woman well-loved?

From the sudden awareness in his eyes, she figured she did.

"Thanks." But he looked hurt, delivering the wounded expression he'd perfected for times when he wanted his way and didn't get it. It was somewhere between puppy-dog sadness and petulant grumpiness.

Again she got that prickling feeling he was working her, plying guilt, dropping hints, worming his way into her life. Waiting for that moment she'd welcome him home with open arms.

"Well, good night, Cal."

He stepped outside. "I'll be seeing you."

Abigail watched her ex-husband walk away, lifting her hand when he looked over his shoulder at her. And then he was gone.

She twisted the lock and switched off the lamp in the parlor, leaving the buffet lamps on the foyer table lit in case one of her guests decided to go for an earlymorning walk. Then she went upstairs to her room, hair still damp, body replete from making love with Leif, thoughts tumbling with relationship parameters, ex-husbands and the fact she had to go to art class tomorrow night.

Yawning, she decided to tuck away the guilt and snuggle beneath her down comforter with the next episode of *Call the Midwife*.

TUESDAY WAS LEIF'S busy day—after working car pool, he had little more than an hour between the end of one job and the start of his part-time gig at the community college nearly twenty miles away. Just enough time to leaf through the photo album Abigail had let him borrow yesterday while choking down a veggie roll.

Not many photos of the cabins used by the artists were included, but there were plenty of the grand house before renovations. Notes beneath the photos acknowledged many of the original furnishings had remained—some of which had been restored and were currently used in the bed-and-breakfast. Before renovations, the staircase bore a broken banister and chipped marble, and as Leif studied the structure, he wondered what had really happened the night Simeon had plunged to his death.

One thing he knew with certainty was his mother was no killer.

Which meant he needed to talk to Bartholomew Harvey.

But how did one bring up that sort of conversation without revealing his true intent? Though he'd told both Abigail and Hilda about his mother and the real reason he was in Magnolia Bend, he wasn't ready for the censure that would likely come when people learned the truth. According to Hilda, many in Magnolia Bend didn't like Calliope, but that had been over thirty years ago. Surely, many had forgotten.

But if some townspeople still called the Civil War the War of Northern Aggression, maybe not.

The South was slow in many ways—both a good and bad thing. Nothing wrong with moseying—a term they used in rotation with lollygagging—but he didn't care for the way many held on to past prejudice.

Leif rose from the couch, moving to the sliding glass door. The sun neared the horizon, casting long shadows on his backyard, one ray spotlighting the fire pit where he'd held Abigail.

She'd felt so good in his arms, and seeing her leave her overactive rationality behind had been rewarding.

God, she'd been beautiful with the water sluicing off her pale skin, the luminous moon highlighting her curves, shadows darkening the valleys. He loved her unexpected boldness, the passion she'd shown. In

the depths of her eyes he'd found a kindred spirit...
if only for a few hours.

But then she'd gone, leaving an empty spot on
the cushion while still sitting with him. He'd felt the
change. Not necessarily regret, but she'd pulled into
herself. Like tugging on a woolen coat for protection.
Abigail was like Mr. Rogers in that old children's
TV show. Taking off what the world expected of her
in order to play in a world of make-believe, knowing she must return to the person everyone expected
when the magic abated.

The dark lanterns swayed in the wind as the sun
took a final bow. His exotic world of make-believe
was a darkened set, awaiting another magic moment.

If only...

Earlier he'd texted Abigail, feeling a bit clingy
but wanting her to know he'd been thinking of her.

Great first date. You're welcome to hang out at my
house anytime.

He'd sent it, and then wished he hadn't. Maybe
it was too blatant. Abigail didn't seem the kind of
woman to dial in a booty call...and his text had
made it sound like that was what he expected between them.

Dumb move.

Or maybe she would see the text for what it
was—a tap on the shoulder, a reminder he wanted

to see her again. Not in the classroom, but alone, in the privacy they'd shared last night.

What they'd shared wasn't just about sex…though that particular activity had been mind-blowing. There was something inside him that craved more. That wanted Abigail to be a part of his life while he stayed in Magnolia Bend.

If only for a while.

He sighed and turned toward his austere—aka empty—living room. Maybe he was lonely. Leif wasn't great at being alone. Oh, he could do it for a while, but it wasn't his ideal. Underneath his "don't nail me down" persona was a human being who thirsted for what he'd had in the commune as a child—a place to belong. This needy feeling was what had led to his string of romantic entanglements. He wanted to be that guy—the one with the lifetime commitment—but he simply wasn't. Each time he approached the final step, each time he faced true commitment, he balked. Ran. Got the hell out of town.

Speaking of which… He glanced at his watch.

No more time to ponder what was missing from his life. He had a class to teach, and Abigail would be there.

How things had changed in a mere week.

Crazy.

An hour later he unlocked the classroom door as Peggy appeared at his elbow.

"Good evening, Leif. I looked up some of your

artwork. You are such a talent," she said, parking a hand on her hip and smiling at him with apple-red lips. She sort of fluttered her eyes, looking a tad unsure at her attempt to engage his attention. At that moment, he felt bad for her. Something akin to loneliness lurked in her eyes.

"Why thank you, Ms. Peggy. I'm proud of what I've been able to do. It's a joy for me." He swung the door open and flicked on the lights.

"You know, I can tell. Shows in your paintings. You sure have traveled around a lot. Me, I've only ever been to Florida to visit my late husband's aunt. I didn't like her much, but Florida sure was pretty."

Leif wasn't interested in making small talk with the older lady, but he didn't want to be rude. "Your husband is no longer with you?"

"Not since last December. Heart attack in the middle of a Saints game. I'm not kidding. He was dead afore he hit the floor."

"Oh, I'm so sorry." He erased the board, turning slightly so he could make eye contact.

"Yeah, he was a pain in the ass, but he was my pain in the ass."

Leif smiled at her comment. He could hear the love in her voice. "He must have been a good guy."

"Only the best for me, honey," she said with a wink.

Leif waved as several other students came in, including the new student, Mr. Cho, whom he'd met earlier in the office. Then he caught Birdie out of the corner of his eye. He raised his hand to say hello, but she didn't look up. Just set her pad on the table in the middle of the classroom no one had used last time and sat without even looking at him.

So that was how it was.

Abigail hurried in, talking low on her cell phone. She caught his eye but immediately looked away again.

And something inside him twanged like a string breaking on his ukulele.

He nodded at Peggy, who had turned her attention to the older black lady whose name he couldn't seem to remember. Wait, Alba. That was it. Leif shook off the slight and readied his supplies as if Abigail weren't the woman he'd made love to last night. If Abigail wanted to treat this like a secret, he'd go along with it. But still, the idea felt like shoving his foot into a stiff Oxford dress shoe a size too small.

Tight fit and not real comfy.

Fact was he was an instructor, so he shouldn't emphasize a personal relationship between him and any student. This was a professional setting for him.

"Okay, everyone, if you'll get seated, I have a special treat for you tonight," he said, clearing his throat and holding up his hands in order to get everyone's attention. The two college girls slipped in late, quickly sliding into their former seats, tugging out their earbuds and pocketing their cell phones with a quick look of acknowledgment at him.

"Is it one of those life models?" Peggy cracked

with a cackle. "'Cause that's what I took this class for—to sketch a real live hunka, hunka burning love."

A few people in the class chuckled, but most, including Abigail, who had gotten off the phone, looked confused.

"I don't think you're quite up for drawing the human body, but I do think you're ready to learn some technique tonight, including adding perspective to the still life you sketched last time. I'm going to pass back the sketches of the fruit, but I want you to take out several clean sheets of paper to practice some of the techniques I'm about to show you. Giving perspective will help you become a better artist. After we practice, we're going to re-create the piece of fruit using what you learned. Any questions?"

Birdie raised her hand. "I did a whole bowl of fruit."

"Which was ambitious."

The child frowned. "Not what I meant. Can I choose just one item?"

Yeah, she wasn't smiling or happy the way she'd been in the last class. He wondered if Birdie knew about him and her mother. "Of course."

Abigail caught his gaze then and he could see the apology in her eyes.

Shoving thoughts of Abigail from his mind, he plunged into the lesson, reminding himself to treat Abigail like any other student. Of course that was easier thought than applied. During the course of the class he couldn't escape the prickling of awareness every time he passed Abigail. He sucked in the scent of her shampoo like some nutcase, noted the way she tilted her head along with the way her eyes narrowed making four small furrows on her forehead. When she bent to erase a line, her hair swished forward, reminding him of the way it brushed his naked chest when he'd held her.

Ignoring her didn't work so well.

His gaze was too stubborn.

And damned if Abigail didn't sense his thoughts. Often her gaze would meet his and suddenly the world fell away. He'd smile at her, forgetting he was her instructor, too lost in the idea he was her lover. On some level it felt very much like junior high— him eyeing the girl across the room, composing poetry in his head, trying to hide the boner he had under his desk.

Thankfully, no one else seemed to notice...except for Birdie.

And it must have pissed her off a little because her green eyes became laser beams. Leif was certain if they actually *had* been laser beams he'd be crawling on the floor hunting his testicles.

Finally the last few minutes approached.

"Okay, good class, everyone. I've seen some real progress in the new drawings. What I'd like for you to do is to take the piece you're working on home with you. Spend some time thinking about the techniques we discussed and see if you can't apply them.

No need to rush this process. Art is about passion and being in the moment, but it's also about taking your time."

"Just like with a woman," Mr. Cho said.

Leif crooked an eyebrow before snagging his gaze on Abigail. Again. "I'd say that's a good assessment, Mr. Cho."

The older man nodded, solemnly accepting the affirmation of the wisdom he'd dispensed. Nearly everyone in the class hid a smile.

"All right, then. I'll see you next Tuesday," Leif said, swinging his hands, giving a brief clap of dismissal. "Have a good one."

The members of the class stood, shoving papers into their portfolios or bags. Abigail tried to help Birdie, but the child pulled her supplies away, pinning her mother with a glare.

This thing he had going with Abigail wasn't going to be easy. Birdie hadn't declared war on them, but she wasn't happy about them dating or hanging out or, the actual truth, having mind-blowing sex.

"Give me a minute, Birdie," Abigail said, turning toward him, trying not to look so interested. The color in her cheeks gave her away, though.

Most of the class had already left; only a few stragglers remained.

"I'm ready to go, Mom. You can talk to Mr. Lively on your next date," Birdie huffed, slapping her pad shut and shoving her chair underneath the desk.

Abigail froze, glancing at Alba and Peggy, who both stood wide-eyed.

"That's enough, Birdie," Abigail said to her daughter.

"It's Brigitte," the girl said as though her mother was the biggest dumb ass in Louisiana before tossing her dark hair over her shoulder and striding to the door. "I'll wait in the car."

Peggy looked hard at Abigail and then glanced at the retreating child before saying, "Hey, hey, Brigitte."

Birdie's steps slowed. She turned. "Ma'am?"

"Isn't she your mother?" Peggy asked, pointing a finger toward Abigail.

"Ma'am?" Birdie asked again, looking confused. Leif glanced at Abigail, who still looked mortified at her daughter's comment and ensuing behavior.

"I said, 'Isn't that your mother?'" Peggy asked again.

"Yeah, she's my mother."

Peggy nodded, giving Birdie a big smile. "I thought so, but the way you just treated her made me think differently."

This time Birdie's cheeks flooded with color. She darted a glance at her mother as if she didn't know what to do.

Well, what do you know? Ol' Pegs wasn't going to take crap from a kid who'd gotten too big for her britches. Leif bit his lower lip to prevent smiling and ducked his head to shift the class syllabus in his hand.

"Uh, yes, ma'am," Birdie stammered. Leif glanced up to find Birdie nearly the same shade of magenta she'd been the night she admitted she'd spied on him. "I'm sorry."

Peggy gave her a knowing smile. "It's hard being your age. I remember my own girls and the way we butted heads, but your mama is your mama. Remember that, sweetheart."

Birdie nodded, her eyes wide. "Uh, good night, everyone. Sorry, Mom."

Then Birdie slipped through the door.

Peggy laughed, looking at Abigail. "I don't envy you. Raised three girls myself. Gets worse before it gets better."

"Oh, Lord, don't tell me that," Abigail said, shaking her head.

"It will be fine," Peggy said, brushing a hand toward Leif. "And don't let her manipulate you. Our daughters have strings attached to our hearts and sometimes they pull them in the wrong direction."

Alba nodded her head. "Mmm-hmm. And that man looks like the right direction to me." Then the older lady cackled, giving him a wink.

Leif couldn't resist a smile.

"Hey, Peggy," Alba said, snapping her canvas bag shut. "Come with me over to the student center. They got good coffee. We'll let these young people chat."

"Sounds perfect." Then the two older ladies

headed out, debating the pros and cons of having fully caffeinated coffees at this hour.

"I can't believe she just called me young," Abigail said, walking around and pushing in chairs while Leif gathered the stray papers peppering the tables.

"Why not? You act like you're ancient."

"Some days I feel like I'm ancient." Abigail pushed in the final chair and regarded him with enigmatic eyes.

"You're embarrassed."

"Maybe a little. This feels a bit unreal." She swiveled her head around, looking for anyone remaining in the hall. "It's probably better if we're not so obvious about what we're doing."

"I'm hoping that means we're doing it more than once," he teased.

Abigail nodded. "I'd like that. I won't let Birdie manipulate me, but, like I said last night, I don't want to flaunt an affair around town. It goes against who I am as a person…who I've always taught my daughter to be."

"Which is?"

"Moral."

Leif stiffened. "So what we're doing is wrong in the light of day but right when we're beneath the covers?"

"Look, I'm not trying to be a hypocrite. If waving the fact we're getting busy together under everyone's noses is what you want, then I can't be with you."

"I may not be moral, but I'm honest."

Abigail swallowed. "So you don't want me to come by later?"

"I didn't say that."

"This is what we agreed to—a little fun. I don't want to hurt when you leave." Her voice broke at the end of her statement.

And like fingers snapping, Leif clearly saw the issue spread before him. Abigail wasn't scared to let go and live a little. She was scared to hold on again.

Because falling in love often ended with a splat.

"You won't. We're good," he said, electing to give her space. He didn't understand his need to push her in the first place...or maybe what he didn't understand was how much it hurt inside that she wanted him only under the cloak of secrecy. Why should he care? His ego wasn't fragile, and there had been plenty of times he'd slept with a woman and never worried about what anyone else thought.

He was probably still messed up over his mother's death and the ensuing quest to find his father. Somehow his skin had thinned or long-seeded emotions had worked their way to the surface, messing with his head.

Abigail was a friend and lover. Nothing more.

"I might drop by tonight. Uh, that is if you want me to?" she asked, color once again flooding her face. He liked that she blushed. It was so Abigail.

Leif walked over and tugged her to him. "That would be awesome, FWB."

She smiled before glancing around. Then she rose

on her tiptoes and kissed him squarely on the chin. "This sneaking around is a bit of a turn-on."

"Yeah?" he asked, bunching up the hemline of her long-sleeved cotton T-shirt dress, brushing the backs of her thighs. Her breathing increased as his fingers walked toward the edge of her panties. "Next time you wear a dress, don't wear underwear. Think you can do that, Ms. PTA?"

"Seriously?"

"If we're going to do this sneaking around, let's do it right. Next time you know you're seeing me in public, ditch the panties."

She licked her lips, pupils dilated. Too tempting. He swooped and caught her mouth, tugging her bottom lip with his teeth so he could taste her. At the same time, he stroked her ass, making her wriggle against him.

With a final slap on her butt, he broke the kiss. "You better go before the custodian shows up and catches us making out."

Abigail stepped back, shifting her dress into place. Through the material, he could see her hardened nipples. His gaze rose to those puffy just-kissed lips before sliding up to eyes full of desire. He almost walked over and locked the classroom door. Yeah, kinky sex with Abigail on his metal desk could be the ultimate in naughty fantasy.

"When Birdie goes to bed, I'll come over so you can finish what you started, Mr. Lively."

"Don't think you're getting an A just because

you're putting out. You're going to have to draw that damn apple better."

Abigail fluttered her eyelashes. "Maybe you can tutor me."

"Oh, I'll tutor you," he said, with another slap of her ass. Abigail gave a little squeak.

Abigail's response was a quick kiss before slipping out the door.

CHAPTER FOURTEEN

A SILENT DRIVE home wasn't as bad as Abigail expected it to be. For some reason she needed only the hum of the tires on the road to accompany her mixed-up thoughts. Normally she would have lit into her kid about the way she'd acted earlier, but some sixth sense told her Birdie needed to think about it. So she let the issue go and focused instead on how she'd nearly screwed things up with Leif.

I don't want to hurt.

Why had she let that cat out of the bag? Made her sound weak, like some clingy girl who might show up one day wearing a wedding dress, holding a piece of cake to toss into his face. She hated being vulnerable, hated letting any man, or person for that matter, have that much control over her emotions.

She could tell herself she was over the pain of Cal's betrayal. She could feed herself lines about being reasonable and taking relationships slow. But the fact was she was full of shit.

Because she was afraid of what she could feel for Leif if she let herself go there.

And he was so wrong for her. Why couldn't she have chosen some regular Joe who had lived in Magnolia Bend his whole life…and never wanted to leave? Why the nutty, sexy art teacher? Why the guy who thought a good date was roasting hot dogs and skinny-dipping? Why the man who dared her not to wear underwear? Why the man who made her...laugh, wear short skirts and drink Scotch on moonlit porches?

Because he was the yang to her yin.

Maybe his being so not for her made him so for her.

Maybe Leif Lively was perfect for her.

But that messed everything up. Leif wasn't staying in Louisiana. And his "love 'em and leave 'em" past proved as much. She couldn't let herself think about something more than what they now had. She had to protect herself from falling in love.

But maybe it was too late?

Birdie sneezed, drawing her attention away from her total failure as a one-night stand. She hoped Birdie wasn't getting a cold. The virus had swept through the lower grades of St. George's last week, rendering a lot of absentees. When they got home, she'd look for an antihistamine for the girl. The motherly knot of concern nearly overshadowed the earlier disappointment she experienced at her daughter embarrassing her in front of Peggy and Alba.

"Alice Ann said she had to run over to Neil's to iron his suit for an interview. She said she'd be back later tonight, though. I forgot to tell you," Birdie said as they crossed over the old mill pond road, still several miles away from Laurel Woods.

"Oh? Well, I guess it doesn't matter. We don't have any guests tonight anyway," Abigail said, a nugget of worry gnawing at her. Business had slowed since the holidays. The only bright spot was that Mardi Gras was a week away and she was booked solid for ten days straight. Then there would be only a few more slow days until the arts festival and tourist season launched in Louisiana. She hoped her business picked up soon.

As she swung into the long driveway studded with twisting oaks, she caught sight of Cal's new truck shining like a penny in her driveway.

Great.

"Daddy's here," Birdie said, straightening, her beleaguered expression melting into a smile. "He said he might stop by to see what I did in art class. I think I'm going to enter one of my drawings in the U15 category of the festival. Mr. Lively said he'd look at my portfolio and suggest the ones he thinks are the best. Can you take it to him when you go over there?"

"I don't know when I'll go over."

Birdie smirked. "I bet you'll go tonight."

Abigail felt as though her daughter had punched her. "I might go over for a drink."

"That's what you call it?" Birdie muttered under her breath.

Panic slammed into Abigail. How could Birdie know she'd slept with Leif? She couldn't. Abigail let the smart-aleck remark slide. "Hey, are you upset I went over to his place for dinner? You didn't act very nice to Mr. Lively tonight."

Birdie shrugged. "It's your life, and I doubt he cares what I think."

"That's not true. He's always been one of your favorite teachers."

"Jeez, Mom, don't worry, I'm not into him if that's what you think. Spying on him was just a silly thing. That's it. I'm not a pervert or anything."

"That's not what I meant," Abigail said, slowing down so she had a little time before Cal invaded their world again.

"I know you're still mad at me for that whole spying thing. I embarrassed you."

"I'm not mad at you. I'm confused."

"Because I want to know things?" Birdie asked, her mouth thinning into mulishness.

Abigail had no idea where the conversation was going. Mothering Birdie was like playing a game where you chose what was behind door one, two or three. Scary.

"You know, I looked at those magazines because I wanted to know things. That's all. You treat me like a baby, never talking about sex and stuff. You always act like a person's body or sex is dirty. But it's not. It's natural."

Abigail felt her legs get weak at the accusation in her daughter's tone. "I don't think you're a baby. Look, it's hard being a mama. I want to protect you, and I probably messed up the whole 'birds and bees' talk. You're right. Being interested in the differences between a man and woman or being interested in sex is normal for someone your age. And, honey, you can talk to me about sex or ask questions anytime you want."

Her daughter looked straight ahead even as she shifted on the seat, wiggling like a worm in hot ashes. Perhaps, when it came down to it, talking to her mom about sex didn't seem like such a bright idea after all. But then Birdie stilled. Jutting her chin out, she glanced at Abigail. "So, I have a question."

Abigail parked the car behind the house. "Okay. Shoot."

"Are you having sex with Mr. Lively?"

Abigail tried not to shrink away, but it was too late to keep her cool. "What?"

"You said I can ask questions about sex, so I am. You told me not to have sex if I wasn't married. So I want to know if you've had sex outside marriage." Birdie crossed her arms and leveled a look at Abigail that would have made a detective proud.

"Frankly, Birdie, that's none of your business."

"That means yes," Birdie said, opening the car door.

"No, it doesn't. It means there are lines in life and you just crossed one."

"But it's okay for you to know everything about me? It's okay for you to tell me what to do even if you don't do the things you preach?" Birdie said, slamming the car door.

"Hey, wait a minute, young lady," Abigail said, trying like hell to find the right words…and not look guilty. After all, she told Leif she'd be over later…to have sex with him. "You can't talk to me like that."

"I'm not being disrespectful. Besides you said I can ask you anything about sex. Remember?"

"Do you really want to know about my sex life? Do you? Because I could make your hair curl with the sex I haven't had because I've been busy raising a daughter. Is that what you wanted to hear? Or maybe you want all the details of the sex I've been having? It goes pretty much like this…" Abigail tilted her head.

Birdie watched her, eyes wide, looking a bit frightened.

After a few seconds, Abigail righted her head. "Did you hear it?"

"No."

"Exactly, because when your father left, I ceased to have any sort of adult fun." Abigail wanted to stop herself, wanted to be the mother she'd always aspired to be for Birdie—careful with her words—but she couldn't stop this time. "You want to be treated like an adult? Well, that's how the mop flops because being an adult means you don't go off and do whatever feels good. You give it up because there's something more important at stake. And for me, that was you. Up until this year, I felt like I was doing a helluva job, but maybe I wasn't because lately you've been rude, disrespectful and selfish."

Cal came around the corner of the house, looking concerned. "Hey, what's going on? Glad you don't have any guests because it sounds like a hen party out here."

"It's none of your concern, Cal. Your daughter is being difficult as usual," Abigail said, brushing past him, heading inside. She needed to calm down before she said something else she'd regret. She'd already done a bang-up job. Things felt so outside her control. Never in a million years would she have expected to lose her cool that way. For heaven's sake, she'd just talked about her sex life with her daughter.

Okay, so she technically hadn't, but she had essentially blamed Birdie for the drought in her love life, which wasn't fair because Birdie had nothing to do with that. The fact that Abigail had used her daughter as the excuse to put off dating wasn't anyone's fault but her own.

Exactly.

And she'd remedied that last night.

Abruptly, she changed directions.

"Where are you going?" Cal shouted.

"Out," she said as she stomped toward the path she'd taken last night. "You're her father. You deal with her."

Moments later, Abigail stood on Leif's porch, breathing hard and wondering if this was a booty call.

Of course not.

They were friends, right? Nothing sexual even had to happen. She just needed someone to talk to… and she wasn't going to think about how before art

class she'd slipped into her second-best set of un-
derthings and sprayed her favorite cologne between
her breasts.

Good Lord. What healthy, reasonably attractive
woman stood on a guy's porch trying to talk herself
out of a night with a sexy man? Especially after having admitted how pathetic her sex life had been to
her twelve-year-old daughter.

She was probably officially cracking up.

Still, she watched her finger press that doorbell,
counting one…two…three…fou—

The door swung open and Leif stood there, looking much the way he had that day over a month ago.
Naked, golden chest, lean waist, karate pants and
bare feet.

He looked like sin personified and something inside her let go of all the drama, trauma and whatever else had plagued her seconds ago. When he
smiled at her like that, the world seemed easier. She
felt stronger.

"Hey," he said, stepping back.

Abigail walked in, shut the door and kissed the
hell out of him.

"Mmm," he groaned, gathering her against him
as he twisted the lock on the door.

Abigail answered with an "mmm-hmm" as she
threaded her fingers through his gorgeous, sexy hair
and lost herself in Leif.

Deepening the kiss, she reveled in the way his

hard body felt against hers. His arms wound tightly around her and he slowed and softened the kiss.

Abigail finally broke the kiss. "Sorry."

"Why? I personally hope that's the way you've decided to always greet me." He smiled at her, a hot flame of passion still flickering in the depths of his gaze.

Abigail thumped her head against his chest. "You just looked so good standing there. I needed…something."

He kissed the top of her head. "Feel free to take what you need. I'm here to please you."

Inside she turned to mush. When had anyone wanted to please her? Not in a long time. A very long time. This was why she needed Leif in her life right frickin' now. Because until he opened that door in December and reminded her that she was still a woman, she'd forgotten what it was like to be in—

No. Not love.

But something.

Leif rubbed her back, making her feel so taken care of. She leaned into him. "Is everything okay?" he asked.

"Birdie and Cal."

Leif didn't say anything, just watched her.

"She's being difficult and, of course, as soon as I pulled into our drive, I saw Cal's truck. I left and came here. I know I'm avoiding the problems in my life but—"

"Sometimes you have to step away from things

that are hard, so you can return to them better prepared. Nothing wrong with needing a break...or
coming to me," Leif said, nuzzling her earlobe.
"Birdie's going through some hard stuff—dealing
with changes in her body, wanting independence,
managing her father back in her life. Now, Cal, well,
I can get all macho and tough if you need me to."

Abigail shook her head. "No, I don't want you involved. Cal's an ass and thinks he should be able to
have what he let go of long ago. He came back because Morgan did to him what he did to me. I guess
he didn't get the memo that I'm no one's leftovers."

"No way are you anyone's leftovers," Leif murmured, making his way down the column of her
neck. His mouth felt so good. She leaned back a little, clasping his shoulders so she wouldn't fall.

"That feels so good."

He nodded against her. "You taste good."

Abigail literally felt her knees go weak. This man
made her want to forget all she'd been so she could
be everything he wanted.

Leif made her reckless.

"You want to talk some more or do you want to
have your buttons popped?" he asked, fingering the
buttons on her blouse.

"My buttons popped? That sounds dirty," she
whispered before running her hands over his shoulders. Then she trailed her fingers down his stomach toward the drawstring. Below the ties, his pants

tented with his erection. "But maybe it's not about the buttons."

She dropped to her knees and tugged the string.

"Hey, Abigail, you don't have to," he said, reaching to cup under her arms. She pushed his hand away.

"Hush," she said, freeing the ties and tugging his pants from his lean hips. She pulled the cotton free and sank her hands into his fine ass. No underwear. There were some really nice things about the freedoms Leif practiced.

"Abi," he whispered, his face slack with pleasure at her touch.

Abigail clasped Leif's erection in her hand, enjoying the control she had on her knees. Leif closed his eyes and dropped his head back as she ran her tongue over the head, trailing her fingers down the length of his erection. Teasing.

"Bedroom," he said as she blew against his sensitive flesh.

Abigail gripped his length again, testing the girth and heft of him. He was magnificent. Built like a model, hung like a, well, not a bull, but he had plenty to work with. Abigail leaned forward and flicked her tongue over the tip of him again.

"Ahh," he moaned, before fisting his hand in her hair and tilting her head. "You better stop now."

Abigail rose. "I'm only pausing. Follow me."

She lifted her blouse over her head as she walked toward the darkened hallway that had to lead to hi·

bedroom. She also unbuttoned the mom jeans, wiggling out of them, pausing only to kick them aside. Her bra and panties were lacy pink confections she'd found in a box she'd packed away a few years after her honeymoon when T-shirts and practical bras became her go-to for lingerie.

"You're such a tease," he said, his voice playful as he followed her, splendidly naked, toward the bedroom.

Abigail looked over her shoulder. "No, I'm a guarantee. Now get your ass in here so I can finish what I started."

"Yes, ma'am."

CHAPTER FIFTEEN

ABIGAIL LOOKED AT Cal and grimaced despite her mother's incredible Sunday lunch efforts. She felt grumpy not only because her ex-husband currently wolfed down turnip greens at the Beauchamp family table, but also because she hadn't been able to see Leif since Tuesday night. Birdie had come down with the flu at the same time a big group celebrating the first parades of Mardi Gras in New Orleans had descended on the B and B. "Can you pass the rolls, Jake?"

Her youngest brother tossed a roll at her. Abigail snatched it out of the air and gave him the stink eye.

"Jacob Douglas Beauchamp, don't throw things at my table," Fancy said, not missing a bite of the chicken and dumplings she'd served moments ago.

Jake grinned in spite of their mother's proclamation. "She said pass it."

Fancy jabbed a finger at him, saying nothing more.

"Sorry, Mom," he said, retackling the food on his plate. A few minutes slid by before Jake looked up at his former brother-in-law jammed in between Birdie and Matt. "So, Calhoun, tell us about Cali-for-ni-ay."

Cal cleared his throat and wiped his mouth with a napkin. "Not much to tell."

"Well, you were out there five years. Surely you did something more than Morgan."

Her daddy must have stomped down on Jake's foot because he yelped. Dan Beauchamp always sat next to Jake in order to pinch, nudge or out-and-out pop his youngest child, who had a mouth with no filter on him. Fancy rolled her eyes and tried to stifle a grin behind her napkin.

"Watch your mouth at the table, son," Dan warned.

"Sorry, Pop." Jake's blue eyes danced and he didn't look the least bit sorry.

Abigail didn't like humiliating Cal, but on the other hand, she took some pleasure in Matt's and John's cool demeanors and Jake's not-so-subtle jabs at the man who had dishonored their sister. She guessed Cal should be glad they lived in South Louisiana and not Iran. Protecting the family honor in some cultures would have resulted in Cal's being spoon-fed for the rest of his life. As it was, a little coldness and a well-placed zinger were to be expected.

Silence descended again before Cal said, "I played one show with Jackson Browne when one of his rhythm guys went down with the flu. That's the highlight. No, wait. I saw Cameron Diaz jogging on the beach once."

"In a bikini?" Jake looked interested.

"We're at the table, Jake," Dan said.

"Pretty girls in bikinis aren't bad language," , winking at Birdie, who still looked wan.

"Today is the Lord's day, son," her father said, his normally jolly blue eyes portraying his aggravation with Jake.

Typical Jake. He loved poking sticks at people... even his own parents.

Abigail felt about as comfortable as a bear in thorns, so she tried to shift the mood by looking at John and Shelby at the end of the table. "So is everything ready for this upcoming weekend?" She hummed a few bars of "Here Comes the Bride."

Shelby, who'd tucked into her food like a starving woman, looked up. John had remained quiet as usual, casting occasional worried glances at his wife-to-be. "Well, that's something we wanted to talk to you all about. My parents can't come next weekend, so we're postponing for a few weeks."

John patted Shelby on the back when she looked a bit teary. "My mother's not the easiest to deal with. She runs a furniture company, and they're in the process of some business dealings. Uh, I'm hoping everyone can still make it on February twenty-eighth. Fancy said we can have the wedding and reception here. It's the only weekend my parents are free. Sorry."

Fancy gave all the Beauchamp siblings *that* look. "Of course we'll all be here. Nothing's more important than family. And we're sorry it won't happen on Valentine's Day, but that's okay. I think February twenty-eighth is a fine day to get married. My aunt Gracie's birthday, God rest her soul."

"Of course, we'll be here," Abigail added, noting Jake's frown.

"I can switch shifts with one of the guys. I'll be here," Jake said after a few seconds.

Matt wiped his mouth and nodded. "I'll make sure Mary Jane can get the boys here. I want them at the wedding."

John looked at Shelby. "See? No big deal."

Shelby's shoulders dropped and finally she smiled. "Thank you all so much. I didn't think I could eat I was so worried about y'all getting aggravated with me."

Everyone, including Shelby, looked at her empty plate.

John started laughing and the sound made every Beauchamp, including Birdie, smile. It had been a long time since John had been happy. That wedding could take place any day and they would all be okay with it.

Abigail glanced at her mother, who regarded the two lovers with an even sappier grin on her face. Jake mimicked sticking his finger down his throat, making Birdie laugh again.

Cal just watched, picking at his corn bread, a wrinkle on his forehead as though he wondered if he should speak up.

No. You shouldn't, jackass. You're not in this ~~~ily.

~~~~ail was still baffled as to what had led her ~~~~ invite Cal. But after her father delivered

a sermon entitled "Obeying God: Receiving Life's True Blessing," all through which Abigail had squirmed, she wished she'd taken a rain check on the family feast.

Yeah, she'd felt a little guilty about sitting in her father's congregation after getting naked with Leif. Teenage déjà vu. At least this time she wasn't hungover. She'd call it Catholic guilt…except she was Presbyterian.

The shame of being a brazen hussy was bad enough. Then Cal had walked into the sanctuary in his Sunday best, big hometown-boy smile in place, shaking hands and looking damn near adorable the way he always had. He'd skipped his parents' pew and settled down right beside her and Birdie.

It made her twitchy because she'd spent many a Sunday the same way, sitting with him, Birdie tucked between them, her father delivering the word. As the rest of the congregation belted out "Onward, Christian Soldiers," she could hardly catch her breath.

And then she overheard her father inviting Cal to lunch.

Wasn't like she could shout "That bastard isn't invited" in the middle of the benediction. Besides, this wasn't her house.

After the strained lunch was over and dishes washed and put away, Abigail went to find her father. She found him in the den watching the Super Bowl with her brothers and Cal. Like little boys they were in the throes of arguing a call.

"Dad?" Abigail shouted over Matt being Matt—insisting he was right about the in-bounds interception.

"Don't care what you say, he stepped out," her father said before glancing her way. "What?"

"Can I speak to you for a minute?"

"Sure," he said, his eyes returning to the big screen momentarily. He nodded his head and slapped his hands together. "Told you. He stepped out."

"Dad?"

"I'm coming," her father said, lowering the footrest of his recliner. When her father stood, slightly stooped with a groan, Abigail's heart skipped. Her father was getting older...even if he still could hang with his younger sons. "What do you need, hon?"

"Can we go out back?" she asked, darting a glance at Cal, who watched her and not the game. He looked uncomfortable.

"Sure, but I want to see the fourth quarter so if it's something that can wait—"

"It can't," she said, walking toward the door. Shelby and Birdie were helping Fancy make cookies to take to Aunt Reva in the nursing home so no one was around when Abigail stepped into her mother's faded garden. The screen door slammed behind her father.

"What's wrong, honey?" His gaze moved over her face with concern.

"Why is Cal here?"

"Oh, that."

"Yeah, that. We're divorced, Daddy. He left me and Birdie, remember?"

"I know he did, but…" Her father looked out at the bedrock of the empty creek bordering the backyard of the big house. "You should know that Calhoun is coming to me for counseling."

"Counseling?"

"He's requested my guidance as he seeks to repair his spiritual life and make amends for his past transgressions."

"Wait. Counseling? Cal?"

"I'm still his pastor, honey. I can't deny him when he needs me."

"What about when I needed him? Did you forget what it was like for me when he hightailed it out of Magnolia Bend with a virtual teenager beside him and our life savings in his suitcase? We ate Spam, Dad."

Dan looked guilty for a few seconds. "I don't condone what he did, honey, and even though I'm a man of God, I'm still a daddy. Daddies don't forget."

"But pastors do?"

Her father frowned. "You know being a pastor is sometimes like being a defense attorney. There are things you don't like about your clients, or congregation, but you're still obligated to do your job. My job is to counsel even those whose actions I dislike. No matter my personal opinion, Cal is still a child of God…and will be connected to our family through Birdie."

"Brigitte."

"What?"

"Never mind. So how does counseling Cal earn him a spot at the Sunday table?"

Her father seemed to think about this for a moment. "He's family."

"No, he's not."

"He's Bird—uh, Brigitte's father. I don't approve of what he did, but I won't be bitter. Maybe you need to let go of some of that bitterness yourself."

"No. My bitterness gives me comfort," she said, wanting to stamp her foot like a child but refusing to be juvenile. She couldn't believe her father had let go of the hate so easily. But then again, hate wasn't something her father felt for anyone. He'd been disappointed in Cal. Maybe even disgusted by a man who would leave his family for some selfish dream and a younger woman, but he never hated. That's why people trusted Dan Beauchamp and the reason he'd stayed the pastor at First Presbyterian for so many years.

"Honey, don't hold on to your anger. It serves no purpose and it makes you brittle. Your mother says holding on to hate makes wrinkles."

"Are you saying I'm wrinkled?" Her shoulders sank as she accepted her father would not be moved on this. And maybe he had a point. Anger and loneliness had been the cloak she pulled around her and they'd left their marks—those damn lines on her forehead that resisted every retinol A product on the market. Maybe she should loosen her hold a little. Perhaps it was time to let go of some of the hate.

Or not.

She'd have to think about Cal and her attitude toward him.

Her father leaned over and kissed her forehead. "You're as pretty now as you ever were, and I, for one, hope that Calhoun Orgeron chokes on regret rather than a dinner roll. He never deserved you, honey."

"But you think he deserves my forgiveness...even when he's never actually said 'I'm sorry'?"

Her father smiled. "That's up to you. I think everyone deserves forgiveness, honey. Love your neighbor. Love your enemy. And love your—"

"I don't love my ex-husband, Dad. Sorry. But I can try to be civil and maybe one day I'll forgive him for throwing me away." Abigail marched up the stairs, spine straight, shoulders back. But she didn't feel as much resolve.

Today she felt hard even though her skin felt thin.

With Leif she'd been a different woman. Being enfolded in his world of warmth had thawed a part of her heart she'd put on ice. So maybe she should stop being such a bitch to Cal. Sure, he deserved everything she gave him and more, but what was it accomplishing? Cal was impervious to his wrongdoing and the negativity wasn't good for her. So maybe—

"Hey," Cal said interrupting her thoughts as she

entered the house. He'd been waiting for her in the doorway of her father's study.

"Cal," Abigail said, unable to soften her tone.

"Look, I'm sorry if I upset you coming today. Your dad's been helping me a lot, and I always liked coming to Sunday dinner."

"My mom's cooking?"

Cal gave her a small smile. "Yeah, and your brothers are fun to watch a game with...or at least they were."

"Well, we're going to be in each other's lives. Might as well try to be decent about it." Abigail nearly choked on *decent*. That word didn't deserve to be used in the same thought as Cal. But her father was right about the anger she expended like Tic Tacs—it made her feel small.

Cal relaxed a little. "We could salvage something—"

"No. I told you I'm not interested in going backward. At all."

"I just meant that at one point we were friends."

"I'm not ready to be friends, Cal."

Cal reached a hand toward her, but she pushed it away. Cal looked at her, his dark eyes swimming with regret. "I wish I could undo it, Abi."

"Maybe so, but what's done is done."

"We had some good times. We had plans, dreams and laughter. Your father is helping me understand why I gave up on my life. I know now I was scared, afraid of being nothing."

Hurt ripped a path to her gut. "How is being my husband and Birdie's daddy nothing?"

"I didn't mean that. I'm trying to explain that giving up on a dream does something to you. When I looked in the mirror every morning, I hated who I saw. I started hating you, the house, my job. Everything. I hated my world."

Abigail held her tongue. All those years ago, Cal hadn't bothered to tell her what he shared now. He had merely said he'd made a mistake, didn't love her and had to leave Magnolia Bend. He'd refused to talk to her or to listen to her pleading. It was as if a light switch tripped, darkening out that part of her life. She'd had no answers and could find no reason for what had happened.

Click.

Her husband gone.

Cal shoved his hands into his pockets. "I hurt you, and for that, I can't tell you how sorry I am."

Abigail nodded, tears suddenly clogging her throat as a dam inside her broke. It was what she'd wanted to hear for a long time, but it had come much, much too late. Still, she and Cal had a past, shared a daughter and before he'd broken her, they'd loved each other. "Okay. You've apologized and you're working through some things, making amends. It's what you have to do and I won't stand in your way."

"Thank you, Abi."

"Abigail. I'm doing it for Birdie, but I'm also doing it for me. I'm tired of being angry. I'm tired of feeling like a victim." She brushed past him because she didn't want him to see any weakness inside her. She'd refused to show the world her pain. She'd stiffened her spine and stuck out her chin for so long that anything softer made her feel odd. Not that she'd forgiven him. Not that the anger had dissipated. But maybe for the first time ever, she had the desire to consider forgiving.

The image of Leif's blue eyes twinkling at her appeared in her mind.

Maybe Leif hadn't popped just her buttons. Maybe he'd thawed her, healed her, made her think about wanting more than what she'd settled for—a lonely bed, a hard heart, a facade of practicality and self-sufficiency. What if her heart had been moved only because she was falling in love? Maybe Leif filled her in ways she'd never imagined.

Stop that right now, Abigail Ann. Love and Leif do not go together. Leif is for big-girl—albeit secretive—fun. So keep your mind off forever, sister.

With that in mind, she went to find Birdie. She needed to swing by the grocery store before heading to Laurel Woods. And then maybe later she could finally spend some time with Leif.

Or not.

That was how casual affairs worked—no rules.

And for now that worked for her.

LEIF HAD SPENT the past five days without a friend who had really nice benefits. Abigail had a full house due to an early Mardi Gras and her nights were spent tending to a sick Birdie, who had contracted the flu. In lieu of her physical presence, Abigail sent him sexy texts.

She claimed she'd never tried sexting before, but had written something about *Cosmo*, and wanting to be "with it" had become a mission of hers.

He indulged it because it was a damn sight better than writing lesson plans.

Sunday morning rolled around and, feeling especially lonely, he got down to work tying up all the loose ends for the judging of the Golden Magnolia Award. The Laurel Woods Art Festival was less than three weeks away. He'd procured the judges, booked their hotel rooms and correlated their itineraries with the other events. Everything had to be Hilda-approved. After sending the last email, he saw an email had come in from Bart—he was out of town for the next week and couldn't meet.

Disappointment filled him.

He hadn't accomplished much in his quest to find his father—he'd been a little distracted. Of course one distraction was delectable. But that was no excuse. And Abigail hadn't been over in days.

Glancing at his watch, he made a snap decision. Leif needed to talk to someone who could give him insight into his mother's life while she was in Magnolia Bend. According to Hilda, there was one person who knew more about the Laurel Woods Guest

Artist Program than anyone else—a woman named Carla Stanton.

Picking up his phone, he dialed the number for the woman who had worked as the director of the program and the chair of the festival for over ten years. With any luck, Carla would remember his mother… and maybe the man she loved.

She answered on the fourth ring.

"Mrs. Stanton?"

"Yes?"

"This is Leif Lively, I'm a member of the Laurel Woods Art Festival committee. I have a few questions."

An hour later, Leif stepped into Carla's patio home south of Baton Rouge. Carla had iron-gray hair, a sad face and a plate of killer oatmeal cookies.

"Gosh, working for Simeon seems so recent. Funny how that is. Years just speed by too fast," she said, passing him a cup of steaming cinnamon spice tea from an old-fashioned tea cart. They sat in recliners, but Carla seemed determined that social niceties prevailed. "So why exactly did you need to see me?"

"I wanted to get a sense of the past artists—a sort of 'looking to the past for our future' direction—in order to set up the exhibition tents for this year's festival. Since I need exact numbers by the end of next week, I figured I'd talk directly to someone who remembered the last few festivals so I can be better prepared." God forgive him, but his excuse was a bald-faced lie. He'd already sketched out what he'd like for the space where the entries would be displayed.

"Well. That's an interesting idea. I like a man who respects tradition," Carla said, her gaze flitting over him again. He could see what she thought of him: what an untraditional-looking fellow.

"I heard all of this started with a visiting artists program. How did that come about?"

Carla rambled on about how Simeon had gone to Europe and met a guy who sponsored artists. He'd returned determined to try the same thing. Yada yada yada. And finally she came to his mother.

"You know, he was so smitten by one particular artist—a girl named Calliope. Shocked us all because we always suspected him to be a little light in his loafers, if you know what I mean."

"As in homosexual?"

Carla's mouth twitched. "We never used that word. So crass."

Leif never thought of it as crass, but, obviously, in the seventies being homosexual wasn't something many people around here were open about. "So why this girl?"

"She was beautiful. Coloring just like yours. Very blonde and she had this beautiful way about her, just the way she'd tilt her head or widen her eyes when you told her something. There was this innocence paired with, well, sexiness. She was someone in a song, you know?"

Yeah, he knew. All too well.

His mother had stood out in their commune, too, no matter how hard she tried to blend in. Her art and the very essence of who she was could not be hidden under a bushel. "So…"

"Oh, well, Simeon fancied himself smitten with this girl."

"Was she into him?"

"Oh, she cared for him. So many people in town didn't like her. It's the way people are. She was from out West, pretty as the day is long with buckets of talent. And she dressed like you." Carla smiled in order to show him she wasn't trying to be offensive.

"I like comfy clothes."

"Me, too, but that comes with age," Carla said, pouring herself another cup of tea. "Calli—that's what we called her—wasn't in love with Simeon. I think she saw him as an odd older brother, like someone in a family some would be ashamed of, but you love them because they're quirky and a good person at heart. Calli had fellows buzzing around her like flies on a cow patty. Goodness, even my husband perked up when she entered the room."

Leif felt something within him tighten and vibrate, like an old-fashioned divining rod. "Like who?"

Carla's forehead wrinkled. "Hmm, let's see. It was so long ago. I think she dated George Dominque. His father owned a garage in town and he drove a souped-up Trans Am, the kind with the eagle or whatever on the hood. And then there was Clyde

Grommet, who raced motorcycles all over the South. He was a good-looking thing even if he did wear his hair too long," she said, pinking a bit when she remembered Leif wore his long, too. "Oh, and she dated Everett Orgeron. He's our state senator and they say he's in line to run for governor in a few years."

"Orgeron? As in related to Abigail?"

"No, he's related to Cal. Everett's his uncle."

An uneasiness crept inside him at the thought of anyone related to Cal dating his mother. "Well, with this woman dating so many men, I can see how her reputation wouldn't be the best."

"Sure made it easier for the women in town to hate her. But anyway, she ended up killing Simeon and then going on the lam so I guess it doesn't matter."

"Killing him? You said she liked him."

"I shouldn't speculate. No one knows if she pushed Simeon down the staircase or not. No one else was there. We have only Bart's word for that, and that's about as good as toilet paper."

"You don't like Bart?"

Carla sniffed and crooked a shoulder. "He's never lost sleep over anyone not liking him. Bart's a single-minded man. He likes money and to be left alone. It's a wonder he didn't figure out a way to get out of paying the prize money for the Golden Magnolia."

"I met him and he didn't strike me that way," Leif said, trying to be fair to Bart, but sensing more and more that Bart was the key to learning what happened that fateful night. Bart had a huge stake in Simeon's death.

"You're right. I shouldn't let my opinion influence yours." Carla set down her tea and picked up a binder. "I found this from my time as the director of the foundation. I think there's a list of artists and logistics about the festival. Since the parade grounds haven't changed, you can do something similar."

Leif directed his attention to the pages Carla thumbed through. He put aside thoughts of his mother and focused on the information Carla provided. Even though his mission had been to learn more about his mother, he did have a job to do as a committee member.

Later that evening when he left Carla's, he carried the binder and a mental list of guys he needed to learn more about.

As he pulled away from the curb, his phone buzzed.

He looked down and caught the text message from Abigail.

Birdie is better. Want to move on to zippers tonight?

Did a bear shit in the woods?

He glanced at his watch. Six o'clock.

Pulling over, he grabbed the phone and texted:

I'm talented with zippers. See you in a few.

CHAPTER SIXTEEN

THE DOORBELL RANG.

He frowned. He'd been home for only ten minutes. When he said *a few* he assumed she understood that as a few hours.

Leif went to the door and opened it, ready to snap his teeth and make a joke about zippers and moving on to hook-and-eye closures.

But Birdie stood there.

"Hey," she said.

He glanced toward the sidewalk. No Abigail behind her.

"Hey, Brigitte," he said, trying not to look confused. "What's up?"

Birdie was dressed in her standard uniform of skinny jeans and vintage rock band T-shirt under a dark hoodie. Her hair was pulled into a messy ponytail and heavy black eyeliner rimmed her eyes. She had a look going. A little grunge, a little metal, a lot angst. He liked it on her—the perfect combination of vulnerability and tough rocker chick.

"I, uh, wanted to talk to you…if you have a sec."

"Okay."

"Can I come in?"

"Probably be better if we talk outside."

"Whatever," she said, sinking onto his steps since

he had no furniture on the porch. Not bothering with shoes, he closed the door and joined Birdie.

"You okay?" he asked after a few seconds of the girl's silence. She seemed to be struggling with how to start the conversation.

"Yeah. Uh, are you really dating my mom?"

Okay. How to handle this? "Uh, we've been hanging out. We roasted hot dogs on the fire pit out back."

"But that's more like a date, right?"

"I guess. We like each other."

"Why?"

"Because we do."

"But my mom's older than you."

"Not by much. Maybe five years or so. Age doesn't matter as much when you're an adult, Bird— Brigitte. Besides we enjoy each other's company." He kicked aside the thought of him and Abigail naked, enjoying each other's company in a very adult way. "You have a problem with that?"

Birdie shrugged. "It's weird. Y'all don't go together. You're, like, cool. And she's my mom. You know. Kinda old and, like, not very cool."

"Well, you don't see her the way I do."

"Obviously." Birdie sounded pissed. Man, twelve-year-old girls were hard to understand.

"So because your mom is a mother, I shouldn't see her?"

"I guess I can't tell you what to do."

"Bingo."

"I just don't get why you're into *her*. She's not

your type." Her voice was firm as though she could convince him her opinion was valid.

"You know my type? Presumptuous of you."

"I call 'em like I see 'em," Birdie said, her delicate face a study in belligerence. "I *was* here when your bride girlfriend shoved cake in your face. That Marcie chick's nothing like my mom. I'm not stupid, Leif."

"Since when did you stop calling me Mr. Lively."

"Since you told me to at art class weeks ago…and since you started 'hanging out'—" she made quotation marks with her fingers "—with my mom."

They both fell silent, staring into the darkening evening. A porch light across the street switched on and a few houses down, old lady McCray dragged her fluffy white dog out to poop on her neighbor's pristine Saint Augustine lawn.

"It's just that my dad is back, you know."

"What does that have to do with me?"

"Guess it doesn't, but I think he's hoping to, you know, make things better with my mom."

"Oh," Leif said, understanding dawning on him. Birdie, like so many other children of divorced parents, yearned for reconciliation. She wanted her family to be whole again. He understood. As a kid who had never had a father in his life, he'd spent plenty of afternoons daydreaming about a handsome man driving up, having spent years trying to find Calliope, thrilled to learn he was a father. And then they lived happily ever after.

Unfortunately, life wasn't a fairy tale…and Birdie had no control over her parents or their hearts.

"So you're asking me to step aside?"

Birdie turned toward him, her eyes narrowed. "Would you?"

"No."

The irritation in those green eyes reminded him of her mother. "Why not? He's my father and you're just some guy she doesn't even really know. She only likes you because you're hot and, like, all the moms like you."

"So you're saying your mom is shallow and only likes me for my body?"

Birdie looked at him as though his question were a trap. "I don't know."

"Okay. So I'm only what I appear to be on the outside? All people who are relatively attractive are interchangeable? We don't have any feelings? Any other worth other than being *hot*."

"That's not what I meant." Birdie wrapped her arms around her legs. "I just wanted to say something because my dad's feelings were hurt. He's sorry about everything he did back then. He wants to make things up to us, but my mom's all distracted… by you. I can tell by the way she looks at you. Like you're candy."

Leif watched as the girl stood, looking a bit lost and at the same time magnificently determined. Damn, she was a remarkable kid, and even though he had no intention of stepping out of the way so

Cal could schmooze his way into Abigail's life, he admired Birdie's gumption.

"I'm not trying to make you sound like you aren't a good person, Mr. Lively. I personally think you're cool. But my mom doesn't go out with a lot of guys and she's not like Marcie. She's normal and, you know…"

"You think I'm using your mom?"

"I read an article about how men don't really want women over a certain age…but they know they're desperate so they're easy pickings."

"What kind of articles are you reading, Birdie?"

"Brigitte. I know I look young, but I'll be thirteen soon. I'm tired of everyone treating me like a baby."

"I don't treat you like a baby."

Birdie softened a little. "Not you. You don't."

"I'm not looking for hookups. I can have those if I want, but I don't operate that way. You can't cover everyone with a blanket assumption. Just because I'm younger than your mom doesn't mean I'm some gross caricature looking for desperate older chicks so I can get laid. Give me some credit."

Birdie swallowed. "Sorry. I didn't mean that."

"Okay."

"So?"

"So?"

"I guess you don't care what I want," she said.

Leif shook his head, a little zap hitting his heart at this girl standing there asking for the impossible. "You know I care about you, Brigitte, but you're

trying to play God, and that doesn't work. Whatever happens between your mother and your father
is beyond your control. You know that. I'm not in
the way. I'm not forcing anything on your mother,
and I don't think the fact your father wants to be in
your mother's life again is reason enough to with-
draw my...interest. If your mother tells me differently, then that's altogether another thing."

"Okay. Whatever. I tried," she said, padding down
the steps in her black Converse high-tops with neon-
yellow laces. Such a tough girl.

"I'll see you tomorrow," he called.

She held up a hand as she cut through his yard
toward the path her mother took when she sneaked
over to Laurel Woods.

"Later," Birdie called, none too happily.

Leif lifted his hand to nosy Mrs. McCray, who
gave him a halfhearted wave before the fluffy dog
laid another turd in the Toups' immaculate yard.

WHEN SOMEONE KNOCKED on the door three hours
after Birdie left, Leif prayed it was Abigail.

It was. And rather than upset her by telling her of
Birdie's visit, he decided to do something adventurous...something that he hoped would make Abigail
lose herself in the night.

"Hey," she said, her eyes widening when she saw
what he wore. "What are you wearing?"

He looked at his charcoal jeans and black faux-leather jacket and grinned. "I'm wearing my badass pleather jacket."

Abigail laughed and stepped inside, wearing fleece pajama pants with little kittens on them. "Pleather, huh?"

"You can't laugh when you're wearing kittens, lady."

"I thought you could play connect the kittens to-night."

"And I thought you were about to make a pussy joke."

Abigail sucked in an overemphasized breath. "You dirty boy."

"You know me so well. Now, if you're brave enough to risk being a little cold, pull your jacket on and follow me to the garage."

"Garage?" she repeated, shrugging on the puffy down jacket she'd just dropped on a beanbag chair and following him past the laundry room toward the outer door. "What's going on?"

"This," he said, stepping back and flipping on the lights. Sitting next to his innocent car was his bad boy of a hog—the restored 1972 Harley-Davidson FLH touring bike. The bright blue paint was original, as was the white leather seat and chrome trim. On second thought, it wasn't really badass as much as a work of art.

"Ohhh," Abigail said, her eyes shining at his baby. "You want to play *Sons of Anarchy* with me?"

"I don't know what that is, but don't sell your kittens short."

Abigail laughed and it sounded like Christmas bells. "Well, then, are we going to ride it or role-play on it. I can shimmy out of these kitten pants and be the bad girl who got pulled over and needs to be punished."

"I'd planned on a ride, but maybe I'll just grab my mirrored sunglasses and the handcuffs I keep in the bedside table," he joked, picking up the two helmets and crooking his eyebrow.

"Oh, let's do this. I used to date a guy in high school whose dad had one of these, but we never had the guts to 'borrow' it from him. But, wait. What about Birdie?"

"I don't have room for her," he replied, deadpan.

"Well, Alice Ann is in the cottage next door. I sent her a text that I was coming here for a drink."

"We can just zip down the highway and back again. But if you're worried we can stay here."

"No. Let's do it. I have my cell phone."

Leif handed her the helmet, straddled the vintage motorcycle and started her up. She roared to life, making Abigail jump.

"Loud," Abigail yelled over the sound of the bike idling.

"Sexy," he called, patting the seat behind him. Abigail fastened the strap beneath her chin and flung her fleecy leg over the seat, clasping his hips with her kitten-covered knees. Warm and solid against his back, she made his pulse gallop when she slid her hands around his torso, resting them against his stomach. And then the minx dipped her hand lower, sliding it beneath the flannel shirt he wore, fingering the snap of his jeans.

He caught her hand and flipped on the microphone in his helmet, turning to help her do the same.

"I'll wreck if you keep that up," he drawled, shifting gears and rolling toward the rising garage door.

"We'll die happy." She laughed, squeezing him tight.

"Well, I would." He turned on the headlight and rolled out the door, balancing them with his boots, which were leather and inherited from the toughest biker he knew—they were his one leather concession. "Hold on."

"Gladly."

Leif shifted gears and took off down the street, clicking the garage shut behind him, smiling at Abigail's little squeal of excitement. She laughed again when he took the curve and hit the straightaway. Seconds later they sped down River Road, the cold air blowing in their faces, the stars winking above and the road before them a curling ribbon dividing the huge swaths of farmland. The levee buffered the wind off the river, but still it was freezing.

"Too cold?" he asked her.

"Yes, but don't stop."

He didn't go far because they weren't really dressed for the night, but he loved the feeling of Abigail's thighs clasping him, the purr of the motor beneath his ass and the sound of laughter in her voice. It was like a gift wrapped up just for him.

Seeing a patch of level gravel to his left, he turned the bike. They hadn't met a single vehicle on the road, making the night seem as if it belonged solely to them.

"I'm freezing, but that was fun," Abigail said.

Leif pulled the bike to a halt, balancing it once again with his feet. He turned, unsnapped Abigail's helmet and tugged it from her head. Her inky hair fell out, swishing around her face, the streak of silver-white gleaming in the moonlight.

No words were necessary. He covered her frigid lips with his. Outside she was icy, inside she was warm and buttery...the epitome of his Abigail.

No, wait. Not *his* Abigail.

Her chin quivered and he broke the kiss. "I want to remember you like this always—windblown, sexy, with a promise in those bewitching eyes."

Her teeth chattered, but she managed a smile. "Such a poet."

"Your turn."

"Huh?" Her forehead crinkled. Four lines. So cute.

"You drive."

"No, I've never driven a motorcycle."

"I'm going to help you. It's fun. Give it a whirl." He slid off, holding the handlebars steady, and flung his leg behind her, then moved her forward with his bulk. After a few quick instructions, he helped her with her helmet and placed his hands next to hers on the handlebars.

"Now, push this," he instructed, covering her hands with his.

"Oooh, your hands are cold." She did as said. He shifted gears and carefully they eased onto the highway.

"Good girl," he said, showing her how to lean. Gradually, she became comfortable and settled against him, increasing the speed. In a matter of minutes, they were zipping along.

"I'm doing it," she said.

The feel of her between his knees was headier than having her wrapped around him. Something about cradling her as he pushed her to be wild and adventurous stroked something inside him, filling him with a feeling he'd never felt before. It was as if he soared above the cracked asphalt, weaving along the river like an eagle catching a current, dipping and looping while defying gravity.

Eventually they arrived at his neighborhood and his house.

"Oh, my God, that was so much fun," Abigail said as they rolled into the warmth of the garage. "Thank you for making me do that. It was incredible."

He pulled his helmet off and combed his fingers through his hair. "It was."

Abigail had pulled off her helmet and blew into her hands. Her chin still quivered. "I'm freezing."

"Then I'll have to warm you up," he said, dropping a quick kiss on her lips and helping her off the bike before shutting everything down.

Minutes later they were in his home, peeling off their jackets.

"Let's grab a hot shower. That will warm us up," he said, shucking his jeans right there in the living room and hurrying to the bathroom to start the shower.

Abigail followed him to the bathroom, dropping her clothes as she went. When she got to the bathroom, she stood splendidly naked, arms wrapped around herself. He peeled his T-shirt off and drew her to him, gathering her body close to his. "You were magnificent tonight, Abs."

"I loved the feeling of that bike. So freeing."

He opened the shower door and the steam boiled into the room. "Come on, let's get warmed up."

"You already do that for me," she said, pulling her head from his shoulder and looking at him. "You make me feel like I'm a different woman. You make me feel stronger."

He kissed her because she made him feel the same way. Not like a different woman, of course, but she made him feel like the man he could be someday. The sort of man who put down roots and grew toward the light of goodness, spreading limbs, sheltering all that was important to him. He could feel himself changing…and it had nothing to do with finding his father.

More like finding himself.

As they stepped in the shower, shivering in delight at the hot water sluicing over their bodies, Leif felt a sweet peace settle over him.

This was right.

Never in his life, with any of the women he'd been with, had he felt the way he felt about Abigail. And it was so odd to find this with someone like her. He'd thought she was amusing when he first met her. All prickly, picky and exacting as she directed her committee to put this here, that there. Buttoned-up Ms. PTA turned out to be surprisingly sensual, delightfully witty and utterly wicked in bed. Who woulda thunk?

"Want me to wash your back?" she asked.

"Only if I can wash your front," he said, running his hands up and down her back, loving the way her slick skin felt next to his. They fit so nicely together, her curves settling against his hard angles. Leif caught Abigail's lips and poured all those tender emotions into a kiss.

Tenderness faded as passion flared.

Abigail ended the kiss, leaning back so she could look him in the eye. "I counted on you washing my front."

Leif laughed and then picked up the handmade goat soap he'd bought in New Orleans a few weekends ago. "Whatever you want, Madam President."

Abigail smiled. "That's exactly what I like to hear."

LATER THEY LAY in the soft glow of the bedside lamp beneath the draped muslin that swathed Leif's bed. The whole room looked like it had been imported straight from Bali. The canopied bed was made of ornately carved dark wood. Sand-colored walls covered with huge canvases of swirling water and palm trees contributed to the exotic atmosphere.

"This looks like a girl bed," she said, pushing up and rolling to her side. Leif lay splendidly naked and spent. His body felt a little sweaty and she liked that. He was a primitive male and she was his mate.

"I like it," Leif said, fingering the airy fabric that hung beside his head. "I have a friend who makes this stuff. She suggested it for the bedroom."

"She?"

"Relax. I didn't sleep with her."

"Well, I have no right to care. You don't belong to me," she said, despite the pain flooding her heart. Leif wasn't hers. What they had between them wasn't lasting. Just mutually beneficial. The way she'd felt on that motorcycle, powerful and loved while plunging into the night, Leif's arms around her, was an illusion. Some kind of adrenaline rush. Nothing to do with her heart.

"Perhaps not, but I still don't sleep with two women at the same time. Guess I'm not that modern."

She shrugged, trying to hide her relief. She wanted him all to herself. She was selfish that way.

"You're beautiful, you know that?" He rolled to face her, stroking a hand down her ribs to her waist.

She shook her head. "I'm passably attractive."

"What? You're crazy. Look at the way your body slopes. Here." He traced her breast down to her nipple, which peaked at his touch.

"Is slope a kind substitution for sag?"

"No, let me show you," he said, hopping out of bed and padding across the room toward a table that held a variety of art supplies. A work in progress that looked like a cross between a landscape and an abstract design sat on his easel, framing the backside of the man she'd just had her way with. Abigail decided she loved the view from Leif's bed.

He returned carrying a large drawing pad and a pencil.

"What are you doing?"

"I'm showing you what I see."

"You're going to draw a nudie pic of me?" Abigail asked, sitting up, a string of alarm unwinding. "I need to go. It's getting late."

Leif gently nudged her back. "Why?"

"Because I left the house unattended and Birdie sleeping inside."

"No guests tonight?"

"No, but tomorrow I'll have two older ladies who are here for a garden tour."

"Do those ladies know it's February?"

Abigail smiled. "I think they're researching formal garden layouts for an article or something. What do I care? I want their money."

"So bloodthirsty," he said with a mischievous smile. "Your cell phone is on, right?"

She nodded.

"And Birdie is asleep?"

She nodded again.

"Then give me a few more minutes before you get dressed and run from me."

Abigail frowned. "I'm not running from you. I have to go home—I have a kid."

"Understood, but it's like dating two different people with you. Here, you're a vixen, shedding clothes, driving me crazy with sexy underwear and your considerable fellatio skills."

Abigail smiled. "I am good."

"Understatement," he teased, tugging the sheet so it covered the juncture of her thighs. He lifted her hand above her head, before pulling the shoulder beneath her forward. "There. But tomorrow you'll be buttoned-up, putting down shelf paper and pretending me away."

"I could never pretend you away."

"You know what I mean. Now relax."

Abigail sank into the softness of Leif's bed, trying to put away her nagging worries about Birdie, Cal and all the heart-shaped boxes she was supposed to make for the St. George's Valentine's Day luncheon.

"See, your mouth has a sensual curve. I love to nibble your lower lip. So sweet. And the way you taste… I'd say cherries, but that's trite. It's unique to you—spicy, yet sweet. Clean, yet sultry."

"Minty, yet garlicky?" she added.

She was certain Leif smiled, but she wasn't sure. Languor settled over her, a sudden need to close her eyes with it.

"I love your hair. So thick, and that swoop of silver so stylish and unexpected. Just like you."

"I almost covered it with color."

"Don't you dare," he said, the sound of the pencil moving filtering through her senses. "And your neck's elegant, another place I love to taste my sweet Abi."

She shivered, thrilled at his soft words of romance. He made her feel so…so…alive.

To Leif, she was a desirable woman. She'd forgotten how powerful being wanted made her feel.

"And here—" he brushed the curve of her waist beneath her breast "—so feminine with the dips and hollows. Makes me want to lose myself in you."

"Such pretty words," she murmured.

"Only the truth," he said, the scratching of the pencil ceasing. She opened one eye a crack to find him studying his sketch before he raised his gaze to her. "Look."

He turned the pad around and she gasped.

The sketch was rough but so lifelike…and she looked like a seductress.

"Wow, that's— I look so different."

"That's the way I see you. Let me finish this. You'd be amazing done in chalk."

Abigail pushed herself up, brushing her hair from her eyes. "But only for you. I don't want anyone seeing me like this. They wouldn't understand. They wouldn't see this woman as Abigail."

"Maybe they should," he said, stroking the side of her face on the paper. Something about him caressing the sketch plucked a chord in her. "I have to go."

"I know." He leaned down and kissed her so tenderly. "One day maybe you can stay and sleep beside me. I'd like that."

Abigail looked around for her lacy underwear. "Sure, you say that now, but wait until I start snoring."

"You snore?"

Abigail gave a soft laugh. "I'm not sure if anyone knows."

Leif wrapped her in his arms. "Next time I'll finish the sketch."

"We'll see."

"No, you're too beautiful not to draw. I knew it the first time I saw you."

Abigail arched an eyebrow.

"Okay, maybe not the first or second time, but definitely by the third."

Abigail scooped up her jeans from the hallway. "Well, they do say the third time is the charm."

CHAPTER SEVENTEEN

OVER THE NEXT few weeks, Leif worked on categorizing the art pieces submitted to the Laurel Woods Art Festival, completing the sketch of Abigail on a larger scale and researching his potential father from the names Carla had given him. Abigail had managed to locate a list of the artists who'd stayed on the property over the years in some files she'd stored up in the attic, but the list didn't tell him much other than who lived in the other cabins while his mother was at Laurel Woods. Leif had tried to make an appointment with Bart, but the man hadn't returned his calls. With the festival right around the corner, his legitimate reason to meet with Bart slipped away.

So he'd started his investigation with George Dominique—the first guy Carla had mentioned his mother dating. He stopped by the garage the man's father had owned and asked a guy with a big belly and grease-stained hands about George. Big Willie seemed willing to chat in order to escape from beneath the hood of the car he was working on.

"Yeah, ol' Georgie boy is an accountant over in Mississippi. Jackson area. Bilked his daddy out of every dime in order to get through school, so I don't think much of 'im. Let me grab my book and see if I got his number. Might still be in there," the new owner said, hitching up his work pants and moving heavily to the garage office.

"Thanks," Leif said minutes later when Willie handed him a slip of stained paper with a number written on it.

"What you want with him again?"

"Just need to ask him something. No big deal." Leif held up his hand and moved toward his motorcycle, which the big man had already asked about. The gleam in Willie's eyes told Leif taking the bike to the shop had gotten him instant respect and the number he needed. Which was a relief since Big Willie had eyed his blond locks and hemp hoodie with suspicion when he first walked in the garage.

"Aw-w-right. Later, man," Big Willie said, tugging his ball cap down on his head and walking away.

Leif hurried to his motorcycle and dialed the number.

"George Dominique," the man said. His voice was smooth, if rushed.

"Hi, Mr. Dominique. My name's Leif Lively and I'm doing a biography on an artist who once lived in Magnolia Bend. Several folks around here said you knew her. Calliope—"

"Oh, yeah. I remember her. She came to town when I was a freshman at Ole Miss. Met her that summer."

"Yeah, well, according to a few of my sources, you two were an item." Leif waved at a woman who stuck her head out the door of the dry cleaners. She gave him a questioning look before waving and returning inside.

"We went out one time, and that's only because she felt sorry for me."

"Then the report someone gave me was wrong?"

"Yeah, she was such a fox. I asked her out, but I could tell she said yes only because she didn't want to hurt my feelings. We went to a place in New Orleans in my new Trans Am. Hot little car."

"So no romance, huh?"

"Not even a good-night kiss. Try Meat Grommet. I think she hung out with him some, and I heard Finch sniffed around a little, too."

Leif froze as the image of the bird on his mother's hand popped into his head. "Finch? I didn't have him on the list."

"Well, back then everyone called him Finch. Now everybody calls him Senator Orgeron. Finch was his middle name or something."

Leif swallowed the excitement. Nothing but a hunch. Meant nothing at this point. But still. Maybe. "Great. I'll check him out. Thanks for the information."

"So when's it coming out?" George asked.

"What?"

"The book you're writing. I want to get a copy."

"Oh, I have to sell it to a publisher first, but I'll let you know."

Leif hung up after thanking George and immediately typed Everett Orgeron in the internet search engine on his phone. The man's official biography popped up immediately—Everett Fincher Orgeron III. Sounded pompous. Leif enlarged the screen and studied the picture.

Hmm. Did the good senator look like him?

Leif couldn't tell. The man had a prominent chin, close-cropped silver hair and light colored eyes. His brow was heavier than Leif's but Leif knew he'd inherited most of his looks from his mother. Oh, and Everett was listed as a Republican.

A Republican?

Leif gave a wry laugh and jammed his helmet on his head, firing up the engine and reversing out of the parking spot. He'd need to check out Clyde "Meat" Grommet before he became too fixated on the senator. But until then, he had a beautiful woman to occupy his time…and some grading to do. The shooting star centerpieces were painted and ready to go for the banquet at school. He'd also closed submissions for the Golden Magnolia last week. The submitted forms were organized into five categories—there weren't as many as past festivals but hopefully word would spread and they'd get more next year.

A tiny pang of regret struck at the thought that he wouldn't be here next year. Maybe he could visit? Or not. Somehow the thought of returning after he and Abigail were done didn't seem like a good idea.

A bigger pang hit him at the thought of him and Abigail being over. She'd become such a part of his life in such a short time, and he couldn't imagine not having her teasing him, laughing at his impressions of his fellow teachers or wrapping her arms around him and making him feel like he was the only man in the world.

This weekend her brother was getting married and the following weekend was the festival gala at Magnolia Bend. Maybe they could take their relationship public. He loved spending time with Abigail, but he hated feeling as if it were tawdry. He wanted to be able to stand beside her, hold her purse when she went to the restroom, fetch her a glass of wine.

Then again, he wasn't sure why the secrecy bothered him so much. He'd never been one to be insecure. But obviously living in a small and somewhat conservative town meant he had to give a little more forethought to his relationships. He'd never lived in a town where something like this mattered. Hell, maybe it didn't matter to anyone else but Abigail. Maybe keeping him hidden was her hang-up.

But that hang-up didn't stop her from coming over almost every night after Birdie went to bed. Some nights they got busy quickly before she hurried home. Other times they'd hang out and talk. And he'd draw her.

Just as he did that night.

Abigail lay on his bed again, twined in his sheets. Candles flickered on his bedside table, permeating the air with a spicy intimacy and bathing Abigail in a soft glow.

"I bet this is how Rose felt when Jack drew her," Abigail said, stretching her arm above her head.

"Who?" Leif asked, narrowing his eyes, trying to get the shading perfect. He was nearing completion of the piece and felt it might be one of his best. It was as if his feelings for Abigail had leeched from his body and dripped down his hand to become one with his creation.

She made a face. "You know. The *Titanic* movie."

"Never saw it. I don't watch much TV."

Abigail smiled. "I love TV. It's always been my escape."

"Mmm," he said, readjusting the sheet over her hips, lingering a bit longer than needed and taking the opportunity to brush the underside of her breast. He wanted to make love to her again but knew she'd have to go soon. Abigail was a stickler for being at the B and B by eleven o' clock, which was her standard lockup time.

"Any luck with talking to Bart?"

"He won't return my calls. I implied I wanted to talk to him about the festival, but still nothing." His usual endless supply of patience was running low.

"He might be a dead end anyway. Bart didn't live here then, I don't think," she said, stretching and messing up his line. "What about the guys Carla mentioned?"

"Well, I know my father is not George Dominique. They had one date. He gave me a few leads and I'm in the middle of checking them out." For some reason he didn't want to mention Everett yet. The senator actually seemed like a good bet—Leif kept seeing that little bird tattooed on his mother's hand, the name *Finch* echoing in his mind. "Next on the list is a guy named Meat Grommet."

"Does he work at the dairy?"

"Yeah, I'm going to stop by his office tomorrow and talk to him."

"Who's the other guy?"

"You know what? I don't want to waste time talking about my potential sperm donor." He set the tablet aside and pulled her to him.

Her eyes flew open in surprise but then she smiled. "I wouldn't call talking about something that's important to you a waste of time. I like being here for you."

"Oh, you do? Well, I like you being here for me, too," he said, sliding his hands down her rib cage to the hollow of her hip. He dipped his head and dropped a kiss on the sweet spot beneath her hip bone.

Abigail sighed. "Oh, man, I love being your booty call."

"You're not my booty call. I'm *your* booty call." He peppered kisses along her jaw, working his way toward her mouth.

Abigail groaned. "It's late. I have to go."

"Let's make out a little while longer," he said, brushing his mouth against her lips. She sighed and he took that as a yes and kissed her thoroughly.

Her hands tangled in his hair before one slid down his back. Abigail broke the kiss and looked at him. "I'm so getting addicted to you."

That made him smile. Mutual addiction. Nice.

Abigail's eyes reflected exactly what he felt—sublime happiness in the time they spent together.

Damn, she looked so fine with her tangled dark hair falling across her bare shoulders, those sleepy green eyes shining at him and those bee-stung lips beckoning. He lost himself in this woman.

He dropped a kiss on her nose. "Making love is a great addiction. Fabulous upside."

"Unless you get genital warts…or pregnant. Could be a very uncomfortable downside. College is expensive," she quipped.

"There's that," he laughed, giving her a little squeeze, knowing she had to go.

Abigail shifted, swinging her legs over the side of the bed. "Birdie woke up last night and I wasn't there. She said something sarcastic this morning at breakfast. I shifted the conversation, but I know she suspects. I feel like at any moment she's going to point a finger and condemn me as a whore."

"Not getting any better with her, huh?"

"There's definitely a wedge between us. I keep thinking time will fix it, but I don't know."

"She's at a difficult age. It's what tweens do—ride a wave of lunacy."

She pulled on a pair of faded jeans and an old Henley shirt that had likely been Cal's. Leif didn't like thinking about that fact. "Yeah, I knew this stage would be hard, but I'd really rather she revert to eating crayons and flushing my socks down the toilet. Birdie still holds on to the delusion of her daddy and me waking up to sunshine streaming into our bedroom window and her bringing in a tray of toast and juice. A freaking commercial for happy-family-after."

"She's a kid. They all want the Beaver Cleaver experience."

"Yeah, and Cal's being 'present' in our lives isn't really helping. Yesterday, I came home to him on the porch with a hammer and nails fixing a loose board. Birdie had cookies and milk on the swing. Another commercial-worthy moment."

Leif tried to dam the jealousy coursing through him. He had no right to Abigail. At the very beginning they'd made it clear—they were friends and lovers with no ties. He had to remind himself. Constantly. "Consider it free labor."

Abigail nodded. "That's a good way to look at it."

Leif didn't say anything as she slid into her UGG knockoffs, looking, for once, like a teenager instead of a mom. Abigail didn't care about fashion when it came to getting to him, though he appreciated the lace and satin waiting beneath her mom jeans or sloppy pajama pants. "Will I see you tomorrow?" He always asked.

"Probably not. We're having a small wedding shower for Shelby."

"Damn."

"And not Saturday, either. That's the wedding and I'll be busy all day."

Something inside him sank at the thought of not seeing her for several days. He craved having her with him. Holding her made his day complete. "You don't need a handsome man to escort you to the wedding, by chance?"

She glanced up, a flicker in her eyes. "It's not a date thing. The wedding is really small with just family and a few close friends."

"Is Cal going?" He hated himself for asking, but nasty jealousy had already knocked down his veneer of not giving a damn about what Abigail did or didn't do.

"Are you jealous?"

Hell, yeah.

But he didn't say that. He remained quiet, his insides reverberating with hurt at the thought she didn't want him to meet her family. Didn't want him beside her as a close friend. It made him feel small, dirty. Hadn't they grown beyond a hookup? He'd thought so. He'd hoped so. "I'm not jealous because I have no right to be, right?"

Abigail's forehead wrinkled. "Look, if you want to go, you can."

But she didn't sound convincing. It was as if she were throwing him a bone she didn't want to give up.

"No. It's not about the wedding. No guys *want* to go to a wedding. I just want to be with you. We don't have to advertise the fact I screw your brains out nightly." As soon as he uttered the words, he wanted to kick himself. He sounded like a needy bitch.

"Come on, Leif," she said, sliding a hand onto his bare shoulder, stroking him in a motherly fashion that annoyed the crap out of him. He shrugged her touch away. "It's not that I don't want you there, it's just that I can't open myself up to speculation. You're going to leave Magnolia Bend, shaking the dust from your shoes, but I'll still be here...with a shredded reputation."

"Who gives a shit?"

"I do. My dad's a pastor and well-respected community member. I have a daughter."

"Oh, I forgot. I'm the son of a slutty murderess."

"That's not what I implied. Don't put words in my mouth." Her tone had hardened and he hated that his insecurity had brought this between them. He couldn't seem to help himself.

"Why are you so worried about what people think? Is it because I'm too weird? Too young? Too much a man whore? Is that it? You don't want people to suspect you're doing the wacky art teacher?"

"Leif..."

"No, I get it. They'd talk about *you*, and you can't stand anyone seeing you as human. Would mess up the whole Perfect Abigail thing you have going."

"People don't judge men. They judge women. You'd leave and I'd be the same pathetic loser who couldn't keep a man…except this time I'd also be a whore. I don't want to be that woman."

"God, you have some major esteem problems, don't you? Do you think everyone in this town is concerned about what you do? Life's too short to worry about this shit," he said, rising and slipping on his drawstring pajama pants. Inside, his anger grew and being naked felt more vulnerable than normal. He needed pants on for this conversation.

"I don't think everyone's watching and waiting for me to mess up. It's not just about my image. I have heart problems. Love has never worked out for me," she said, her words falling like the first flakes of snow, a stinging harbinger.

For a moment he felt regret. Abigail had been hurt and embarrassed. Still, her past was no excuse for avoiding a future. She wanted to protect herself, hiding what she felt from the world because if no one saw her vulnerability, they couldn't see her world fall apart when love didn't work out for her.

That was a chickenshit way to live. Sure, his relationships hadn't worked out so well to date, but at least he jumped in with both feet expecting them to work out for the best.

Leif stared at her, trying to figure out how to shelve his hurt and help her through her insecurities. But he couldn't stop the emotions rollicking through his body.

Her attitude about him hurt.

Abigail released a pent-up breath. "Look, I don't

want to leave like this. Maybe I am being selfish but I like what we have. This has been good. Why change it?" She waved her hand, turning her head to look around their exotic getaway that cloistered them from reality and tucked them into the fantasy they'd created just for themselves.

On one hand he was an enabler. On the other he didn't really care because being with Abigail had been so easy. "So you like sneaking around, screwing me and then showing up at church the perfect mother, daughter and sister?"

She recoiled as though he'd slapped her. "Is that what you think?"

The tangled sheets and sweet intimacy they'd experienced moments ago evaporated. Suddenly this thing they'd avoided for weeks was out there. The idea that Abigail wanted to keep getting action from the resident—what had she called him the night Cal had come home? Lothario. Yeah. In Abigail's mind he was good for one thing…but not good enough to stand beside her in public. "Well, babe, the old adage of 'actions speak louder than words' comes to mind."

"I'm not using you. You know that. We agreed on this arrangement from the beginning, so why are you upset now?"

"I'm starting to feel dirty from this. You come over, under the cloak of darkness, to sleep with me. We had one date that might be considered halfway public. The rest of the time we've spent together has been strictly on the down low. Which, hey, is cool. I mean, I like getting laid."

Abigail's eyes grew icy. "It's more than some sordid rendezvous. We're friends, too. You know that."

"Do I? You seem pretty comfortable with what's going on between us. Slightly more than acquaintances on the surface but getting nasty every time the lights go out."

"Leif, why are you doing this?" Abigail asked, her voice trembling.

"Because I'm beginning to understand the way my mother might have felt. Am I really that different from the other men in town? Are you embarrassed of this?" He lifted a hank of hair brushing his shoulder. "Or because I play the ukulele, dress differently and meditate?"

"You're twisting this around. If you want to come with me to John and Shelby's wedding, you're welcome to. I just didn't think you'd care. I thought this was what you wanted, too—the whole 'let's hang out and have a little fun' thing."

Leif shook his head. He didn't believe her. "Know what? It's fine. I don't care about the wedding. I just wanted you to treat me as something other than your plaything."

He couldn't seem to take the hurt from his voice. Honestly, up until he'd uttered the words, he hadn't known he felt this way—or at least, not so strongly. The past few weeks had been sweet and intimate as they'd gotten to know each other, enjoying the hell out of each other's bodies but also finding laughter and commonalities.

Maybe looking for his father had brought these feelings to the surface. Inside he felt about as stable as gelatin, wriggly and messy. He'd thought it would be so easy—find his father, tell the man he had a son and then move on in life knowing he'd carried out his mother's last wishes. But this? This was complicated. He'd grown too attached to the community, too attached to Abigail. And deep down he worried about what his father would think of him. What if he, too, rejected him? Leif had never felt so needy or out of control before. He hated what he'd become.

He didn't think he could do this anymore.

"I'm sorry if you felt that way," she said, her expression sincere. "Maybe I *have* been content with the way things are. And, yeah, you're different than any other guy I've ever been with. But that doesn't mean I'm ashamed of you."

"Yeah, guess there's not much diversity in the dating pool around here. I know I'm different. I like that I'm different," he said, staring past her, not wanting her to see any residual hurt that might be lingering in his gaze. Part of him was embarrassed at letting his true feelings show, the other part resigned to owning those feelings of inadequacy. "All the dudes look the same—plaid button-downs or camo. Just trying to bring some variety to Magnolia Bend."

Something seized him. He couldn't end it just because he'd come down with a case of clinginess. He needed to throw himself a life preserver and pull himself to safe ground. Make light of their first disagreement. Turn the situation to something that wouldn't feel like it could drown him.

Abigail walked to him and brushed her hand over his naked chest. "Don't be mad. Okay? You've been so good for me."

He couldn't resist asking "How?"

"You've made me feel like I'm worth loving again."

"Love?" he said. At that word his heart gave a jolt. He couldn't love Abigail. Care about her? Sure. But not the L word. He couldn't fall in love because he wasn't that kind of guy. Time and again, he'd proved he couldn't stay with just one woman. This was something he'd accepted about himself, mostly because the panic attacks he'd suffered while engaged to Marcie had proved he wasn't a normal guy who could settle down. He couldn't commit. That was what every woman he'd ever been with screamed at him eventually.

Besides, Abigail wasn't looking for a forever guy.

If she were, she would have found someone already. Plenty of staid, family men around town. Hell, she had Cal sniffing around, nailing shit and trying to be useful again.

Leif was her boy toy, a virtual emotional handyman, patching up her esteem and improving her morale. Yeah, that was him in a nutshell—"easygoing, good for a roll in the hay" Leif.

But maybe that wasn't enough anymore. Maybe he now wanted more for himself.

And that scared the hell out of him.

Abigail's eyes had widened at the L word. "Wait, I didn't mean love. I know we're not going there. I meant you have given me back a piece of myself I had put away on the shelf. These past few weeks of laughter, flirting and feeling absolutely daring and desirable, have been so good."

He pulled her to him, resting his chin on her head. "I'm glad for you."

But what had Abigail given him?

He'd come to Magnolia Bend in order to find the truth, but instead the empty hole in his life had grown wider. He'd seen the small-town closeness, the way the community supported its own, and feared a faceless man who wouldn't want him. He'd known he had a void—he just never knew he longed to fill it with anything like what Cal had thrown away.

God, who had he become?

Leif didn't have an answer for that.

Because he couldn't move forward until he found his father...until he knew his past. Nothing about Abigail could change that.

So maybe, as much as he wished it wasn't true, being with Abigail wasn't good for him at this point. Her pretending him away in the light of day made him feel marginalized, reinforcing the fear of rejection he had with regard to his father. He didn't want to be a rent-a-stud. He didn't want to be whiny and pathetic. He didn't want to fall in love.

So if all he and Abigail ever had between them was sex, then why bother continuing?

At some point, he and Abigail had stopped being about fun, and teetered on the precipice of something that could hurt. Maybe it was time to retreat and reassess. Maybe it was time to think about what he needed.

He'd given Abigail what Hilda had originally suggested her cousin needed—button-popping and panty-dropping.

Mission accomplished.

Abigail pulled back. "Birdie's going to stay with my parents Saturday night, and Alice Ann will be minding the bed-and-breakfast while I'm at the wedding. Maybe when I get back we can take another moonlight swim?" Her eyes teased, tempting him to dump his last few thoughts.

Instead he dropped his arms, stepping away. "You know what? I think taking a little break would be a good thing."

"What?" she asked, before wrapping her arms around herself. "What do you mean?"

"We should take a step back. Reassess."

"Reassess? Wait, are you saying you don't want to see me anymore? Because I didn't invite you to my brother's wedding?"

He swallowed. "No, I just don't like feeling the way I feel right now."

"How do you feel?"

"Look, I just need some space."

"Oh," she said, her face reflecting hurt. He'd seen that look before. This was how it always felt when he pulled himself away from a relationship...except this time he held the same pain inside himself. Abigail hadn't changed the rules, but he'd changed how he felt. Maybe it wasn't fair of him, but he couldn't help it.

"Look, I'm not trying to be a little bitch over my feelings. And I'm not taking my toys and going home. But some time to work through what's going on in my life would be good. So let's give each other some breathing room. Okay?"

She swallowed. "Sure. Breathing room."

"So I guess I'll see you in class tomorrow night? Then we can see about—"

"No," she said, shaking her head. "I get it. This has been good, but we knew it wasn't going to last. Don't feel like you have to, uh, uphold some kind of commitment to me."

Leif didn't know what to say. He wasn't even sure how things went south so quickly. It was like a bitter last bite of pecan pie with nothing to wash the taste from his mouth. "So..."

"Let's do a clean break. You're wrapped up in finding your father, Birdie's being a pain in the ass, Cal's just Cal and we've got the festival. Things are complicated. Let's undo one of them. Besides this was getting...I don't know."

But he did. They were both getting too attached to each other.

"So let's just, um, stop before things get hard," she said.

Something tore inside him, but he knew she was right. They'd been dancing too close to the flames. If they didn't step away, they'd catch fire and burn. "Maybe this is for the best."

But it didn't feel that way.

A horrible heaviness sank in his gut and the back of his throat ached.

Abigail turned her head away. "So this is it. I don't think I've ever really done this before. The last guy who dumped me sent me a text and the one before that just left. I've never actually broken up with anyone before."

Leif rubbed his hands over his face. "But we're still friends, right? I mean, we have to see each other."

"Yeah. Sure," she said, but her chin wobbled a little. "I gotta go. It's really late, and—" She sniffed, turning toward the doorway. "I'll see you later."

"I'll walk you out."

"No," she barked, not turning around. "I know the way."

And then she hurried from his room, her soft-soled boots swishing a goodbye on the hardwood floor of the hallway. Leif clutched his chest, fingernails digging painfully into his skin as the front door opened...and then closed.

The shutting of the door made the whole nightmare that had just played out final.

He'd just called things off with Abigail.

God, he was a freaking dumb ass.

He jogged down the hall. He had to catch her and tell her he had been wrong. So what if they got burned? Wasn't the journey worth it? That's what all the songs said, right? So he had to make her come back. He had to make her see he'd been insecure and stupid and...

As he opened the front door, he caught sight of himself in the mirror. His gaze reflected desperation.

Right.

This was what he'd been worried about—he'd gone off the rails. He was in Magnolia Bend to find his father...not mess around with love.

He watched Abigail disappear along the path to Laurel Woods, the tall lanky grasses closing behind her as if she'd never been there. Never been part of his life.

He could see his breath in the cold night and very slowly he stepped inside and closed the door.

It was for the best.

Had to be.

But his heart didn't believe him.

CHAPTER EIGHTEEN

ABIGAIL BARELY MADE it off Leif's porch before the tears started falling.

Part of her was shocked at what had just happened, the other part hurt. How could he think so little of her? To think she was embarrassed of him? To dismiss what they had like it was nothing.

Sure, she knew they would end things someday. There was no other recourse.

But, God, it felt as if her heart had been ripped from her chest.

She pressed a hand against her mouth and stopped, leaning against a rough tree, trying not to fall apart. So much for being a modern woman who slept around and didn't give a rip about the guy. Massive fail.

Her breath puffed into the night as she struggled to swallow the grief threatening to flood her.

You don't love him, goose. He's just a guy. He's just a stupid man. You were using him for sex. That's it. He wasn't going to stay. This wasn't love. Get a grip.

She said all the right things to herself, but her heart was having none of it. Her heart seemed to firmly believe she'd fallen totally and emphatically—right down to the exclamation marks—in love with Leif Lively, artist, teacher and tofu-weenie roaster.

Damn her heart.

Abigail wiped the dampness from her cheeks, determined to deal with it. No other avenue was open to her. She didn't have the luxury of going to bed with a box of tissues, a pint of ice cream and her DVD copy of *Pretty Woman*. She had stuff to do. A daughter to raise, an ex-husband to chase off her porch, her brother's wedding to attend. She still had to find a gift and get her nails done.

Exactly. Abigail had plenty to do. She probably wouldn't miss Leif at all.

A sob escaped and she pressed her hand tight against her stomach, battling against the emotion. She could do this. She had to do this.

So she pulled away from the tree and took one step. Then another. Then another. Away from Leif.

As she reached the end of the path, where the view opened up to reveal the grand house, she inhaled deeply, remembering who she was. The moonlight fell softly on the massive columns of Laurel Woods and on the naked branches of the trees, a sort of mysticism enveloping the grounds. The house had survived the Civil War, a fire and neglect, defiant against all that tried to bring it down. A grand old dame shaking a proverbial fist at fate.

So, too, would Abigail survive.

She'd heal from her failed attempt at conducting an affair…from falling in love, or whatever it was, with Leif.

They were just friends now.

Could she even handle seeing him in that capacity?

She'd have to. But not tomorrow. Or the next day. Or even the day after that. By Monday, she'd be fine.

SHE CLUNG TO the belief that she'd be fine by Monday. Despite her determination, on Saturday night after watching John and Shelby exchange the vows given to them by her father, she felt far from okay.

Maybe it was the gorgeous ivory Empire-waist dress Shelby wore that was so similar to Abigail's own gown. Or maybe it was seeing her brother's tears as he tenderly took Shelby's hand and promised to cherish her always. Or maybe it was the fact she felt both deliriously happy for her brother and madly melancholic at the same time. And her mental state wasn't helped by having to deal with Birdie's refusal to wear a dress or the fact her daughter had sweet-talked Shelby into letting her bring her father. *Pretty please, Aunt Shelby?* It was the "aunt" part that had sealed the deal. So Abigail spent much of the reception—held at her parents' house—hiding from Cal.

"Hey, you look like you lost your best friend," her mother said, finding her almost concealed by the damask drape in the dining room.

"Huh?" Abigail asked, jarred from her contemplation of the dormant bushes outside the window. She glanced toward the formal parlor, where most of the guests stood chatting with one another. "What best friend?"

"I meant you look troubled. Or are you sad about marriage in general?"

"No, nothing like that. I'm just dealing with... stuff."

"Is it the art teacher? Leif?"

"What?"

"Birdie said you've been seeing him."

"We're friends." *And we had fabulous sex. And I may have fallen in love with him.*

But she didn't say that, of course.

"Oh," Fancy said, tracing the condensation collecting in the corner of one windowpane. "I had hoped."

"He's not my type."

"You have a type?"

"Everyone has a type. Besides, he's not staying in Magnolia Bend."

"Well, no one said *you* have to stay in Magnolia Bend."

Abigail jerked her head toward her mother. "Don't be ridiculous. I have a business here and this is where Birdie goes to school. It's where you and Dad are. I'm not giving that up for a chance at—"

"Love?"

"I'm not in love," Abigail said as fresh pain throbbed within her. Like a cut she'd thought healed, her wound reopened to throb anew. Then the anger came. She'd done this to herself. Waded into a shallow pool, thinking she'd be safe, then grabbed help-lessly for something to hold on to when the earth beneath her feet shifted, sucking her into a vortex. Despite her strong efforts to remain casual, cool and collected, she'd been pulled into love, was mired in desperate emotion.

Hell.

"Well, Leif hasn't left town yet," Fancy said with a soft smile. "Nothing is hopeless."

"I'm not a starry-eyed girl. To act like it is silly."

Fancy narrowed her green eyes. Her wispy red hair was perfectly coiffed for once, complement-ing the emerald dress that accented her curves and camouflaged her tummy. Nestled between her age-defiant décolleté was the single ruby pendent Dan had given her on their twenty-fifth wedding anni-versary, telling her she was indeed a prize above ru-bies. This woman was a true steel magnolia and she didn't bullshit when it came to her children. "Love is supposed to be silly, Abigail Ann. Don't you dare miss out because you're worried about looking fool-ish. That would be stupid."

"Who wants to be a fool, Mom? I've been there and done that with Cal."

"And you're letting him win again."

"What are you talking about?"

"Honey, there's not one person in this town—outside his own mother, maybe—that doesn't think Calhoun is the stupidest man in all of Louisiana. What he did, well, people don't forget that easy. But you're letting *his* insecurity and foolish choice to let you go keep you from living and loving. I've sat by for years, biting my tongue—"

"Ha," Abigail sniffed.

"—waiting for you to have the guts to shuck him off your back. But you let that memory cling to you. You wear it, and last week when I saw you at the grocery store, your eyes were sparkling, your cheeks were pink and you looked like a woman who'd been well-pleased. I came home and told your father that you'd finally kicked that asshole to the curb."

Abigail looked around. "Mom."

"I don't care who hears me. I don't even care if Cal hears me. You deserve to fall in love, to laugh, to have a future beyond being everyone's servant. You live for everyone else and not yourself. And that, my dear, is unacceptable. Now, I must go save Shelby's parents from Uncle Carlton. He's telling them about his hemorrhoid surgery."

Her mother walked away before Abigail could say anything more on the subject.

Abigail sighed and leaned her forehead against the chilled glass. She should go home. She didn't feel like celebrating and her mood wasn't fair to John or Shelby. She'd just turned to leave when her father, still wearing his vestments, tapped his champagne glass. The talking quieted.

"Usually the best man makes the toast, but tonight I want to be the first to lift my glass to the happy couple. Both John and Shelby walked a difficult road to get to this moment. Despite the potholes, dead ends and the proverbial rocks in their shoes, they have persevered in finding love again. The good Lord knew what each of you needed."

John and Shelby looked at each other with such tender intimacy, it made tears well in Abigail's eyes.

"Here's to John, Shelby and the triumph of love," her father said.

"Hear, hear!" several people said, lifting their glasses. Abigail swiped a glass off the side table and lifted it, too. Taking a huge gulp of chilled fizziness, Abigail caught Birdie's eye.

The girl smiled for the first time in forever and raised her glass of grape cocktail toward Abigail. Fancy always had fake champagne for the grandkids at any special event. Seeing her daughter's smile was like balm on the wound that ached inside her. Birdie might be difficult but she was worth it.

"She's looking more and more like you," Cal said from behind her.

"Well, I am her mother," Abigail said, turning to the man who had occupied her thoughts only moments ago. "She looks like you, too. That stubborn chin and those long fingers. Too bad she's not a boy. She would be a great wide receiver."

"Or guitar player."

Abigail didn't want to spend time with Cal. "She's a good artist. I think she's found her thing."

"Are you okay?" He looked at her with a yearning that made her shuffle backward.

"Fine. Just a lot going on."

"You going to the committee meeting this Thursday?"

"I have to. Hilda knows where I live," she said, giving the woman in question a nod when she glanced this way. Abigail dreaded seeing Leif again. Maybe by Tuesday, she'd feel stronger. Maybe she'd be over this infatuation with him. After all, she couldn't have really fallen in love so quickly. So, yes, what she felt was infatuation. That's it.

"Could we step outside for a moment? I need to talk to you."

Abigail blew out a breath. "Fine."

She went where she always went when problems plagued her—the rose garden. Fancy had strung white Christmas lights around the perimeter, which would have been cheerful if the rosebushes had been full instead of spindly. She started walking the brick path. Cal fell into step beside her.

"Cold," Cal said, rubbing his own arms. He was over six feet and still as broad as he had been in the days he played football. His rugged jawline made him even more masculine, yet the lines around his eyes lent him some vulnerability.

"That's to be expected. It is the end of February. But I'm guessing you didn't ask me out here to discuss the forecast."

"No," he said, frowning at her sarcasm. "I had hoped you might come to better accept me in your life."

"You're not in my life. You're in Birdie's."

Cal made a noise in his throat and looked out at the dry creek bed at the rear of the property. "You remember the day we bought Laurel Woods?"

She didn't know where he was going, but she would shelve the prickliness for the time being. "Of course. In April. Those daffodils had sprouted by the back door."

"One of the happiest days of my life."

"Really?" she said, trying to keep the bitterness at bay.

"You wore that pink dress—the one with the white flowers on it. You looked good in that dress, and I kept thinking I'd have to be careful so the men who stayed at the inn didn't try to whisk you away from me."

"Oh, please. I can see you brought your charm with you tonight."

"That's not my charm working—it's my eyes." He jabbed a finger at the brown eyes she used to tell him were the color of chocolate chips. "You were always beautiful. Why did I ever think what we had wasn't enough?" He stopped and took her elbow, looking at her with a mixture of regret and hunger.

"Cal, we've been over this. We can't go back. What's done is—"

Cal's mouth descended, capturing her protest. He wrapped his arms around her, drawing her to him.

Abigail didn't resist, but allowed the kiss. Maybe she needed to see if there were something there, or maybe she needed the closure, but either way, she didn't push him away.

Cal tasted familiar. His lips were warm, not too demanding but not the least bit brotherly. She felt something stir inside her, a gentle awakening, before the realization that this embrace was wrong broke through.

Carefully she ended the kiss. She studied the man she'd once loved, the man she'd given herself to, the man who'd tossed her away.

"Abi," he whispered, lifting a hand to stroke her cheek. "We were so good together. I still want you, baby."

Abigail caught Cal's hand in hers, and pulled it away. She stepped back still holding his hand a moment before dropping it. "The key word in that statement is *were*, Cal. We're not together anymore. I know you thought you could come home and convince me to give you another chance. But I won't. You have to move on."

"But what I did wasn't about you, babe. It was me. I was screwed up."

Abigail nodded. "I know. But I've learned some things about myself. I allowed what you did to me to happen because we were never equals in this relationship. I gave too much of myself. I sacrificed what I wanted to make you happy. No more."

"Just give me another chance. I can make you happy."

"You can't because I don't love you anymore, Cal." Abigail looked him in the eye. "And you don't really love me. If you did, you never would have left. Love isn't selfish."

"I'm sorry."

Abigail twirled around, spreading her hands. The moon above cast a luminous, almost magical glow on frosted grass. "Look at this. All of this has been here for centuries. People have loved, laughed, cried and grieved on this land. We're no different, Cal."

"What do you mean?" he asked, looking at her as if she'd sprouted wings.

"I mean, this is how it is. You don't always get what you want. It's the ebb and flow of life."

"I don't—"

"This time you're not getting what you want. I'm not yours anymore. You had me and you tossed me away."

Cal watched her as she lowered her arms and walked toward him. She took his hands, making the first move to touch him in over five years. He looked at their linked hands. "My daddy told me to let the anger go. I didn't want to because it still hurt to see you and know you didn't want me. But you know what?"

"What?"

"I'm over you, Cal. I've truly healed from the pain, and so I want to forgive you. Oh, there will be times it will be hard because I'll always remember, but I want to let you and what we had go. Finally."

"But—"

"No buts. We will never be in love again, but we can do as you suggested a few weeks ago—we can be grown-ups. I don't want to be bitter anymore."

After a few seconds of silence, he murmured, "Okay."

"And that means you can no longer manipulate Birdie into thinking you and I have a shot."

"I didn't…" His protest died when she arched an eyebrow.

"Okay, I was jealous over that Leif guy and said things about him not being right for you. I didn't help things for you. I exploited her wanting a family again."

"You told her he was wrong for me?" Abigail asked, pissed, but also incredulous that Cal had admitted to being wrong.

"Only because I wanted to be right for you again. Look, I'll fix this. I'll tell her I shouldn't have done that. But I'm not sure I can ever give up on you, Abi."

"Abigail. And you'll have to."

For a minute or so they stood there, breath puffing white in the chilled air. The moon shone over them, a silent witness to the true end of Abigail and Cal.

"I'll try. Like you. I'll try," he said finally before jerking his head toward the house. "Let's go inside and warm up. I'll drive Birdie home and talk to her. She'll come around and adjust to all of this."

Abigail felt relief flood her, along with something she hadn't expected when it came to Cal. Peace. Forgiving Cal and gaining some form of closure had allowed her to…see who she'd been? Or maybe it was like having the stitches removed from a wound. The scar was there, but the acute pain no longer was.

She followed Cal inside, telling herself this was what she needed. Clean break with Leif. Closure with Cal.

She already felt stronger. And though her heart still ached over the most recent breakup, she knew she could heal. She'd done it before.

Just stiffen your lip and pretend the emotion away. Worked before. Will work this time. You don't love Leif. It was sex. Nothing more. Say it enough and you'll believe it.

But as she slid her coat on, Matt called, "See you Monday morning."

"What?"

"You're subbing for Mrs. Dyson, right?"

Shit fire. She'd forgotten that she'd promised to substitute for the pre-K teacher so she could go to a doctor's appointment.

Which meant Abigail would be at St. George's bright and early Monday morning…and she would see Leif…and it would not be better. Her shattered heart would still throb, pulsating pieces scattered at her feet. But on the surface, she knew how to play the part.

Chin up, don't show the cracks.

Come Monday, she'd be heartbroken…but the world wouldn't know.

CHAPTER NINETEEN

LEIF LEFT MAGNOLIA BEND for the weekend. He couldn't stay because the Beauchamp wedding, small or not, was the talk of the town. He couldn't risk bumping into Abigail or any of her family.

Leif didn't want to see, hear, feel or think about Abigail.

He wanted to drink.

So he'd driven to Houston to visit a friend who had been doing sculpture work for several large companies in the downtown area. Daisy Reynolds was much in demand and the perfect person to buy him a drink, tell him to suck it up and get over the bourgeois concept of commitment.

Daisy didn't believe in marriage or any other convention that said she had to follow rules…like making vows or obtaining a license or sitting in a certain place. For a woman with such a girlishly innocent name, she was fiercely defiant and always the first in line to lead protests or marches against tyrannical, narrow-minded bigots.

This meant the moment they bellied up to Daisy's favorite bar in some high-class suburban area and Leif explained the situation between him and Abigail, Daisy didn't hold back.

"Love? That's total horse crap. We've gone over this before, but obviously you can't comprehend that it's impossible to be happy with just one woman. Men aren't made that way."

"Says the queen of one-night stands," Leif said.

"So? I know myself, but you, my friend, are walking dangerously close to being stupid."

"It's stupid to want to fall in love?" He motioned to the bartender and ordered a Scotch.

"I'll buy," Daisy said, sliding out her credit card. "Open a tab, buddy. It's gonna be a long night." She looked at Leif. "And, yes, it's stupid. For one thing, love is a concept people buy into in order to justify their actions."

"You're messed up."

"I'm not the one with a broken heart, am I?"

"You have a point." Leif took the glass filled generously with Johnnie Walker Scotch. They sat and drank, comfortably silent for a long while.

"I've never met a man who wants to fall in love as much as you. You're like the antithesis of every man your age. You *want* to be tied down. It's like something is broken inside you," Daisy said when he was on his third drink, this one bought by a group of women wearing bridesmaids shirts. One had already asked him to give the bride a night she'd never forget.

Their silly antics made the concept of hating marriage that much easier for Daisy. She barely restrained herself from showing them her teeth. "How do they know you're not with me? It's not like I'm wearing my lesbian ID."

"Maybe because you bought that woman at the end of the bar a drink and you keep growling at me?"

"I'm not growling. I'm lecturing."

"One and the same," Leif said, smiling at his old friend. Daisy might be a militant feminist lesbian, but she was his favorite militant feminist lesbian. "Maybe you're right. Maybe something's broken inside me," he said, hoisting the drink toward the women and nodding his thanks. "It's my mother's fault. It's always a parent's fault, right?"

Daisy nodded. "I'm screwed up because of my dad. Yeah, it's always someone else's fault. That's my MO."

"She never told me about my dad and then she leaves me that cryptic plea while on her deathbed. I thought I was happy. I tried to make the thing with Marcie make sense, but a piece inside me was missing."

"You definitely couldn't fill it with that crazy bitch. Maybe you're trying to fill it with some*one* and that's the problem. You don't *need* a woman. You *need* to find this guy who made the sperm donation, blow that town and come stay with me. Fill the hole with work...with beauty. You shouldn't be teaching—you should be focusing on your art."

But he didn't want to focus on his work or move to Houston. He wanted to stay in Magnolia Bend. With Abigail. It wasn't the same as it had been with the other women. There was something different between them, something more. It was as if they both needed each other. When he was with Abigail—hell, even when he wasn't with her—he felt as if he'd found where he was supposed to fit.

But that was crazy.

Maybe Daisy had it right—he needed to do what he'd said he'd do, then get on with his life. He'd probably subconsciously attached himself to Abigail, glomming on to her as an additional reason to stay in Magnolia Bend, imprinting his desire to belong to a mixed-up emotional woman who was an integral part of the community. What he felt wasn't real love, just a misplaced need to know his father.

Or something like that.

After all, he hadn't taken psychology in college and had only a few episodes of talk shows to base that assumption on.

"I like Magnolia Bend," he muttered.

Daisy snorted, her nose piercings catching in the light reflecting off the bar. "Why in the hell would you stay in some backwoods Louisiana town teaching snot-nosed brats when you could be here working with me? Or, hell, you could open your own studio and get a shit ton of contract labor."

"I don't know. Maybe I need to settle into my career more," he said, concluding that Daisy, while fun to hang with for a weekend, didn't understand him well enough for him to trust her advice. Daisy had already shifted her attention to the woman at the end of the bar, who was nursing the beer Daisy had bought her. The blonde wore a shirt thin enough to reveal she wore no bra. Daisy loved hot lonely women and chances were if the blonde played for Daisy's team, he'd be heading to her apartment alone.

Two hours later, he went to Daisy's apartment alone. He met Daisy and Felicia, the hot blonde, for breakfast the next morning before heading to Magnolia Bend.

"Forget that chick," Daisy yelled as he reversed out of the drive. With a wave, he left, heading east, ready to focus more on finding the man who had fathered him and less on his heart.

But when he saw Abigail outside the teachers' lounge Monday morning, trying to carry too many empty tissue boxes, his vows went out the window. Her scent crashed into him, awakening the hunger, and totally destroying the crap he'd told himself that weekend.

"Oops," Abigail muttered, scrambling to catch the box falling from the top.

"Here," he said, grabbing the plummeting boxes and taking another from the top of the stack. "Let me help you with these."

Abigail straightened as the lounge door shut behind her. For a full second she froze like an animal catching the scent of a predator…or like a woman who hadn't expected to face her whatever-he'd-been-to-her first thing in the morning.

"Uh, thanks," she said, her gaze shifting left then right…but not falling on him. Like she couldn't stomach looking at him.

"Sure," he said, turning so he stood beside her. No need to act like two teenagers who had just broken up. They were both adults who had agreed to stop meeting for secret hookups. No big deal. He shoved the hunger for Abigail into its cage and allowed reason to take its place. "So where are we going with these?"

"Uh, the lower school building. Mrs. Dyson's room. I'm subbing for the morning." Her words sounded like an apology.

They started walking, Abigail looking about as comfortable as a missionary in a whorehouse while he pretended this was any other meeting. Just a normal day for two people who were acquaintances, nothing more.

"How was the wedding?" he asked, playing his part.

"Oh, very nice. Shelby looked pretty and John smiled a lot."

"I would hope so." He toed open the door leading to the walkway between the buildings, smiling at a few students standing outside. Two rushed to open the door of the adjacent building. Not snot-nosed brats. Just good kids.

"How was your weekend?" she asked, dutifully playing her role, too. Nothing to see here. We're both just fine.

"I went to Houston to see a friend. She's doing some work for one of the big places downtown and they were unveiling the sculpture."

"She?" Abigail asked, turning toward him before addressing the students. "Thanks, Lauren and Jordan."

The students waved and jogged toward their friends, leaving him and Abigail alone.

"Daisy Reynolds. She's becoming well-known in art circles. Lots of lucrative contracts so I made her buy the drinks."

"Didn't take you long," she said, the hurt fuzzing the edges of her sarcasm.

"Come on, Abi. I don't move that fast. Daisy and I go way back. I needed to get away, okay?"

"It's none of my business," she said, moving around a library cart left in the hallway. She'd thrown her shoulders back, assuming that same no-nonsense armor she'd had in place the first day he'd seen her in the office.

"Hey, Abi—"

"Abigail," she said, turning stricken eyes from him. He caught the sadness within the green depths and it made him want to sweep those damn boxes from her arms, pin her against the wall and kiss the hurt away.

But he couldn't because he'd broken things off… and they were in the middle of the pre-K wing.

"I want us to be okay," he said.

She searched his face for a few minutes before her gaze hardened. "We don't always get what we want. I learned that long ago."

"So cynical."

"It's how it'll have to be. You wanted space. I can now see that was a good decision. In fact, my good sense is finally in place."

"What do you mean? You regret us?" Pain struck like a flash of lightning.

She thought they were a mistake?

No wonder she'd readily accepted his suggestion for a break. Hadn't even tried to talk him out of it. All along she'd had regrets...wished they hadn't started.

"I don't know." Abigail twisted the doorknob of the kindergarten room. "Look, I have to go. I think it would be best if we keep distance between us. We have the festival next weekend and after that it should be easier. Let's just get through this."

"I understand. I'll keep my distance," he said, nodding toward Mrs. Dyson's room, "just as soon as I deliver these for you."

He didn't wait for her response. Instead he walked into the room, flipped on the lights and deposited the boxes on the nearest worktable. He wanted to get out of there before she saw the truth.

Fact was that after dodging all those women who had fallen in love with him in the past, he'd fallen for the one woman who didn't love him, who didn't think he was worth the effort.

Irony really *was* a bitch.

"Thanks," she said, without looking at him.

"No problem," he said, wishing things were different, half of him recognizing Abigail's coldness as a measure of protection, the other half too hurt to care.

Abigail regretted everything.

But what was he missing out on, really? She'd hidden him as if he weren't worthy, content to keep the relationship within the parameters of sex only. Abigail hadn't wanted to try anything different. She hadn't wanted him beyond the bedroom, so maybe she *was* right. Maybe they shouldn't have started at all because the ending was damn near crippling.

"Have a good one," he said.

But what he really wanted to say was "Why am I not good enough? Why can't you give me what you gave that dickhead Cal? Why can't I have your days and your nights? Why can't I have all of you?"

But he didn't say that. Instead he pushed out the heavy door as the bell rang, sending students scurrying around like cockroaches. Time to face the day and forget about his wounded pride and busted heart.

"Morning, Mr. Lively," called one student.

Another called, "Hey, Mr. Lively. Bitchin' boots."

Leif waved and said, "Watch it, Mr. Salindas. Younger students will think it's okay to use that language."

"Sorry, Mr. L. I'll watch it," the high school senior replied with a shamefaced grin.

And thus began Monday morning at St. George's Episcopal School. Another day, another dollar, no room for regret.

ABIGAIL SPENT THE morning faking happiness because to give fifteen four-year-olds anything less would be unfair.

By the time Muriel Dyson arrived to take over, Abigail felt as if she'd been ridden hard and put up wet. Her hair had fallen out of the bun she'd fashioned that morning, her sweater had a huge glop of glue right over her left boob and a dull roaring headache had sneaked up on her.

She'd like to blame it on the four-year-olds, but the tears she'd cried the night before paired with the pain at seeing Leif again were most likely the culprit.

But she'd made it through seeing Leif for the first time after their breakup without crying.

So there was that.

Leif had looked at her as if he wanted to say something more than "I want us to be okay." She wanted him to tell her to stop being an idiot, to give them a second chance, to come over and have makeup sex.

But he'd uttered nothing beyond common banalities.

His casualness had been a hot poker plunged into her gut. But what had she expected? Leif knew how to play this game. To him, seeing her was no big deal. He'd used a soft voice, the same sympathetic one she'd heard right after Cal left. It was the "let's be careful with Abigail" voice.

Leif probably used that apologetic voice often. After all, he was a man who got out when things got serious. Commitment wasn't his thing. Hadn't he used that same voice when the last woman he'd broken up with had appeared wearing a wedding gown?

One day you'll see breaking things off was the right decision for both of us.

Same voice, same sorry expression in his eyes.

Just keep putting one foot in front of the other. That's the plan. The ache will dull. You've done this before. Hey, at least this time everyone in town won't see your utter humiliation. You got this, sister.

The bell rang and classroom doors exploded open as kids poured into the hall, high-pitched laughter mixed with shouts. Nothing like the middle-grade hallway at class change to make a person glad she wasn't a full-time teacher. Abigail caught sight of Birdie at the exact moment her daughter saw her.

And the little turkey did a total about-face and headed the opposite way.

Yeah. Every time Abigail showed up around school, Birdie disappeared. Somehow today it hurt worse.

Like kicking a sick pup.

Abigail tried to ignore her heart and focus on the errands she needed to run. The next week would be busy with the festival gala and ensuing events. Between now and then, she had to see Leif in flippin' art class tomorrow and again at the final committee meeting on Thursday. All she had to do was pretend he was Hitler or something.

Or she could throw her dignity off a cliff and crawl to him, begging his forgiveness for whatever she'd done…which, as far as she could tell, was refuse to make them an official couple.

And what was so wrong with that?

It wasn't as if she were ashamed of Leif. On the contrary, she still couldn't believe he'd been so into her in the first place. No, it didn't have to do with Leif. It had to do with her.

Why couldn't he understand that she didn't want the whole town to know her business…to watch her fall apart when Leif left? She couldn't bear glances of pity any more than she could ones filled with censure. Being pathetic wasn't her bag. Not anymore.

Damn it all. She was worth love. She was worth staying for.

Abigail wove through the remaining middle schoolers and found Birdie in Mrs. Peavy's English classroom. All the students were in the process of pulling out journals, chatting with one another while Dawn Peavy scratched something on the overhead projector.

Birdie looked up, saw Abigail and froze.

I am not pathetic and I won't be treated as such.

"Hey, Birdie, I just wanted to tell you I'll pick you up after school. Don't ride the bus. We've got to get your dress for the Spring Fling. Girl time!" Abigail declared, giving a little clap.

Birdie turned an indescribable color before ducking her head.

"Y'all have a good day," Abigail said, cheerfully, giving a little wave to Dawn.

That's right, sister. I'll teach you to act like I'm gum on your shoe.

And then Abigail left St. George's, brokenhearted, but empowered to do something in regard to Birdie's behavior.

CHAPTER TWENTY

BARTHOLOMEW HARVEY POURED gin in his glass before topping it off with a dose of tonic. Mixing the drink with a glass stir stick, he took a large gulp and eye-balled Leif. "Sure you don't want a drink?"

Bart leaned back and crossed his legs. They sat beneath the large palm on the patio of his impressive home on the golf course. Evening approached, and though a chill hung in the air, the temperature had been atypically warm for the beginning of March. Bart had called and suggested they skip the last meeting of the festival committee and have drinks at his home instead. Since Leif had ignored the search for his father in order to nurse a broken heart and going to Bart's meant he wouldn't have to see Abigail, he'd agreed.

"Not really my poison," Leif said.

At that moment, Bart's Hispanic housekeeper interrupted. "Phone for you, Mr. Harvey," she said, her accent as heavy as her makeup. She was likely in her twenties, with a curvy body and eager-to-please demeanor, making Leif wonder for the second time whether she was truly the housekeeper or Bart's mistress.

"Hold all calls, Bonita. I've been remiss in speaking to Mr. Lively here for the past few weeks, and he deserves my attention. Take a message, please." Bart nodded a dismissal, but his eyes held possessiveness toward the woman who had not been the least bit covert in checking out Leif when he'd arrived.

"So what do you require from me, Leif? I'm rather inept when it comes to judging art."

Leif launched into the criteria for judging that upcoming weekend and what role Bart would have in the process.

"I honestly don't see why it's critical for me to be involved. It's my uncle who liked art," Bart said once Leif finished.

And just like that, Bart opened the door for Leif's real reason for sitting on the wealthy man's patio. "And this was the uncle who was killed?"

Bart flinched. "Oh, so you've heard the accounts of my uncle's murder?"

"People like to talk. So do you think Calliope did it?" Leif tried to look casually interested. He'd tracked down Meat Grommet, and the man swore he had been only friends with Calliope. He claimed she'd done nothing more than help him with a piece of art he wanted to give his girlfriend, who had since become his wife. Another name struck from Leif's list.

"I do. She was after the Harvey fortune. I have no doubt about that," Bart said, lifting an unaffected shoulder even as his hand trembled slightly. It seemed he wasn't necessarily uncomfortable speaking of his uncle's death, but he didn't seem eager to share the story, either. "But that's all water under the bridge."

"But if she killed your uncle, why wasn't she held accountable?"

"She ran before the sheriff could question her. I gave my statement and when they went to find her, she was gone. You know those people. They're like migrant workers—fake names, dark alleys to disappear in."

"But by all accounts she was small and harmless." Leif led the questioning much like a defense attorney, trying to lull Bart into security.

"My uncle was both feebleminded and delicate in constitution. A child could have tipped him down those stairs. Besides I saw her with my own two eyes."

"So you were actually there?"

"Yes. My uncle had asked me to come by," Bart said, setting the empty glass on the small table beside him. "Why are you so interested?"

"It involves the founder of the festival. Suppose my curiosity got the best of me." Leif gave the man a sheepish smile before looking out at two golfers about to tee off. "But why do you think she wanted his money? He'd already endowed the artist program."

Bart laughed. "Shit, everyone wants money, son. Uncle Simeon had plenty of it, too. He was a typical tightwad Southerner, though. Didn't like to part with it. Kept damned tinfoil and storage bags like he couldn't afford more. But when it came to art, he tossed money away like it was nothing."

"Must have driven you crazy."

"It'd drive anyone crazy. He had me on a strict allowance. Getting more out of him was like squeezing blood from a turnip."

"I know the type," Leif said, though he really didn't. Most of the people he surrounded himself with were generous in nature and reusing, renewing and recycling was expected. "Must have been a relief to inherit the money and have control over how it was spent."

"Yeah, but it was a hard thing to lose the old bag. Of course, not having to beg was nice. I closed down the artists' program. Why spend money on something I had no interest in continuing? No offense but I didn't see the point."

Leif shrugged. "It was a good program."

"Which led to my uncle's death," Bart said, looking a bit more relaxed. "So why are you so interested?"

"Because Calliope was my mother."

Bart froze, his gaze shifting from his pool to Leif. "Your mother?"

"Yeah."

For a few moments Bart seemed to mull over how to handle this wrinkle. Leif, however, felt an enormous sense of relief at finally coming clean about exactly who he was with someone other than Hilda and Abigail.

No more secrets.

Finally, Bart looked at him. "I can see the resemblance in you. She was a beautiful woman, and if I may say, you're likewise as pretty." He gave a small nervous chuckle.

Leif, however, didn't respond.

"So I suppose one of the reasons you're here in our little town is to clear your mother's name?"

Leif answered with a slight lift of his eyebrows.

"Well, I can give you no help there. I stand by what I saw."

"You saw my mother push Simeon down the stairs?"

Bart averted his gaze again, and at that point, Leif knew the man wasn't telling the full truth.

"You're lying about it," Leif said.

"Not lying. Look, I saw my uncle at the bottom of the stairs. Your mother stood over him and I asked her what she'd done. She said, 'This wasn't supposed to happen.' Honestly, she scared me—it was as if she was capable of anything. Perhaps she was on drugs. Acid makes people see and do crazy things. That particular drug was popular among her crowd."

"My mother never dropped acid."

"That you know of. Kids don't know what their parents did because Mommy and Daddy don't want their reputations sullied, right? Besides if your mother hadn't killed my uncle, why would she run?"

Bart had a good point—one Leif couldn't answer. Calliope had never spoken about Magnolia Bend,

Simeon Harvey or Leif's father, so in this quest for the truth, he was crawling around on the floor, blind and groping his way. "My mother didn't have a motive."

"Why don't you just ask your mother what happened?"

"My mother died last summer. She never told me about Magnolia Bend. Or Simeon."

Bart picked up his empty glass and shook it, the ice cubes tinkling against the crystal. "I'm sorry about your mother, but perhaps since she's gone, you shouldn't bother with unearthing that whole mess. Sometimes the past should stay in the past for good reason. It's like picking up a log in the woods only to find crawly things beneath."

"Maybe so, but with her last breath Calliope begged me to set things right. Obviously she'd been haunted by what happened here, and I can't ignore her final wish."

A myriad of emotions crossed the older man's face—guilt, anger and resolution. Leif would get nothing more from Bart regarding Simeon's death, but perhaps he could get a clue as to his father's identity. "One more thing, if you don't mind?"

Bart didn't look excited but said, "Sure."

"Was my mother close to anyone besides your uncle?"

"I'm not the right person to ask. I didn't live here and only met your mother twice, the final time being the night of my uncle's death. I didn't know much about her, other than she was a sculptor and her work was very sensual. There was a rather evocative sculpture of Diana the Huntress sitting in my uncle's room the night he died."

Total strikeout.

Bart stood. "Well, if you don't mind…"

Leif rose and extended his hand. "No hard feelings, Mr. Harvey."

Bart took his hand and gave it a brief, hard shake. "Of course not. I wish I could give you better news."

"Thank you for your time," Leif said, moving toward the open doors of the patio, where Bonita stood smiling like a good hostess. Leif spun before exiting. "Oh, and I hope you'll keep this in confidence."

Bart nodded. "I'm many things, Mr. Lively, but a busybody is not one of them. Your business is your own." He turned to stare out over the golf course at the sun sinking low in the sky, casting fingers of light over the newly greening lawn, looking much like Jay Gatsby.

And, perhaps, like the infamous hero of *The Great Gatsby*, Bartholomew Harvey held his dirty little secrets close to his vest.

Or perhaps his guilty expression throughout their discourse was over something entirely different. Either way, it didn't matter. Leif had gained nothing from his visit with Simeon's nephew.

He struck Bart off his mental list, leaving only one name—Everett Orgeron.

And something told him that was the name he should have started with.

LEIF WALKED UP the drive to Hilda's with mixed emotions. He wasn't the kind of guy who marched to another man's drum, but he pulled his weight. He should have attended the meeting earlier but after enduring Abigail in art class earlier this week, going to Bart's sounded like an escape hatch being tossed in front of him. He opened that bad boy.

In art class, Abigail had been more autobot than human, never asking questions, refusing to make eye contact, and seeming to exist in her own bubble. Her coldness froze any heat he'd tried to generate by smiling her way or teasing her about her lopsided vase of flowers.

Stone-cold Abigail.

Brrr.

But he missed her so much, and this search for his father wasn't nearly as meaningful without having someone to share in the progress. He'd gone to see the old groundskeeper, but the man couldn't remember what sort of art Calliope created, much less who she dated…though he could remember lots of meaningless facts about Simeon and the way the wild violets bloomed about the cabins. Essentially Leif's trip out to the Desadier house had proved a waste of time.

So that left Cal's uncle Everett.

Leif had done research on the senator, trying to

decipher from the publicity photos on the internet if he looked anything like the distinguished politician. Other than the fact they had the same height and build, Leif couldn't find any clues as to whether the man could possibly be his father.

"Well, I wondered about you," Hilda drawled, answering the door wearing an expensive-looking pantsuit and small gold ballet flats that bore a designer's logo. She turned without saying another word, leaving the door open. He followed her into the parlor and found her sitting on the pink settee, long arms draped over the back, making her look all-knowing and all-powerful. "Why weren't you at the meeting?"

"None of your business," he said.

"Huh, well, that could mean a great many things— you had a bad case of flatulence, things are going smoothly with the art judging, you're close to finding your father…or you're avoiding Abigail. Tell me. Which is it?"

Leif smiled. "None of your business."

She laughed and picked up a goblet of red wine from the side table. Then she studied him, her dark eyes assessing before giving a toothy smile. "I do like you, Mr. Lively."

"So you've said," he replied setting the papers she needed to sign on the coffee table. "I need some signatures on the hotel check."

"Avoiding the question, I see," Hilda said, picking up the folder and leafing through. "By the way, Cal was here."

"Was he? Smashing," Leif drawled à la Hilda.

"And Abigail."

"Of course she was. She likes meetings and colored tabs and making spreadsheets." Even though he was flippant, jealousy rose in him. He could see Abigail and Cal sitting together, looking like they fit each other, both with dark sleek hair, prominent jaws and a sense of belonging to the world around them. Oh, and there was that whole "having a daughter together" thing that united them.

Maybe he should have done as Birdie suggested— step aside. Abigail might have accepted Cal's renewed interest. Without Leif popping her buttons, she may have relented. He'd trod into Abigail's world as if he belonged in it. She had known he didn't. That's why she hadn't wanted anything more than sex.

And though his heart and body craved a different ending, his mind could sift through the facts and conclude that staying away from Abigail was for the best.

Hilda cleared her throat. "So if I get nothing on Abi, why not tell me about the search for you father? Or is that, too, none of my business?"

"Well, I've pared the list down to one name. After that, it will be back to the drawing board...or perhaps I'll just forget about it."

"And who is this final possibility?"

Leif hesitated for a second, then decided Hilda's reaction might be telling. "Everett Orgeron."

"Whoa. Now that's something," she breathed.

"He's the only other guy Carla Stanton mentioned my mother knew or dated."

"Does Abigail know?"

"No, why would she?"

"Because she loves you?"

Leif gave a wry laugh. "I don't think so, Hilda. But nice try. Abigail and I are no longer engaging in the undoing of buttons, zippers or snaps."

"Oh, dear. You must tell Auntie Hilda what in the hell is going on."

Leif shook his head. "Nothing to tell. I'm essentially at the plate with an oh-two count."

"That's a piss-poor attitude from a determined man."

Leif looked at the dog, who ambled in wearing a duck sweater. "Hilda, no offense, because I really think you're the bomb diggity, but you don't know me. As much as I want to belong, I know I don't. And even if I wanted a future for me and Abigail, I know there isn't one. I'm not made to stick."

"Bull to the shit," Hilda said, lifting her chin. "That's a bunch of malarkey piled on malarkey. I knew the minute I saw you there was something special about you, and being around you, watching you work on this festival and generously giving your time and charm to Abigail, I knew you fit this town like a glass slipper."

Leif gave a humorless laugh. "Hilda, that slipper was dropped and shattered weeks ago. I fit this town like a pair of too small Birkenstocks. Look, I've loved my time here, but when the school year is over, regardless of whether I've found the man who fathered me or not, I'm heading west. Abigail's better off sticking to what she knows."

"Like Cal?"

"Or a man who fits her world better. We had fun, but that's all it can be."

"Well, shit on a shingle, you fell in love with her."

It felt as if she'd punched him. Not love. Anything but love. Daisy had talked him out of that, right? He simply missed Abigail right now. That was it. "Remember how you said approval's given too easily?"

She nodded.

"Well, the concept of love is brought up too easily these days."

Hilda's brow wrinkled much like her cousin's did when confronted by something with which she disagreed. "So you're discounting love because…?"

"It doesn't lead to anything."

Hilda tilted her head. "Did I ever tell you about Sherburne? My late husband?"

Leif looked desperately toward the front door. He needed to get home and crack open a beer, not get a lecture about love from Hilda.

"Well, he was a horrible man."

Leif made a face. "So why did you marry him?"

"Because he was rich as hell and spent almost all his time at the office."

"You could be doing more harm than good here, Hilda."

"Anyway, Sherburne worked incessantly to make money, never really caring what I did with my time as long as I attended his business and family functions in New Orleans. When he died, he was a millionaire several times over with absolutely nothing to show for his life aside from his picture hanging on the wall of the firm he slaved years working for."

"And your point is?"

"I was the moron who thought I didn't belong here with Denny Trosclair. Denny was a plumber and wanted nothing more than a snug little house in Magnolia Bend, a bunch of babies and me in his bed every night. My mama told me I was too good for Denny. She told me Magnolia Bend was a Podunk town full of backward, fashion-challenged busybodies."

"And it isn't?"

"No, this town *is* full of the fashion-challenged, but my point is I believed what someone else told me about myself. Do I like having Sherburne's millions at my disposal without having to look at his sour face every night over dinner? You betcha. But I'm jealous as hell of Kathy Trosclair with her cute window boxes and three pretty grandbabies. Who in the hell was my mother to convince me I was this?" Hilda waved a hand over her silk pantsuit, the large diamond rings catching the light from the crystal chandelier above them.

Her intense gaze caught his. "Don't let anyone tell you that you don't belong somewhere...that you are destined to be their image of you. You can take that however you wish, but just because you're pretty and you've left a string of broken hearts doesn't mean you are only that."

Leif watched the strong emotions storm across the face of a woman who normally reveled in her own bored indifference. He saw through to her pain and regret. There was nothing left to do but hug her.

"Oomph," she wheezed as he gave her a squeeze.

"Thank you for sharing that with me. You're a remarkable woman who smells fantastic."

"Well, I can afford good perfume," she said, giving him a squeeze before releasing him.

"I know I'm more than what most people think of me, and I don't suffer from low self-esteem. But lately, I've felt like I'm walking across a sheet of thinning ice. I can't find my footing, my heart is in my throat and any second I'm sure it will end in disaster."

"Yeah, sounds like love to me," Hilda said, catching one of his hands. "I would have loved a son like you. You're one of a kind, honey."

As Leif left Hilda's, he wanted to think he had a better grasp of what he needed to do, but he didn't. He felt more confused because his heart and his mind were at war, and sitting between the two was the search for his father. Perhaps if he could settle all that, he would have a clearer picture of where he belonged in life. He didn't know why he thought this way, he just did.

But the road ahead lay obscured by indecision, fear of rejection and all things Leif Lively was un-accustomed to being.

ABIGAIL PULLED UP to Leif's house the morning of the gala and stopped the car. "I contacted Mr. Lively—"

"You mean Leif?" Birdie's tone showed how little progress Abigail had made in modifying her daughter's behavior.

"Yes. Your art instructor. His text said he left your matted prints on his workbench in his bedroom. Use the key in the birdhouse and make sure you relock the door."

"Why didn't he just take them with him and save us a trip?"

"Because I told him I'd pick them up last week, and I forgot. He took the other piece days ago. It's my fault."

"Well, then why don't *you* go inside and get them? You've been in his house before."

Yeah, and that was the main reason she hadn't picked up the two pieces he'd volunteered to mat and frame. She'd been doing her best to remain strong and that meant staying away from Leif. Any glimpse she caught of him made her feel as if her heart were being filleted. So she'd turned into something she'd never been—a procrastinator. Lately she'd become the queen of avoidance, a shadow of herself. "Do you want to enter the contest or not?"

"I do."

"Then go get *your* art pieces. You want to be independent? This is how we start." Abigail motioned toward Leif's house, déjà vu washing over her as she recalled months ago sending Birdie up the same steps to apologize to Leif. So much had happened since then. Abigail had changed so much...opened her eyes to a bigger world.

"Fine. Jeez, you're as uptight as ever," Birdie said, sliding from the car.

After Abigail had embarrassed Birdie in her English class, they'd had a heart-to-heart. Hadn't been easy, but Abigail had laid out how much Birdie's attitude hurt her. Thankfully, Cal also had taken the time to talk to Birdie, telling her that he and her mother were over. Since then, Birdie had gone back to being a normal mercurial preteen. At times she settled into almost pleasant. Emphasis on *almost*.

"I'm not being uptight. Go. We're on a schedule."

"We're always on a schedule. I can't believe you're waiting to the last minute. Not like you, Mom."

Well, maybe that was because she was an emotional wreck. She'd tried to be distant and hated every moment of playing the ice queen. Seeing Leif's reaction made something wither inside her. This was not who she wanted to be...again. So she'd had a come-to-Jesus meeting with herself, looking hard at the woman she'd clung to being. "I've been preoccupied."

"Because you broke up with Leif? I get it." Birdie's eyes flashed with sympathy. "It's always hard."

"Yeah, but we're still friends." But not really. Friends didn't avoid one another. Friends also didn't cry themselves to sleep from missing the other person.

"At least you tried, Mom." Birdie jogged toward the front porch.

Yeah, she'd tried. Crash and burn.

Abigail gave a heavy sigh. A week ago, she'd decided to hell with protecting herself. She would tell him she'd do whatever he wanted as long as they could be together...for as long as he stayed in Magnolia Bend. Twice she'd started down the path to his house, only to turn back.

The whole thing was stupid, really.

She didn't know how to undo the hurt between them. Did she merely apologize for making him feel like she was embarrassed about being with him? Did she hurl herself into his arms and beg for forgiveness, inhale his scent and the strength he always gave her? Or did she lay it all out on the table, logically giving the reasons he should take her back?

But the old fear of rejection, of the crunch of tires as yet another man drove away, reverberated in her gut.

Why couldn't she let go of the fear?

She had to stop clinging to past hurts and step into the light. Dance near the fire. Take a leap…toward Leif.

Before time ran out.

Abigail looked at her watch. She had forty minutes to get Birdie and her entries to the judges' table before her hair appointment. The gala would be held at the newly renovated country club and the attire was dressy for once. Hilda insisted they move toward more black tie than work boots, so Abigail had dragged out an old bridesmaid's dress of inky blue, cut the skirt off to midthigh and bought a pair of silver stilettos that matched the streak in her hair. When she'd tried on the outfit last week, she'd nearly tossed it for her standby modest black dress with the satin bow. But then she imagined Leif seeing her in the blue one, and she'd decided to be bold.

She wanted to be sexy tonight…because she'd decided tonight was the best opportunity to change things between her and Leif.

Birdie came out carrying her two pieces and an additional piece that looked to be hastily wrapped. She slid both in the back before sliding into her seat up front.

"What's that?"

"Mr. Lively left a note asking me to bring it. He must have left it behind." Birdie clicked her seat belt, then stared straight ahead, shoving her earbuds into her ears.

Abigail pulled the left earbud out. "Are you sure? The committee has already placed all the items to be judged in the storage area."

"I don't know, Mom. I'm just being nice and taking it for him." Birdie shoved in the earbud, sealing Abigail out.

"Guess we can do that," Abigail said, pulling away from the curb, heading for the subdivision exit. Birdie's mood had once again changed. Weather conditions ten minutes ago—balmy. Present conditions—freezing drizzle.

After several minutes, Abigail tapped Birdie's shoulder. "I'd love to see how your drawings turned out."

"Why? I won't win. Nicholas Severson's stuff's much better and he's in my division."

"Don't think that way."

Birdie started tapping on the new iPhone her father had bought her last week, ignoring Abigail.

"Birdie."

"How many times do I have to tell you? I don't want to be called Birdie anymore."

"Sorry."

Her daughter grunted, still staring at the damn phone.

"Come on, it's hard being a mom sometimes."

Birdie didn't move. "So you remind me all the time. If I'm so hard to deal with, maybe I should go live with Dad."

Abigail's heart dropped into her stomach and bounced several times. "Do you want to live with him?"

"Maybe. I'm tired of living in a hotel."

Abigail wanted to punch the steering wheel. "I thought you loved Laurel Woods."

"I do, but I want a house like a normal kid, and it's obvious I'm in your way. You don't want Dad but you want some man in your life."

"That's not true."

Birdie looked up. "You were hooking up with Leif."

"Leif and I were friends." Not a total lie. Just a half truth.

"Just friends?" Birdie asked, her voice dropping in temperature.

Abigail didn't want to lie to her daughter, but she wasn't going to admit to sleeping with her art teacher. The way Birdie said *hooking up* made what Abigail had shared with Leif sound sleazy when it had been anything but. But maybe Birdie, like so many others, would see only black or white. They would never see the healing the relationship had given Abigail, and they would never see the tenderness, the laughter and the sheer goodness of being with Leif. "I told you that my love life—or lack of one—is off the books. Now, we need to get to the festival grounds and then to Fancy and Pops's house."

"Nice avoidance tactic," Birdie muttered, again

tapping on her phone, "but as you remember, I'm not a little kid. I know the score, Mom."

Abigail fought against quizzing her daughter on exactly what she meant, mostly because she didn't have time for the usual drama. She'd been reading books for the past year on dealing with rebellious teens and last week she'd spent time visiting with another mother who had a daughter Birdie's age. She'd assured Abigail the surging hormones were normal for a nearly teenaged daughter. Pairing that with Cal coming home and the fact Birdie seemed to have withdrawn from her friends meant a rockier-than-normal ride for a while.

God help her, but Abigail felt plum tired when it came to being a parent these days.

So she remained silent while she drove the last few miles into town. Pulling up at the gate to the fairgrounds, she shut off the car. "I'll wait here while you go enter your work."

"You're not going with me?"

"As a not-so-little kid, there are things you can do for yourself. Here's the check for the entrance fee. It's only enough for two entries. If you want to enter more, you'll have to use your own money."

Birdie stared at her for several seconds before saying, "Okay."

Abigail sat there for a full fifteen minutes before texting Birdie.

Come on. I have an appointment in ten minutes.

RayAnne, her hairdresser, had squeezed Abigail in last-minute and there wasn't time to spare. She'd have to see if Fancy could meet her at Salon 86.

Birdie replied:

Coming. Had to take Mr. L's art thing to Jolene. BRB.

Abigail drummed her fingers on the steering wheel, trying to decide whether to go with an updo for her hair, or leave it down. Probably the latter.

Finally, Birdie hurried to the car.

"Sorry. I had to find the chick cataloging the art going to the country club," she said, sliding inside.

"Oh, guess that was one of the pieces they're displaying tonight during the gala. Glad you were able to get it logged in for Mr. Lively." Abigail started the car and pulled out, while dialing her mother.

"Yeah, lucky for him," Birdie said, turning her head to stare out at the dreary afternoon.

"You okay?"

"Sure."

Abigail shrugged off the weird vibe sleeting off her daughter as Fancy answered. After settling things with her mother, Abigail headed to the salon. Definitely hair down so it brushed her shoulders. That would make her more approachable.

Hopefully, Leif wouldn't avoid her and she would get the opportunity to reopen the dialogue between them. All she could do was be honest about her fear of being hurt again. She would tell him about how she'd started down the path to his house several times. About how she missed him and the way he made her feel. Then she would ask him to consider a different relationship, one that was in the open. She would tell him he'd taught her to love again.

Because she would rather have Leif to love for a little while…than not at all.

She said a prayer for guidance as she parked the car, waving at her mother, who had just arrived wearing yoga pants and a breast cancer awareness T-shirt. She looked hard at her mother, a woman who had fought cancer years ago and won. A woman who had been scared of her hair falling out and people looking at her. A woman who had feared death no matter how many times she'd nodded in agreement with her husband in the pulpit when he declared eternity with God the ultimate reward. Her mother had taught Abigail to fight, chin up, shoulders back, while wearing fabulous shoes.

No, Fancy hadn't raised Abigail to be scared.

She hadn't raised her to allow the pain of betrayal to sideline her from life.

Tonight Abigail was letting go of her past.

And reaching toward her future.

CHAPTER TWENTY-ONE

LEIF TIED HIS tie for the third time, finally getting the length right. He'd spent the past few hours overseeing the delivery of the art to the gala, leaving Jolene Marks, one of the committee members, in charge of arranging the last few donations for the silent auction. He'd contributed a piece he'd done of a California beach portraying a lone figure against the sinking sun.

Giving his tie one final tug, he turned to make sure Birdie had indeed grabbed the framed pieces he'd left atop his drawing table. The spot was empty, and the girl had even remembered to lock up and return the key to the birdhouse.

Like her mother, the girl didn't miss a beat.

He'd sent Abigail several messages regarding the artwork, but she'd put it off. The woman was good at keeping her distance.

Trying to pull his thoughts from Abigail and the dark clouds that surrounded her, he hummed an old Stones' tune, pulling on the dinner jacket he'd borrowed from Hilda's late husband's closet. As he adjusted his collar, a realization hit him between the eyes—the sketch he'd done of Abigail. He'd left it…where?

Oh, shit.

He had completed the chalk, unable to put it aside

half-finished. Those lonely nights when he ached to touch her, the best he could do was lovingly trace her high cheekbone or shade the underside of her luscious breast. He'd set the chalk only a few nights ago, leaving the piece propped beside the table.

He walked over to his large drafting table and sifted through the few pieces he had there. The one featuring Abigail was missing.

Huh.

Leif rounded the bed to look there just as the doorbell rang.

Damn.

The doorbell sounded again, disrupting the panic growing inside him. The sketch had to be here somewhere. But where?

A horrible feeling knitted around the panic. Surely Birdie hadn't taken the rendering of her mother to the gala. Birdie was at the age where nothing was more embarrassing than having your mother half-naked on display for everyone to see. He knew. His mother had been painted, sculpted and captured on film in the buff. He'd cringed every time he saw images of her hanging in museums across the Southwest.

The bell sounded again, and he wrenched open the door hoping Birdie would be on the other side, holding the rendering of her mother, ready to apologize for nearly giving him a heart attack.

But it wasn't Birdie.

It was Bart, dressed in a tuxedo.

"Bart," Leif said, confused at the sight of the man on his porch.

"Good evening," Bart said, glancing around and nodding at the neighbor and the damn dog that pooped on everyone's lawn but its own. "Can I have a word with you before this evening gets under way?"

Leif had no clue why Bart was on his porch. He didn't have time to spare. "I'm kind of in a hurry."

"I understand, but this is important," Bart said, stepping inside and shutting the door behind him.

Leif gestured toward the sofa. "I need to make a call first."

"Go ahead. I'd rather stand. Too pent-up."

Leif grabbed his cell phone and dialed Jolene. She didn't answer. He sent a text asking her to call him. Immediately. No need to alarm Abigail yet.

Then he turned to Bart, who looked as nervous as a goat in a room full of cheetahs. Leif sank onto the couch, trying to give Bart some breathing room. Yeah, Leif and his goddamned infamous breathing room.

"Look, after you left, I couldn't get that night out of my head," Bart said.

"Makes sense. I dragged it up again, but now isn't the time—"

"No, I have to do this. I couldn't go there tonight without clearing this off my mind. I can't sleep or eat or—" Bart paused, setting a hand to his chest.

"Fine." Leif glanced down at his cell phone. Nothing from Jolene.

"See, Uncle Simeon wasn't the easiest guy to love, but he was the last of my family. He cared for me, though I exasperated him greatly in those days." Bart paced toward the fireplace before turning toward the door again. "This thing is just ripping at me and I can't keep the truth buried any longer."

"What truth?" Leif asked, the concern over Birdie and the sketch fading as Bart's words hit him.

"I lied."

"About...?"

Bart rubbed a hand over his face. "Your mother didn't push my uncle. She wasn't even upstairs when the accident happened. I was."

"You?"

Bart threw up his hands. "Look, I didn't push him, but I was scared someone would think I did. Uncle and I had been arguing because he wanted to give his money to the foundation, appointing your mother the custodian of the endowment. He was tired of me wasting money and wanted to wash his hands of me. I, of course, was against this, so we argued about the foundation and the endowment."

"So how did my mother even—"

"She interrupted. We were upstairs, where my uncle stubbornly kept his bedroom. With his health he should have been on a lower floor, but the silly man didn't want friends to think him infirm. Your mother called out from downstairs and he tried to go down. His foot missed the top step. I don't know if he was looking at her or at me, but somehow he just missed. He landed nearly at your mother's feet."

"Why did you say she pushed him?"

Bart inhaled as he paused at the window. "I'm not proud of myself. I knew what my uncle wanted to do with the family money, knew he'd already contacted his attorney, so I told your mother if she didn't pack up and leave, I'd tell the police she pushed him. I told her the authorities would believe me over her. She literally ran from the house and I searched my uncle's papers and destroyed any evidence of his plans for the endowment fund. His attorney had no other recourse but to drop it because there was nothing official. The money went to me."

Leif sat a moment, reeling at what Bart had revealed. Anger burgeoned within him at the bullish tactics the man had used to chase a no doubt terrified Calliope away from Magnolia Bend. She'd left thinking she'd be arrested for a crime that never existed.

"I'm sorry. Ever since you told me she was your mother, I've been sick with worry—"

"That people would know what a greedy bastard you are?" Leif rose, moving toward Bart.

"Yes, but guilt had burrowed inside me for years. I couldn't undo what I did to your mother, so when Hilda came to me and asked to revive the art festival, I donated the money."

"And that makes up for what you did?"

"No, but I can help you. Whatever you need, I'll

give you. You can tell the truth. You have that right. And I won't stop you…even if it means I go down as the bad guy. I wronged your mother." He took a deep breath, releasing it. "The truth is finally out there."

"How do I know you didn't push your uncle? Why shouldn't I call the police?"

Bart jerked back. "I'm not a murderer, Mr. Lively. I'm greedy and weak, but I wouldn't harm anyone."

"You harmed me."

Bart looked confused.

Leif helped him out. "My mother left pregnant. Because of you, I never knew my father. Because of you, my father never knew I existed."

"What?" Bart shook his head. "I didn't know. Wait, you don't think it was my uncle? No, couldn't be. So who is your father?"

"I wish I knew."

"You don't…oh. Well, perhaps that's how I can help. Maybe hire an investigator and do blood tests? No expense spared."

"I'll take care of it my way, Mr. Harvey. You've done enough."

Bart nodded, still pale but his features reflected a measure of relief. "For what it's worth, I'm sorry. If you need my help, you have it." He turned and walked out the door.

Leif let him go because he didn't trust himself not to kick the man's ass for being such a manipulative bastard. If his mother hadn't felt so threatened, if she'd felt like she had some support in this town outside of Simeon, she might have stayed. Leif might have had a father to toss the ball with, to teach him to drive and to share his first beer with.

As Bart's headlights swept over the front windows, Leif shook himself from the past. His phone vibrated in his pocket.

"Thank God," he said, answering.

"Leif, what's up?" Jolene said, sounding out of breath.

"Birdie Orgeron brought some entries for the junior sweepstakes today. Did she bring something for the auction, too?"

"Uh, yeah. And it's stunning. So—"

"Is it a picture of Abigail?"

"Abigail?" Jolene sounded confused. "Wait. Oh, crap. That *is* Abigail. The hair. Don't know how I missed it."

"Take it down. Now."

"It's already up. Have you looked at the clock? We opened ten minutes ago."

Leif glanced at the clock. Holy shit. He grabbed his keys and lurched out the door. "Go take it down. I don't care if it causes a fuss, go get it."

"I can't—"

"Do it," he said, pressing End and finding Abigail's number. "Pick up, pick up, pick up," he said as the phone rang…and rang…and rang.

He didn't leave a message. Instead he texted for her to call him and ran to his car. The gala had just started. If he could hit all green lights, he might make it before anyone realized the sketch was of Abigail.

His lateness made him want to punch Bart.

Then perhaps turn Birdie over his knee…though he didn't truly believe in corporeal punishment.

Because any chance he had to get Abigail back had disappeared like a sand castle in the surf.

ABIGAIL HAD JUST entered the country club, feeling prettier than she had in years, when Cal grabbed her arm and pulled her out onto the stone patio.

"What are you doing?" she said, jerking her arm away.

"Trust me," he said, his breath forming a cloud in the dark night. "You don't want to go in there."

"Why not? What's wrong?"

Abigail pulled her thin wrap tighter around her shoulders and tried to figure out if something was really wrong or if Cal were playing at something.

"Do you really trust this Leif guy?"

"What in the hell are you talking about? That's none of your business. It's mine."

"No, I don't think it's just yours anymore," he said, looking as if he'd run over a puppy or broken her mother's best china. "Your business is very much out there."

"Tell me what you're talking about or get out of my way. Hilda wanted me here by seven-thirty for the committee introduction."

"Abi, there's a—"

The door opened and a few people came out reaching for cigarettes. One was a guy from the bank who looked stunned to see her. "Oh, hey, Abigail."

Was the man blushing?

"Hi," Abigail said, giving him and two other men with him a smile. They literally raked their eyes over her.

Inside a little thrill shimmied up her spine. She'd looked good in her bathroom mirror and they'd just validated the reflection.

"See you later," Abigail said.

Cal gave her a pained look but nodded.

The warmth of the club along with the hum of conversation greeted her as she moved inside. Cal trailed behind her. As she walked through the hallway toward the main ballroom, people stopped their conversations and stared.

Abigail discreetly looked to check that her boobs hadn't tumbled out or that she didn't have her dressed tucked into her Spanx. A terrible feeling unwound inside her as she walked into the room.

About 70 percent of the people inside turned to look at her. At least the band didn't stop playing.

She spied her brother Matt at the bar. He set down his drink and walked over to her. Dropping a kiss on her cheek, he said, "You look pretty tonight."

"Thanks. Why is everyone looking at me?" she asked.

"Come with me," her brother said, sending a fierce glare to those staring at her, making conversations resume as if on command. He tucked her hand into the crook of his arm. "Have you seen Leif?"

"No. Not yet. Is something wrong?"

Matt made a sympathetic face. "Look, Abi, I want to prepare you for something—"

"This feels familiar, Matt." She tugged her arm from her brother's grasp. Something was up and she didn't need a man to lean on, like some weak-assed female who needed protection from…whatever awaited her.

She moved to the boardroom holding the silent auction. When she stepped inside, it felt as if all the air had been sucked out of the space. Her smoking-hot heels sank into the new plush carpet when she saw it.

The painting Leif had done of her.

Her first thought was how absolutely gorgeous it was.

Her second thought was at how absolutely naked she was.

"Oh, my God," she whispered.

"Yeah," Matt breathed behind her as everyone in the room, Hilda included, watched her.

Abigail swallowed the shock, the hurt, the out-and-out horror, scrambling for how to handle the sight of herself tangled in sheets, nude and sated… on display in front of friends and family. In front of her cousin, who was the mayor. In front of her first-grade teacher. In front of…

Oh, God.

Her father.

Dan stood with a cluster of people he ministered to every single week.

Abigail thought she might faint again. Matt pressed an arm in the middle of her back, keeping her from sagging.

Her father came to her, a smile on his face. "Hey, baby, you look pretty as a bluebonnet."

Dropping a kiss on her cheek, he gave her shoulders a little squeeze. Matt's hand dropped away.

"Daddy," she managed to say, her eyes still on the painting.

Her father turned, his arm around her shoulders. "I think the piece is simply stunning. Like something Michelangelo might have painted. Just has such an intimate, surreal quality to it. Honestly, I've never seen you look lovelier," her father said, holding her firmly so her trembling couldn't be detected.

Abigail took a breath and tried to talk without breaking into tears. She tossed her hair over her shoulder and said, "You know, I love it."

"Just so you know, I've already bought it," her father said, his voice loud enough to be heard by everyone in the room.

Abigail managed a nod and a blistering smile. She couldn't look her father in the eye. If she did, she'd break, shattering into a million pieces.

And it was at that exact moment Leif arrived, looking like a contestant on *The Amazing Race*, jacket open, eyes wild, breath coming in great spurts.

LEIF BARRELED INTO the silent auction room, trying to look as if he hadn't sprinted from the other side of the tennis courts, where he'd parked. A fresh speeding ticket poked out of his breast pocket and he knew sweat trickled down his face.

But when he saw Abigail standing there clasped against her father's side, pale and also quite stunning in a short navy dress, he nearly dropped to his knees.

Sitting in the middle of the room on a large easel was the piece he'd done of her.

"Oh, God," he breathed.

Everyone in the room grew so quiet he could've heard a mouse fart.

Abigail merely stared at him, disappointment mixed with shock shimmering in her green eyes. And there, too, he saw the accusation—she thought he'd intentionally entered the intimate rendering of her in the auction.

Didn't she know him better than that?

"Leif," she said finally, a tremulous smile on her face.

Hilda crossed the room, smiling at him and then her cousin. Turning to the picture of Abigail twisted in his sheets, she said, "You really ought not to have been so modest with this one, sweetheart."

Her remark was teasing, her eyes sparkling. Her approval, along with the good reverend's nod, broke the ice and the other people in the room returned to their wine spritzers and polite conversation.

Leif moved next to Abigail, his heart in his throat. "Can I talk to you, please?"

Her father gave him a stern look. "Maybe later, Mr. Lively." His mild tone tempered his expression. "My daughter has to take a phone call from her mother."

Leif glanced at Abigail, who stared at his buttons and said nothing.

"Please," he whispered to her.

Abigail shook her head and moved past him. "We'll talk later." And then she turned and walked out of the room, effectively dismissing him. Her family closed ranks, Reverend Beauchamp and Matt leaving the room behind her. Abigail belonged to them. She belonged to Magnolia Bend.

He had no one.

Bullet to the chest.

"Chin up," Hilda whispered, taking his arm. "You need a drink stat, and then you need to tell me why in the hell you did this."

"I didn't."

Hilda arched an eyebrow, but kept smiling as they passed other attendees. She maneuvered them toward the bar, where she bought him a double whiskey. He didn't hesitate in downing it promptly.

"Slow down and tell Auntie Hilda what that whole thing was about. Did you draw that?"

"Of course, but it was for my eyes only."

"Then how did it get here?"

Leif shook his head. "I don't want to talk about it. I need to talk to Abigail."

"Not yet. Give her some time. The poor girl looked like she'd been strip-searched and then asked to eat a beetle. The bug kind, not the rock group."

"Shit," Leif breathed, rubbing a hand over his face.

At that very moment, a man tapped Hilda on the shoulder. When Leif caught sight of Senator Orgeron, he felt pretty sure he lost every bit of color in his face. Things were happening too fast, spinning out of control. He couldn't deal with this now.

"Hilda," Everett said, bestowing a kiss on Hilda's cheek. "Someone mentioned you were looking for me."

"Ah, Finch, you old rascal. I'm always looking for handsome men," she replied with a genuine smile.

"So I see." Everett turned to Leif, his hand extended. "Everett Orgeron."

"Leif Lively," Leif said, shaking the man's hand. His grip was firm, not crushing. "Nice to meet you."

"Likewise," he said, before returning his gaze to Hilda. "So what would an accomplished lady such as yourself want with an old tramp like me?"

Hilda batted her eyelashes. "Well, actually I wanted to introduce you to my friend Leif. He's an artist."

Everett's eyes widened. "Oh, he's the one who did the boudoir portrait of the preacher's daughter? Now that was quite a bold one, son."

The way he said *son* made Leif's heart ache. Could this man be his father? He searched for similarities but could find none. "I'm not sure I should say thanks. Seems to have caused a scandal."

"It's art, for pity's sake." Everett waved a hand. "So why was Hilda so intent on our meeting? I'm assuming it has to do with a bill on the arts? Something I need to bring to committee? I'm always ready to listen."

"Not really," Leif said, catching the encouraging gleam in Hilda's eye. "I actually had some questions for you about my mother."

"Oh?" Everett said, his eyes narrowing a bit.

"My mother was Calliope. She was—"

Everett did a double take. "Wait… Calli was your mother?"

Leif nodded.

"My God," Everett said, shaking his head, a warm expression on his face. "I can't believe it. I knew your mother well."

Leif's pulse kicked up. "Did you?"

"We dated the entire summer she was here. Guess you could say she was my first love. Then one night she just disappeared. Not even a letter left for me. Damn near broke my heart." A small dimple appeared in his cheek as his smile widened.

And that's when Leif saw it.

Everett was the man he'd been looking for.

"Well, I'm happy to meet you," Leif said, glancing at Hilda, who nodded, a knowing look gracing her features. She held up her hand indicating she had to go say hello to someone else and left them.

"And I'm happy to meet you. So tell me, how is your mother? Where is she?"

"I'm afraid she passed away last summer," Leif said.

Everett literally paled, his eyes filling with deep sadness. "Oh, I'm so sorry to hear that. I would have loved to talk to her. So much was left unsaid between us." He paused then ran a hand across his brow. "Wow. I'm sorry to seem so shaken. I looked for your mother for a long time. Telling you we were close is a bit of an understatement. We had actually planned to marry. It was a secret, of course. I had a girlfriend in college and I wanted to break it off with her face-to-face, but, Jesus, this is…"

"Would you like to sit down?" Leif slid a stool over to the man, who was becoming less polished by the minute. "A drink, perhaps?"

"Scotch will work," Everett told the bartender.

After sipping a good single malt, Everett lifted a sheepish gaze to Leif. "Sorry about that. Just hit me out of the blue. Calli meant a lot to me, and this felt so…I don't know. I'm glad you told me, though. There's been this hole in my life all this time, you know?"

The butterflies in Leif's stomach had turned into fighting cats, scratching and twisting with a mixture of dread and hope. It wasn't the best time. Things were so…effed up, but Leif was tired of not knowing. "Thing is, when my mother left Magnolia Bend, she was pregnant."

Everett set his near empty glass on the bar with a thump, which sounded like a gavel. "Pregnant?"

Leif nodded. "With me."

"Oh, Christ." Everett looked at the people around him, talking about things like the weather and the food they'd be selling at the festival. So mundane in the midst of the biggest revelation Leif had ever laid on anyone.

"I don't understand," Everett said, shaking his head, looking ashen and sick. "She never told me. Why would she do that? Was it because of Simeon? I'm having a hard time understanding what's going on. Why you're here."

Something shriveled inside Leif. Suddenly he understood his mother's propensity to run. He felt the urge to get out of Louisiana. Leave the hard stuff behind.

"My mother never told me who my father was. On her deathbed she pleaded with me to correct that wrong, so I've spent the past few months researching her time here in Magnolia Bend, trying to set things right. You were the last person on my list."

Everett looked at him. "You look like her."

"Almost exactly like her."

Everett turned away, blinking tears, looking scared. "Are you telling me I might be your father?"

Leif didn't say anything. The night had literally shredded apart right in front of him, littering the ground with regret, uncertainty and shame. He wasn't about to compound it.

"Like right here at this shindig…you're telling me Calli was pregnant with my son. And I never knew?" Everett said.

His voice had risen so Leif pressed a hand in his direction. "I'm not sure of anything. I didn't know she'd been in Louisiana until she told me on her deathbed. I'm just…" He picked up the glass the bartender had filled when he poured Everett his shot.

"I'm sorry. I need some air," Everett said, rising suddenly, sending the stool skidding backward. Charging toward the huge bank of French doors off to the left, Everett ran, leaving Leif feeling empty, that age-old fear of rejection rearing its ugly head.

No hugs. No smiles. No pride.

Just emptiness.

But what had he expected?

Finishing the drink, Leif stood, avoiding those around him who seemed to want to talk about, no doubt, the Abigail nudie sketch, and got the hell out of the gala.

No one stood in his way.

Not even Cal, who seemed as if he were about to say something, but turned in the other direction instead.

Leif strode into the night, heading toward his car, not even caring at this point that he'd downed three shots of whiskey and shouldn't drive.

Hell, he'd add that to the colossal speeding ticket in his pocket.

What did anything matter at this point?

Everything was shit.

He'd crossed the tennis net, bumping his hips against the crank, when Abigail appeared beside him, jogging in her high heels.

He skidded to a stop.

"Jesus, I thought you'd never slow down," she said.

CHAPTER TWENTY-TWO

ABIGAIL STRUGGLED TO catch her breath because, for a laid-back, easy-living guy, Leif moved awfully fast when upset.

"What?" he said, his voice laced with pain.

"I want to talk to you," she said, hobbling beside him because the new shoes, while totally sexy, pinched the hell out of her toes.

"I thought you didn't want to talk," he said, stopping again, glaring at her.

"I changed my mind."

"Well, too late."

"Is it?" she asked, an extra layer of meaning coating her words. "Listen, I know you didn't put the artwork of me naked in the auction."

"No shit. That was for me alone," he said, his jaw still set, his eyes flashing anger and pain intermittently.

"Birdie told my mother what she did, but it was too late to pull the piece. They'd already opened the room and people had seen it."

Leif shrugged one shoulder but said nothing.

"It's beautiful," she said, pressing her lips together so she wouldn't cry or have her voice break with emotion. "It really is. I could feel...well, it just took my breath away."

"I'll bet," he said, pulling his gaze from her,

looking as if he might cry. And that killed her. She wanted to fix things, she wanted to make everything right again.

She'd spent the past fifteen minutes on the phone with her daughter, who'd cried, begged and pleaded with her for forgiveness. Abigail couldn't believe the child she'd cherished her entire life had done something so cruel.

"Why?" she'd asked Birdie.

"Because you lied. You said you were just friends. Just hanging out. But you were having sex with him. You let him draw you, like pornography. Like the stuff you told me was dirty."

"That was not pornography. That was something he made for me, and you showed it to the world. I don't understand why you'd do that. Do you hate me so much?"

Birdie stayed silent for a few seconds before saying, "You know I don't hate you."

"So this was to punish me? Embarrass me?"

"I don't know," Birdie cried, sniffling into the phone. "I guess I wanted you to hurt the way I did."

"The way you do?"

"I don't know, Mom. I'm so mad all the time and I don't know why. I wanted everything to go back like it was…when Dad was here. But you didn't even give him a chance. You were too busy screwing around with my teacher. Do you know how messed up that is?"

"No. Tell me."

"It just is. I tried to tell you. You're a mom. And you're not acting like my mom. You're acting like you're…I don't know. You said all that stuff about love and sex. You said you have sex with someone you love, someone you're committed to. But when I saw that picture of you, I knew you were a liar. It made me so pissed. I wanted to hurt you."

"It's fine to be angry. It's not fine to do what you did. You embarrassed our entire family, including your father, with this antic. Your grandfather had to pay the full amount for the painting just to keep some wacko in town from buying it. And, thanks to you, everyone now thinks—" Abigail took a deep breath. "You know what? I don't care what they think. What I had with Leif wasn't like that. Not that you would understand. Truly, baby, you're still a little girl and you don't know what love is. But one day you will, and you'll feel ten times worse than you do right now when you recall what you've done."

Birdie didn't speak.

For a moment, sitting in the club manager's office, Abigail felt such an absolute failure as a mother, as a daughter…as a person.

All she had planned for the night—talking to Leif, being more open and honest—had been swept away. She'd left Leif in that auction room, feeling hopeless.

But five seconds after walking out, she'd wanted to kick herself. Leif hadn't put that picture in the auction. Why had she doubted him for even a sec-

ond? Why had she let the old ghost of herself come
out again?

"Mom, I'm sorry. I really am. Please don't be mad
at me."

"Doesn't work that way, Birdie. We have some
things between us we have to fix, honey, and that
might take some help from a therapist who can help
me, you and Daddy understand each other better. I'll
talk to you later. Go to bed."

"Mom, I love you."

"And I love you. But that doesn't mean you won't
have repercussions. I'll talk to you tomorrow."

She'd hung up, briefly told Cal what their daughter had done and then apologized to her father, who
gave her a kiss on the cheek and told her she'd never
embarrassed him.

Abigail had never loved her father more than at
that moment,

Then she'd gone to find Leif…only to catch Everett Orgeron leaving him, looking stricken. Leif had
risen and hurried away as if a demon nipped at the
rather quirky Converse high-tops he'd worn with the
dinner jacket. Something told her Leif had found his
father…and it hadn't gone as well as hoped.

Now Leif stared at her as though she was too late
to apologize…too late to declare her love. "I'm sorry
the whole town saw the painting."

"I'm not."

Leif crooked an eyebrow. "So where did you put
the Abigail I know? 'Cause she'd have a shit fit at

the thought of anyone seeing her completely vulnerable…almost naked."

"Maybe I've changed."

"Do you still have a label maker, a triple-pocketed agenda and sticky notes in every color? Do you still fear everyone knowing you're human? Are you still scared to love?"

"Well, yes. I mean no. What I meant is that I don't mind being naked. I don't mind everyone knowing that you are my, uh, whatever you were."

"Well, ain't I special?" he drawled, heavy with sarcasm and hurt before turning toward the parking lot beyond the chain-link fence. "I've got to go."

"No."

He ignored her, kept walking.

Abigail clacked behind him and grabbed his arm, spinning him toward her. "I was wrong. I shouldn't have said yes to a break. I didn't want freaking breathing room."

"It wasn't entirely up to you," he said, shrugging off her grasp.

Abigail reached for the side zipper and unzipped her dress, shimmying her shoulders so the dress fell forward.

"What are you doing, Abi?"

"I'm taking off my dress."

His mouth fell open a little. "Why?"

"Because I have no shame. I want you to understand that I no longer care what anyone thinks." She kicked the dress off, and stood on the tennis court of the Magnolia Bend Country Club wearing only her strapless bra and a pair of nude Spanx.

"You're crazy," he said, moving toward her, casting a glance around to see if anyone might be watching. A beam of headlights swung past them, reminding her of the night when Leif first kissed her. She'd been so paranoid. And now she wasn't...because she'd toss her dignity under the bus if it meant proving to Leif she needed him in her life.

Abigail reached around and unhooked her bra. "Yeah, crazy for you."

"Stop," he said, catching her hands as she released the krakens. Wrapping his arms around her, he dragged her into the shadows. "Your father's a preacher. And you have a daughter."

"But what does that mean if I can't have you? Let everyone know I have lost my mind. That's what this feels like. I've been miserable since that night we broke up and I don't want to live that way."

Leif pressed her bra cups against her chest, placing her hands over them, while he went to fetch her dress. "You said we weren't about a future. I thought that's what you wanted. Friends with benefits."

"Well, I say a lot of things. I'm good at saying things, drawing lines, but problem is, I fell in love with you. So I'm—" She dropped to her knees, still holding the bra close to her not so much out of modesty, but because it was pretty damned cold.

"Abi, get up," Leif said, looking exasperated. When she didn't, he dropped to his knees. "You're freezing and talking out of your head. It's probably the shock."

"Nope. I love you. I fell in love and violated the whole unwritten contract we had. I couldn't help it, and so now I'm here to beg you to spend whatever time you have left in Magnolia Bend with me. I'll take what you can give me."

Leif pulled back, looking deep into her eyes. "You're serious."

"As a heart attack…and those can kill a person. I'd never joke about a life-or-death situation."

Leif kissed her. He tasted of whiskey and his lips were cold, but his arms were warm as he wrapped her in them. For a good minute, they reveled in the taste and feel of being in each other's arms. Finally Leif eased away. "Tonight has been about as shitty as they come, but you've just handed me the golden goose. You've changed everything."

Abigail felt her heart squeeze when she looked at him. "Are you calling me a goose?"

"Yes. But a golden one. The one I want to keep forever. But when did you change the way you feel? You've been so cold. Not cold like you are tonight but—"

"It was the only way I could be around you and not cry. I left your house that night knowing I'd been an absolute fool for agreeing with you. I didn't want a break. I was just too afraid to take what I wanted. It was my fault. Not yours."

"But I share in the blame. I got insecure—

something I never am—and I pushed outside the lines. Things just spiraled out of control and I opened the door to go after you, but you'd already gone."

"I hate to quote a movie line but we've been so stupid."

Leif kissed her again, sliding his warm hands over her chilly back. "But not so stupid that we didn't find a way. Thank you for taking that leap of faith. I love you, Abigail."

Abigail sank into him, laying her head on his shoulder. "I love you, too, Leif. You make me so much better than I ever thought I could be. You helped me let go."

"And you helped me hold on," he said, dropping a kiss on her head. "As much as I want to stay here and enjoy this moment, I'm really afraid of you getting hypothermia. Let's go home and warm up."

"Okay, but I'm going to need help getting in that dress. And we need to ask someone to grab my wrap from the coat room. And maybe—"

"Hush," Leif whispered, dropping another kiss on her mouth. "Everyone will survive without you… except me."

They rose together, still intertwined beneath the moonlight. Abigail concentrated on the breaths Leif took, reveling in the security she felt in his arms. She took her final leap and whispered. "Don't leave me."

Leif squeezed her tighter. "No chance. I've finally found where I belong."

"Me, too," she said.

And she meant it.

If anyone had told her months ago that she'd be half-naked on the country-club tennis courts with a man who burned incense, never ate meat and played the ukulele, she would have locked that person in an asylum.

But at that moment, she knew she'd finally found the man who fit her better than anything she'd ever worn.

Maybe this being-naked thing wasn't so bad.

In warmer weather, of course.

"Let's go home," she said.

Four months later

THE GOOD-SIZE crowd gathered around the gazebo in downtown Magnolia Bend held familiar faces, which made Leif relax slightly in the chair perched next to the fancy podium. Several news cameras from around the state clustered at the back of the crowd, preparing for an announcement.

The microphone squealed slightly as Everett Orgeron bent it to the correct height.

Abigail squeezed Leif's hand as his father cleared his throat.

"Good morning, friends," Everett said, smiling gently at those gathered. Abigail's family sat in the middle section, and even Cal had shown up, bringing Birdie to the press conference because she'd promised her mother she'd be more supportive of Abigail's relationship with Leif. The kid was trying.

"I know many of you came because you believed I was going to announce my bid to run for the next governor of Louisiana, and I'm not saying that's off the table. But today's not about my future in politics. It's about the past."

Everett turned and looked at Leif, a glimmer of tenderness in his eyes. "When I was young, I fell in love. As a college junior, I wanted a great many things, but I'd never wanted anything as much as the beautiful artist I met one summer. She made me see the world in a whole new way. Things happened, as they are wont to do when you're young and stupid, and I lost contact with this woman. I mourned her loss, but moved on in life, finding a wonderful wife and making a good life here in Magnolia Bend."

His father then glanced toward his wife of twenty-eight years, a woman who, despite Leif's fears, accepted what had happened between Calliope and Everett and had treated Leif with great kindness.

"We were never blessed with children, though we enjoyed watching our nieces and nephews grow and blossom. Several months ago, I discovered life is still full of surprises. A most unusual gift was laid at my feet."

A rumble in the crowd started as many began to whisper.

Everett ignored the buzz and continued. "I learned my first true love, who had left Magnolia Bend under misconstrued circumstances, had taken with her a child in her womb, a child who was my son."

One woman gasped and the hum of conversation amplified. A few cameras snapped photos.

Leif thought he might vomit, and if it weren't for the steady pressure of Abigail's hand, he might have bolted off the platform. As it was, he tried not to look like a hunted animal. His smile felt stupid and he kept licking his lips.

"For thirty-four years, my son and I did not know each other, but a final gesture from a dying woman put my son on the road to Magnolia Bend, to the place where his mother and I fell in love. Many of you might think it sinful or shameful I conceived a child out of wedlock, and I can't change your opinion. I can only tell you my life has been blessed by this incredible gift. I was given a son, and I want the world to know him as part of me. He's incredibly talented, generous and conscious of others' feelings. His kindness is the measure of a true man."

Leif felt a ball of emotion well inside his chest at his father's words. The past few months had been difficult, but through much patience—and a blood test—Everett had finally embraced the idea that Leif was his son and had spent several days a week with Leif, getting to know him, sharing their pasts, edging around an official commitment of being father and son.

Everett had asked Leif to attend a small press

conference several days ago. He'd said it was to announce his intention to run for state office.

The man had lied.

"So today I want to introduce you to my son," Everett said, motioning to Leif.

Abigail gave him a nudge, smiling at him with
eyes that sparkled as much as the diamond engagement ring he'd given her on her birthday last month.
"Go."

Leif stood and moved toward his father. Everett
placed an arm around Leif, squeezing him tight. Leif
blinked away the sheen of tears in his eyes.

Everett wrapped him in an embrace as a smatter-
ing of applause broke out. Releasing him, Everett
turned to the crowd. "I'm so proud to be this man's
father. Some people hide the mistakes of their past,
and I won't lie, at first I wanted to sweep this all
under the rug. But then I saw the goodness in my
son. I saw Leif was meant to be in my life. He was
a second chance for me to do the right thing."

Leif swallowed hard and looked out at the people of Magnolia Bend. Many smiled, a few ladies
swiped their eyes with wadded-up tissues. Birdie
looked bored.

"All I have left to say is welcome home, son."

Leif swallowed the emotion threatening to sweep
him away and managed to say, "Thank you…"

He wasn't sure what to call the senator.

Everett leaned forward and said clearly into the
microphone, "Dad."

"Dad," Leif said, catching Everett's gaze. Smiling he looked at Abigail, who wiped her eyes with the back of her hand.

And just like that, Leif Lively found something worth holding on to. He'd found who he was meant to be.

He'd come home to Abigail…and Magnolia Bend.

* * * * *

Look for the next
HOME IN MAGNOLIA BEND *book*
by Liz Talley!
Coming later in 2015
from Harlequin Superromance.

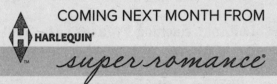
Available March 3, 2015

#1976 THE COMEBACK OF ROY WALKER
The Bakers of Baseball
by Stephanie Doyle

When Roy Walker left his professional pitching career, he was on top...and had the ego to prove it. Now, with a much smaller ego, he needs to make a comeback—something he can't do without the help of physiotherapist Lane Baker. But first, he must make amends for their past!

#1977 FALLING FOR THE NEW GUY
by Nicole Helm

Strong and silent Marc Santino is new to the Bluff City Police Department. His field training officer, Tess Camden, is much too chatty—and sexy—for comfort. When they give in to the building attraction, the arrangement is just what they need. But, for the sake of their careers, can they let it turn into something more?

#1978 A RECIPE FOR REUNION
by Vicki Essex

Stephanie Stephens is tired of people not believing in her. So when Aaron Caruthers comes back to town telling her how to run his grandmother's bakery, she's determined to prove herself. Unfortunately, he's a lot cuter than she remembers him being...and she definitely doesn't need her heart distracting her now!

#1979 MOTHER BY FATE
Where Secrets are Safe
by Tara Taylor Quinn

When a client disappears from her shelter, Sara Havens teams up with Michael Eddison to find the missing woman. The strong attraction between them complicates things. Michael's strength is appealing, but his young daughter makes Sara vulnerable in a way she swore she'd never be again.

LARGER-PRINT BOOKS!

GET 2 FREE LARGER-PRINT NOVELS PLUS
2 FREE GIFTS!

HARLEQUIN®

Romance

From the Heart, For the Heart

HRLP13R

LARGER-PRINT
BOOKS!